LOVE ME
Like that

RENEE KENNEDY

Renee@author-reneekennedy.com
Editing: Flaming Pen Editing, http://www.Flamingpenediting.com
Cover Design: Allusion Graphics, LLC/Publishing & Book Formatting, http://www.allusiongraphics.com
Photographer: Kristy Rogers, https://www.facebook.com/KristyLouisePS
Interior Design: Jovana Shirley, Unforeseen Editing, www.unforeseenediting.com
Book Trailer: Back Cover Clips, http://www.backcoverklps.weebly.com/

ISBN-13: 978-0-9967490-1-5

Dedication

This is dedicated to my Granny and Papa. Without them this book would not have been possible. They really were that great. To know them was to love them. Some of the things in this book about **them** are true with a few little embellishments, but the story Papa tells, in the hospital, is one hundred percent true. I've heard it all of my life.

I miss them both more and more each day. Life isn't the same without them, and I wish I could pick up the phone just one more time to call my Granny to hear her say, "Why haven't you called me?" She was my best friend and the person I turned to a lot in my life.

To hear one of Papa's stories again would be so welcomed. You truly don't know what you have until it's gone. I wish I had recorded them all. If only I could write a book filled with the little stories he told from his life. Some about his childhood were so heartbreaking, but he would laugh about them. I would give anything to be able to take him and get him one more milkshake or C.F. Penn's Hamburgers.

I will always hold you both in my heart ~
Alan Eugene Stricklin: September 5, 1921 - January 16, 2011
Addie B Stricklin: December 25, 1926 - January 26, 2010

Married December 8, 1942 (That's the reason I picked December 8, for my release.)

P.S. He really did cut my hair when I was in my late twenties. I told him I paid good money for those blonde streaks.

Someday someone will walk into your life and make you realize why it never worked out with anyone else.

– Author Unknown

Prologue

Just when I thought I had everything figured out, Murphy's Law reared its ugly head and smacked me right back in my place. I never expected to voluntarily give up a scholarship and a life I've always dreamed about. But dreams and plans are made to withstand being…altered. They aren't broken, nope. They've merely been put on hold. My ultimate goals are still achievable. I know I can accomplish them, in the future because I have my hope, no one can take it away from me. This is simply a detour, not an end.

Life was hard growing up but now that I'm away at college my future has never been brighter. I never thought I would have the opportunity to go the University of Alabama. Woohoo, Roll Tide! Go Bama! I'm still amazed I made it.

I had a dream. I wrote my dream down. I made action plans on how to achieve that dream. Everything had been right on time and going so well. Then I get a call that unexpectedly changes my life, or at least, puts everything on hold.

The last time I went home, my family was great. We all got together out at my grandparents' little house, and I had a great time hanging out with everyone. I miss them, but I want something different for my life. I want to live without worrying how I'm going to pay the bills. I want to have things that I will never have if I stay in my little hometown.

Mom called earlier to tell me about Granny and Papa. Those two people right there are my life. They've been there for me when no one else was. Now they need help, and I've decided I will be the one to help them. A decision didn't need to be made. They need someone. I'm closest to them, and I want to be the one who takes care of them. Now, I have to tell Hendrix. He will be over in a few hours and I've planned an intimate sexy night for us. I do this in hopes that the news is well received.

Last night, before the bottom fell out of my well-ordered life, I had so much fun at Omega House's spring formal. Hendrix was the sweetest guy ever. He arranged for me to be pampered all day with spa sessions to get ready. He paid for Lizzie to go with me, even though they're always at each other's throats. He really went out of his way to make the day special for me. I really thought he might ask me to marry him. He hadn't, but in hindsight the time wasn't really right. I still have another year of school.

We've been talking about our future so much that I know he has been thinking about marriage too. I can only imagine being on his arm for all the charity events he has to attend. We've been dating for nine months, and he has been my knight in shining armor. He took me from eating cheap microwave noodles and barely paying my rent to dining in the finest restaurants. Me. Bailey. In five star restaurants. Unbelievable, I know. This little country girl would have never thought a guy as classy as Hendrix would be interested in her. I feel like the luckiest girl in the world.

I wished Lizzie could see what I see in him. She thinks he is changing me, but she doesn't realize how much I want to change. That's fine. They'll eventually grow on each other.

Hendrix arrives on time, and he looks as handsome as ever. He's always so polished even when he is dressed in jeans and a polo shirt. Peeking through the blinds, I see he has a small gift bag in his hand. My sweet guy is always surprising me with thoughtful gifts. I open the door to the apartment I share with Lizzie.

"Well, hello beautiful. You're looking mighty fine tonight," Hendrix says.

"Hello yourself, lover boy! Have I got plans for us tonight," I tell him, sinking into his arms. His strong arms wrap around me, holding me tightly, providing the security I need right now.

"I like the sound of that. Maybe I have plans of my own for us too." He kisses me softly. "What is all this about, Babe? Don't get me wrong, I love when you plan nights like these. They're just very rare. How did you get rid of your pest?"

"Hendrix, be nice." I take his hand and lead him into the kitchen. I have lit candles everywhere, casting a romantic ambience around us and dinner for two on the table.

"Awe, Babe, you outdid yourself." Hendrix leans over placing a kiss against my sensitive lips. Then he reaches over and retrieves the bag he brought. "I have a little something for you, Sweetheart." He pulls out a box and opens it showing me a beautiful diamond studded watch.

"Hendrix! What is this for? I love it!" I jump out of my seat, going to him, throwing my arms around him.

"This is to remind you how much I enjoy our time together." He picks up my arm and places the watch on my wrist. He lifts my hand to his mouth and kisses it.

I stare at the watch for a few seconds. What did I do to deserve this great guy? "I don't know how to thank you. This is so thoughtful, you're the best."

He flashes me his gorgeous smile. I need to let him know of my new plans for school. I dread doing this, he graduates next month. I really think he's going to be upset. He likes to have me all to himself. "I got some news from home today that wasn't so good." My gaze focuses on my lap as I collect my thoughts.

"What is it, Bailey? Is everything alright?" He pulls me to my feet and wraps me in his arms.

"No, everything isn't okay. Remember me telling you about my grandfather having dementia? Well, he is getting to be too much for my granny to handle on her own. She gets out of breath just doing their laundry." Tears fill my eyes.

"That's horrible, Bailey. What can I do to help? Do you want me to take you to go visit?" He kisses my temple.

"That's what I want to talk to you about. I want to go take care of them, Hendrix, because they mean the world to me. They've done more for me than my own parents."

"What are you saying, Bay? Are you doing this for summer break?" He pulls back a little, with his eyebrows pinched together.

"I'm going to stay until I'm no longer needed, I'll put college on hold for a while." My smile is weak. I know he doesn't understand. No one understands our family dynamics. My family is extremely close knit, but the bond's really more than that. My Granny always tells us your family is all you have. That your family will be there for you when no one else will be.

"Why do you have to be the one who takes care of them, Bailey? You have plenty of family that can help out with them."

"Because I'm the one who they count on. I'm their favorite. I'm the one who they kept from the time I was born until I left for college. It's my place to take care of them. Besides, everyone else is either too young or works."

"What about a nursing home? There are plenty of great—"

"NO! They will not be placed in a home. I've heard horror stories about the treatment of the elderly in those places. As long as I'm able, I will do everything in my power to keep them in their own home. They gave me and the rest of the family so much when I was growing up. They sacrificed and went without to provide for me."

"That's what they are supposed to do, Bailey, that's kind of the law," he says, laughing a little.

I lift my chin up so I can look into his eyes again. "That's what your parents are required to do, not your grandparents. They didn't have to practically raise me, to provide for me like they did, Hendrix."

He drops my arms and turns away, "What about our plans, Bailey? Do we just forget about them? I wanted to take you to the beach after graduation." He turns back to face me and rubs my arm. "I wanted to sit on the beach with you and watch the waves roll in, stay up making love to you all night until the sun rises. It was going to be just the two of us."

"I know and I'm sorry, but we can still do things like that every once in a while. Taking care of my grandparents won't be forever, Babe."

"So when are you leaving? When will this all take place? How much time do we still have together?"

"Hendrix, we'll still be together. I'll actually be closer to you there than I'd be here at school. I'm going to finish out this semester so I'll be here through your graduation then I'll move in with them."

"I say we make the most out of the time you have left here at school. What do you say?"

"I say that sounds like a wonderful idea. Why don't we start that right now?" I pull him toward my bedroom.

"I like the way you think." He pulls up his shirt before we even get to the door.

Bailey

Isn't life really about creating yourself? Sometimes you have to do what is best for yourself and not worry about everyone else. I'm Bailey Reynolds and I'm shallow. At least that is how I've been feeling lately. Really, the only person who is being deceived is myself. I'm the only one who can be hurt by pretending to be something I'm not. If I'm the only one who gets hurt, it's not so bad, right?

How am I shallow, you might ask? I have let someone change me into his idea of perfect. I love most of the changes. I've dropped old habits for newer higher standards. Seriously, how many girls would balk at the spoiling Hendrix has lavished upon me? He facilitates those services that keep me impeccably polished, from spa treatments, to keeping my hair, nails and toes perfect. You name it and he pampers me with it. It's the life I want, or at least I think it is.

The truth is I want out of this small, one-horse town.

I'm not cynical or a pessimist. I'm not desperate for a relationship. I simply want a better life. That's it. Doesn't everyone want a better life? I have dreams of being able to make ends meet without struggling.

But I'm feeling very confused about this choice I've made. I think I really do love Hendrix and he loves me, but sometimes I feel like I need to move on from him.

Hendrix has changed since I left college to take care of my grandparents. He isn't as sweet and things are strained between us. I have two forces pulling me in opposite directions. One is my head and the other is my heart. My heart tells me, dating Hendrix is okay because I love him. My head has a hard time grasping the way he has been treating me. Haven't you ever been confused about love? I need help figuring all of this out before I make a mistake I can't easily change.

Journal Entry: Here I sit, waiting on Hendrix to let me know when he's coming to pick me up. I'm keeping one eye on the window, in case he just shows up, and the other on my phone.

I've been ready for a couple of hours because he can't stand for me to delay him. Lately, we've been just hooking up at his apartment. He seems to only be up for a little fun. I'm up for anything, as long as we are together. I'm a better person with Hendrix, I'm Bailey 2.0! He makes me want more from my life. Lizzie says this makes me shallow. So what! She can stay in Mt. Hope, Alabama forever, but not me. Audios muchachos!

Hendrix's not keen on coming here to my grandparents' house because the drive is a twenty-minute "never ending journey." He wanted me to move in with him when he graduated a couple of weeks ago, but I have to be here to take care of Granny and Papa. I will always put their needs before my own. I am who I am because of them.

Because my mom got pregnant with me when she was about to graduate from high school, she didn't go to college. Instead, she got married and went to work. She has always worked long, hard hours, still does. That's why she can't take care of Granny and Papa. She also has my little brother to take care of and my dad travels a lot with his job. The rest of my family is in similar situations. Besides Papa has dementia and doesn't do well with change, so the ideal arrangement is for them to stay in their own home.

My grandparents did everything for me that parents would do for their children. Papa not only taught me to drive but also cosigned on a loan so I could get my beloved Jeep. He paid the down payment and insurance until I started making enough money to pay for it myself. If not for Papa, I would have had to rely on Lizzie to teach me, and she's a crazy driver. She likes to give me flack over my "flawless" parking skills, but when I'm tired of hearing her complain about them, I remind her that Papa taught me to drive. This effectively shuts her up because Granny and Papa have helped her as much as they've helped me. They are this way with our entire family. They might not have two nickels to rub together, but if someone needed those nickels, they would gladly hand them over. I'm thankful to be raised

by them and staying here taking care of them is minuscule compared to the multitude of things they've sacrificed for me.

While I've told Hendrix all these things, he still can't grasp why I feel like I'm the one who should take care of them. I want to do this. I'm not being forced to do it. His lack of gratitude for all that they have done for me irritates me. I guess, when you're born with a silver spoon in your mouth, you have a hard time understanding the working class.

We've never been what you call dirt poor, but that is about all you can say about our financial state. Dad didn't go to college until much later so he and mom both had entry-level jobs, most of my life. Dad finally got his degree in business management five years ago. Most of the time Papa worked two jobs at once while Granny took care of me. Papa did this so we could have a few extras, like everyone else. They both wanted to help their kids when they needed it.

They consider all of us their kids. This comprises the honorary kids too. The honorary kids are the ones we bring home, our friends who seem to stay at our house more than they do at their own. Granny never minded us bringing one more mouth to feed, and Papa was always at work. If one of those kids had a problem, Granny or Papa would take it upon themselves to help them out as best they could. That's why everybody loves them and calls them Granny and Papa. Everybody but Hendrix. He says it is undignified.

The low rumbling of an engine, followed by a honk, alerts me of Hendrix's arrival. I slip my journal into my purse as I glance at my phone. No, I didn't miss a text.

My best friend / sister from another mister, Lizzie, is here visiting with us. Our moms grew up together. Her mom Kate is almost two years older than mine, but they are best friends. Kate lived with mom and my grandparents while growing up—an honorary kid. Since Papa and Granny raised Aunt Kate, Lizzie is more like blood. Papa and Granny tried to adopt Kate, but her dad refused to sign over custody. I don't know the whole story, but I do know Kate feels like Papa and Granny are her parents. Lizzie has always called them Papa and Granny, since Kate doesn't communicate with her own father.

"Has 'A Joke' resorted to just blowing his horn for you now? Is he too good to come to the door?"

Lizzie doesn't bother hiding her dislike for Hendrix. Unfortunately, Hendrix has the same aversion to Lizzie. I roll my eyes at her. I wish she could keep her opinion to herself, at least in front of Granny. Where three months ago they were at least civil to each other, now they've resorted to a verbal death match. "Shut it, Lizzie!" I say through gritted teeth.

Granny looks at her confused, "A Joke?"

"Don't pay her any mind Granny, she has evidently lost hers." I give Lizzie the death glare, which she ignores on a regular basis.

"He isn't a real man, Granny. He's 'A Joke' of a man. Get it?"

Granny can't contain her amusement. Even if she hid her smile, her eyes would still give her away with their sparkle. They are having an awfully good time at my expense.

"Bailey, it's not respectful for 'A Joke', I mean a boy, to just toot his horn and you go scampering off, baby."

See what Lizzie started? Granny meant to use that name.

"I've hardly met Henry, and I don't like you dating boys who won't come to the door and pick you up. He needs to be bringing you flowers."

Granny really is the sweetest little lady you'll ever meet, but when she thinks someone's doing one of her kids wrong she becomes a miniature spitfire. I don't want her to get upset so I tell a little white lie. "Oh, we're in a hurry. I told him to just honk his horn and I would run out." Giving her a kiss on her cheek, I remind her, "I have my cell with me, if anything happens you can call me and I will come right back, okay?" Papa is already asleep in the recliner, which is his favorite pastime.

"I'm leaving too, Granny." Lizzie gives Granny a kiss then adds, "I'm only a call away too, love you."

"I love both of you girls, but you don't have to worry about us, I've told you that I can take care of myself just fine. Lizzie, come back soon, but not to take care of me, I'm the Granny and I'm the one who does the taking care of people."

She throws her hand in the air, that's her way of telling us to go and leave her be. We both laugh, shaking our heads, at her. Hendrix lays on his horn, making it known to God and everybody he is waiting.

"I guess you better get out there, Bailey, before he wakes up the dead." Granny sighs.

She looks over to see if the horn woke up Papa. He is still sleeping away. It takes a lot to interrupt his sleep. "Bye. Love you, Granny." I'm out the door and off the porch as fast as I can go. I hear Lizzie right behind me. *Shit.* I don't want to have to deal with Lizzie and Hendrix trading insults tonight. It's bad enough that it's eight pm and still in the high eighties. Summer nights are sweltering here. Gotta love it.

"Hey there, Dickwad. Show some respect for my grandparents and my girl by coming to the door. Or are you above good manners?" Lizzie leans into the passenger side of his car. "By the way, why don't you stick that horn up your ass after you jack off tonight?"

Here we go with the insults. Sometimes this gets intense and being the peacemaker gets old fast.

"Fake Ass Hoe, not working your street corner tonight? What, are you on antibiotics for another yeast infection?" Hendrix throws right back at her, and furrows his brows.

"Guys, stop it, can't you two get along for five minutes?" I ask.

"Bay, when asswipe shows you some manners and behaves toward you, like you're a lady, I won't have any problems with him," Lizzie says.

"Get in the car and close your door, Bailey. Let's go, babe."

"Bye, Lizzie, I'll call you tomorrow." I get in and shut the door.

Hendrix slowly backs out of the driveway.

I turn to him and put my arms around his neck. "Hey, babe, I thought you were going to call me to let me know when you were going to pick me up." I give him a kiss on the cheek. He smells so good, so manly. I love this cologne. I swear it has pheromones in it.

Once he's off the gravel driveway and onto the road, he punches the gas. My head snaps back from the jolt.

Great! He's pissed.

Again.

"What's wrong, babe, did you have a bad day? I bet I can make it better." I smile and sound as sexy as possible.

"Why do you allow Lizzie to talk to me like that? I thought you were in love with me. How can you let a redneck like her say stuff to me like that? Don't start the shit about her being family because y'all aren't family." He forces out a rush of air then starts up again. "I hate you living all the way out here. I'm not going to get my car scratched in that gravel driveway."

I sit in shock because he has completely blown my mind. Has he gone off the deep end? He and Lizzie always dig at each other, but I've never seen him lose it like this at her insults. He knows how close Lizzie and I are. We were raised together for God's sake. Granny kept both of us while our moms worked. That is family in my book.

"Hendrix, I don't know what has happened today but you are obviously in a bad mood. Lizzie *is* my family and I've told you before how much I love my family. If I had to choose between you and my family, you would be shit out of luck. This isn't a forever living arrangement for me. When it's over, we can go back to being us again. Until then, please understand I have to do this for them. I love you, babe. Let's just have a good night. I will come to you from now on, okay?" If only he could grasp this. Isn't family important to everyone?

He still has an intense look on his face and the muscles in his face are flexing. I roll my eyes. When he starts this shit, it pisses me off. When I can keep him and Lizzie away from each other, everything is great. He never acts like this unless they go at each other's throats. Lizzie only has my best interest at heart. She thinks Hendrix treats me like a dog turd. I don't know what to think myself.

"Well, if we ever get married, they will not be welcome in our home," he snarls.

Oh, I know he didn't just go there. My family is a hard limit for me. So before I rip him a new asshole, he needs to take me home. "What has gotten into you lately? Where did my sweet boy go? You know, Hendrix, I can't take this tonight. If you are going to be mad the whole night, just turn around and take me back."

I want to be with Hendrix, but I know how rough he can be when he's mad. Sex isn't good when he's mad. As it is, he doesn't take the time to make sure I have my own happy ending. I want to go home so I do not have to deal with all of this.

He slows down and carefully pulls off the road. "Are you done, Bailey?" He looks at me with a condescending sneer then shakes his head. "Come here, Sweetheart." He pulls me over the console of the car and onto his lap, having me straddle him.

His whole tone changes to the sweet, loving Hendrix I adore.

"I'm sorry for talking that way to Lizzie, I'm really just kidding around with her. That's our thing, we call each other names. You know how much I love you, I just want to be with you." He points to my head. "I hate for anyone else to be in here but me."

He kisses me and slips his hands under my skirt to rub me through my panties. He loves me in short skirts and barely there lace panties for this reason. I feel him getting hard and he is pressing into me.

"Feel how much I want you, Bailey? You know I can make you feel good."

He tears my panties.

Wanting me right now, here on the side of the road. The road that all of my family travels down frequently. I don't want to do this here. I love how much he wants me, but not here, where we can be seen by anyone passing by.

"No, Hendrix, let's go to your place, not here, please."

He rips off my panties and rubs my nub.

Waves of pleasure roll through me. "No, come on, I know a dirt road that isn't very busy and I'll do anything you want there."

"See how wet you are, Bailey? You want this right here, right now."

All this will be is a quickie because there isn't any room in his car. I need more than a quick wham-bam thank you ma'am. I have an inner kink goddess, dammit! But I'm getting hot. He knows exactly how to push me to the point where I forget he never brings me over the edge into ecstasy. He licks up my neck as his other hand slides under my shirt and unclasps my bra. He likes when I wear front clasp bras so he can undo them easily. He pinches my nipple with one hand, palming my breast with the other. I've lost a lot of the sensation in them from getting my implants so I give him the right reactions.

"These were the best two things I've ever spent my money on."

Hendrix loves my boobs now. He wanted me to get double Ds, but I talked him into regular Ds. I only weigh 115 pounds so I thought I would topple over if I got double Ds. "You were right, I did need them. I look so much better with them."

He puts two fingers inside of me, and my breath hitches, I move against them. That does feel good. I kiss him, and my arousal grows. I kiss him harder. I want him, dammit. I can't control myself when he does this and he knows it. He counts on this reaction from me. I muster up all the self-control possible, "Not here, Hendrix. I enjoy you letting your twisted side out to play, but this road is well traveled."

"Ugghh, where then? I'm not driving twenty miles back to my place and then turning around to bring you back to babysit."

I nibble on his ear, putting forth my best effort to get him out of this funk. "I know. What was I thinking?" I'm going through every solution possible to come up with a venue to his liking. "So the dirt road is out?"

"To get my car dirty? I just had it detailed, Bailey."

I wanted us to actually go out, do something fun tonight, but all our relationship has come to over the last few weeks is hooking up. There isn't any of the romance we had back at college. He doesn't try to woo me anymore. "I don't know, Hendrix. Let's go get something to eat, I'm hungry." I slide over to my seat. Flipping down the visor, I check to see how much damage has been done to my makeup. None! This shit is good!

"Just forget it." He does a one-eighty in the middle of the road, scaring the shit out of me, and heads back toward the house, "Look, Bay, when you finally have time for me, why don't you let me know." He looks over at me sulking.

I have to pick my jaw up off the floorboard. What. The. Hell. So he didn't get his way, and now he doesn't even want to be with me at all? Unbelievable!

He pulls in front of the house, not in the driveway, "Look, sweetheart, I've had a long day and it looks like you did too. I'll call you tomorrow and we will have a real date." He gives me a quick kiss, "I promise to make this up to you. I should have cancelled tonight. I knew I was already in a horrible mood."

He does sound contrite.

"You know I love you, right? Here, take some money and buy some sexy new panties for me to tear off of you." He reaches into his wallet and pulls out several one hundred dollar bills and hands them to me.

This feels more like a transaction than a date, and humiliation blankets me. "Yeah, Hendrix, I know," I limply show him the cash, giving him a smile. "You show me all the time."

"That's my girl."

My cynicism is lost on him, and I feel frustrated. He's already gone. His mind is anyway. Times like this is when I question the longevity of our relationship.

After I get out of the car, I stand at the head of the driveway and watch him speed off. I try to calm myself down, but my frustration is at an all-time high.

The cab light of a truck goes on across the road and I see the outline of a guy. I guess he is one of our new neighbors. I take a few deep breaths, saying, "Breathe in through your nose, and out through your mouth. In through the nose, and out through the mouth." I hear a soft chuckle. Damn, I didn't know I was being that loud.

I turn down the driveway, feeling like I am taking the walk of shame. I feel horrible I let Hendrix treat me this way. If anyone, other than Lizzie knew this, I would die of embarrassment. It's bad enough she knows. My family would be so disappointed in me for allowing this.

When I walk inside the house, Granny is all smiles, and Papa is even awake. I'm about to get the Spanish Inquisition because I've been gone for less than an hour and Granny is intuitive.

"Well, hey there Bailey, come on in and have a seat," Papa says. With his dementia, he can't always remember I live with them. "You just missed meeting our new neighbors."

Papa loves to have company. He actually wakes up and talks to them. He might not remember them tomorrow, but that's okay, he still loves having people around. I inwardly sigh as I contemplate his failing health. He still remembers us right now and that is what matters to me.

I look over to Granny for verification and she nods. "Margie Wilson and her son Cash. They seem real nice, Bailey, you need to meet him."

Geez. "Is that so? That wouldn't have anything to do with you and Lizzie not liking Hendrix? What kind of name is Cash anyway? Is that like Johnny?" I laugh. I give them both a kiss on their cheek, "I love you guys, I'm going to go settle down for the night, that way I can get up early and work on your roses for you Granny."

She beams. "Cash said he would mow the yard for us tomorrow, too."

Good. One less thing I have to do. I can focus more on my job and make a little more money. "Alright, I have the monitor on so I can hear if you call for me, do I need to help get Papa in bed?" I look at him.

He shakes his head. "I can take care of myself, I don't know why you worry about me." He holds up his crooked finger to me.

His scolding and stern look gets me in my heart every time because he truly doesn't realize how sick he is.

The family was told he is still in the early stages, that things will only get worse as time goes by. We are researching everything we can find on the subject to prepare ourselves. We give him the best care we can at home, to keep his schedule and routines the same, to avoid putting him in a nursing home. He deserves the love and care we can give him here.

"Have you both taken your nightly medicine already?" Granny nods and I look over at Papa. "Did you take yours or did you spit it out?"

He grins, "I always take my medicine."

"Goodnight, sleep tight, don't let the bed bugs bite." I chime out of habit.

"Sweet dreams, baby, love you," Granny says.

CASH

I'm not sure who just left in that little fancy car, but I hope they aren't around a lot driving like that. Thankfully, they probably don't live around here because they only dropped someone off at the Jackson's place across the street and left.

Mom and I just came back from meeting the Jacksons. She'd insisted on meeting them right away. I have a hard time telling her no because she's been through so much. If meeting these new neighbors was going to make her happy, then that was going to happen, one way or another.

First impressions mean a lot to me. I instantly liked the Jacksons, and I'm glad to have decent neighbors. They're an elderly couple who look like they can barely get around. Mrs. Jackson is a sweetheart. I can see mom and her getting along fine. Mom can use a friend and maybe a little guidance. Mr. Jackson is a funny fella, I can already tell, he likes to tell stories. I hope he doesn't drive that Jeep Wrangler himself. If so, I'm staying off the roads, whenever I see it's gone.

They sent us home with muscadine jelly, which Mrs. Jackson told me is a wild berry that tastes like a grape. I've been raised in the country and already know that, but I let her tell me all about the process and how much she loves teaching her granddaughters. She seemed proud that she taught her two granddaughters how to make it.

Mom is back in the house putting things away. She constantly calls me in to ask where I want things. Honestly, I don't care. She can arrange this house any way she wants, because this will be her house anyway. I plan on building another one as soon as I get this one the way she wants it. She doesn't know that yet.

When I signed the deed on this fifty acres and little ranch style house, I knew my life was going to change forever, but what I didn't know was my father had been planning to leave my mom. My one bedroom apartment suddenly became tiny when she moved in with me. Since then, I've been hurrying to get things done to make this place livable. I wasn't planning on having mom live with me, but she is my mom and I wasn't about to throw her out like yesterday's trash. She has had enough of that the last twenty-five years. I can't think about all of that again without getting angry, though. Besides, dwelling on something that can't be changed is counterproductive. I've worked hard, saved most of my money, my company is doing well and taking care of my mom is what I want to do. I don't want my mom to worry about payments or someone coming home and making her cry.

After heading inside for the night, I grab a beer, and settle back for some old sitcom reruns. Why is it that I can watch this stuff a thousand times, and still laugh every time I watch them? The beer helps take the edge off the stress that has become my life. Twenty-somethings aren't supposed to be this stressed, or feel this ancient. At least that is what I'm told. I feel so much older than my twenty-six years. That may be because I've been working my ass off since I was sixteen years old. All through high school and college, I worked for a firm that did computer system analysis. I saved every penny I could along the way and when Paul, the owner, told me he wanted to retire, I invested all of my savings and financed a loan for the remainder to buy the business. I changed the name and developed new products and services. Now, Cashco is making more money than it ever has and I'm finally breathing a little easier. I have a staff of really good people that I trust which has afforded me the time off to work around here.

Mom comes into the room. "I'm getting a shower and going to bed. Is there anything you need before I do that?"

I've been on my own since college, until Mom moved in with me, and she's been hovering.

She yawns.

She's been working hard the last few days, too. "No, ma'am, you just take care of yourself, mom."

She looks at me with red-rimmed eyes. "Cash, I know I've told you already, but son, I appreciate you doing this. I know it isn't what you wanted to do, or had planned. I will get a job, as soon as I can, and be out

of your hair." She puts a hand up over her mouth, trying to control her emotions.

I get up and amble over to her. "Mom, I can't think of anything else I would rather do. You're my mom. It's my job to take care of you. If I was in the same circumstances, you would do the same for me." I give her a hug. I hate to see her hurting over my dad.

"You are a good person, Cash. You have always had such a good heart and I'm so proud of the man you have become. I just don't want to become a hindrance to you finding happiness in your life. Not all relationships are like your dad's and mine. They can be exceptional and there is a soul mate out there for everyone." She sighs. "One day you are going to meet a girl, she is going to smile at you or laugh and you will know she is the one. She will be your best friend, the person you can tell anything. When you find her, hold on tight. You tell her how important she is to you, and make her feel special."

Mom has never been philosophical, however here lately she has been telling me stuff like this and she has been so sad. I give her another hug and a kiss on the top of her head. "Mom, I will find someone one day but, I'm not in any hurry." Laughing, I add, "She just better know how to cook as well as you do." That makes her smile.

"Oh, Cash. Is food all you ever think about? There is some leftover meatloaf and some shrimp and grits in the fridge," she says as she leaves the room.

I take off my boots and stretch my muscles. I've missed my daily workouts the last few weeks because I haven't taken the extra time to get them in. Working out tomorrow won't be possible either. I've got yard work to do and I told the Jacksons that I would get their yard while I was doing mine. They said their little granddaughter who lives with them mows their lawn, most of the time, but little girls shouldn't have to do that. Their lot isn't very big so it won't take me very long anyway.

I do need to get out and meet people in town. Although my work is only forty miles from here, seventy-five miles from where we did live is far enough that we have a whole different town to get used to. I plan to get an early start in the morning so I can do just that tomorrow night. I have enough done around here that I can have a social life again.

In my room, I turn on my TV and set the sleep timer. I like to fall asleep watching reruns of Friends, but it isn't on yet. Any sitcom will do, though. I just need noise. I set my clock for 6:30 because I want to be working by 7:30. The Jacksons said they get up early and 7:30 would be okay for me to mow.

As I settle in, I think about everything mom said tonight. I've been in serious relationships, but not the kind she's talking about because it never bothered me to let the girls go. I've never been truly in love, even if I thought I was at the time. I'll take Mom's word that I will know my soulmate when I meet her. Maybe now's the time I settle down. I would have to be physically attracted to her of course. I really like short women. Something about picking them up and holding them in my arms heats my blood.

Looks aren't everything though, not at all. I'm all too aware of how looks can fade over time. Physical beauty may be only skin-deep, but someone can be ugly to the bone. She would have to have a good heart, to really care about people. Another thing, she can't wear too much makeup. I hate women who look like they used a spatula to put that shit on. It makes me feel like they're hiding something underneath it all.

I drift off thinking about this ideal woman I have all made up in my head. She has long brown hair and is a little sassy. She takes me off to dreamland.

Bailey

What in the hell is that noise? I pull my pillow over my head to drown it. My god, the racket is so loud the pillow doesn't help. I look over at my alarm clock with my blurry eyes. Sounds like our "wonderful" new neighbor is mowing the yard at freaking seven thirty. On a Saturday morning. What in the crap is wrong with this picture? I normally get up around eight, but I was up a lot last night with Papa. He didn't have a good night.

Since I'm already awake, I go ahead and get up. It's too early, but who can sleep with all of that noise? I slip on my cut-offs and a tank top, and pull my hair up in a high ponytail. I drag myself to the kitchen. Granny and Papa have already had breakfast. They don't need me to cook breakfast for them. I was getting up to eat with them until I gained five pounds in the first two weeks. Granny's breakfasts are simple, but homemade biscuits, bacon and eggs add on the pounds, especially when she insist you put her jelly on your biscuit. Oh, don't get me started on her chocolate gravy—a thick, rich chocolate syrup or a thin pudding heaped over your biscuits. This delicacy is irresistible. After having that on your biscuits, you can die happy. But, you can't eat like that and stay in a healthy weight range so I eat healthier, now—a bowl of Special K and a piece of fruit. But how I do crave that chocolate goodness. It has milk in it and that's healthy, right?

Other than their breakfast, I try to make sure they eat healthy. I keep plenty of fruit all cut up and on hand. The same with the fresh veggies for salads and snacking. The easier I make things for them to eat, the more likely they are to eat it. They are kind of like kids, in that regards. Feeding them is the easy part of taking care of them. Granny is easy all together. I get her medicine ready on a weekly basis, so she will remember to take it. I do the grocery shopping and clean the house. I roll her hair up in these old fashion rollers a couple of times a week and she is happy.

Papa is a different story. Bless his heart; he can't help it. He gets agitated if anything changes in his schedule. I'm constantly watching for signs that he may be getting upset so I can deflect as much as possible.

He is full of mischief these days. Sometimes his behavior is comical and sometimes it's very frustrating. He hides things from me, like my car keys and his medicine. He thought the highlights in my hair were gray hairs once. While I was really into watching a movie with Granny, he cut off a chunk of my hair. I try so hard to not lose my temper with him, but I did that day. That's when I started learning deep breathing exercises. They don't always work, but they help some. I've also learned to do the hiding of things. Things like my purse, my phone, and every pair of scissors in the damn house.

"Good morning," Granny calls out in her singsong voice.

I scoot by her. "Mornin', Granny, did you manage to get any sleep last night?" I mumble, barely awake.

She shakes her head.

Poor thing, I hate that for her. "Maybe you can take a little catnap later." I open the fridge and take out the sweet tea. Sweet tea is my form of coffee. I crave my caffeine fix. I have to have my delicious nectar as soon as I wake up. I sip on a glass all day long. I really don't drink many sodas, just my sweet tea. If a restaurant around here doesn't have sweet tea, I don't go there. If I go there by mistake, I just have water. You just can't sweeten tea right after it's already cold. Give me sweet tea over any glass of wine, or godforsaken beer. I'm supposed to love beer because I'm country girl, but I hate that nasty ale. Lizzie, on the other hand, can drink some beer. She has been known to get a little wild and crazy, going home with everyone and anyone who asks. But that was our first couple of years of college when we were both a little wild.

"Is there any reason why we are having the yard mowed so early?" I sit at the table across from Granny. She likes to sit with me and sip on her coffee while I eat my bowl of cereal. I enjoy this time we always take to be together.

"Oh, he wanted to get our yard and his yard finished before it got too hot with humidity. I heard on the news the temperature is going to be close to a hundred today." She grins over her cup of steaming coffee.

I'm waking up now. "Did he ever stop to think some people like to sleep in a little on a Saturday morning?" I raise one eyebrow then laugh.

She covers her mouth with one hand. "Baby, that's my fault. I told him that would be okay, I didn't even think about you wanting to sleep in today."

She comes across apologetic because she takes everyone's feelings into consideration. Who could ever be mad at her? "I needed to be up anyway, I want to work in those flowers out there." I give her a little wink and a grin, so she knows I'm not upset with her.

We sit and talk for a little bit before I get up to clean up the breakfast dishes. She asks me again about the family reunion coming up. "Did you ask Henry last night about coming to our picnic?"

I let out a sigh as I wash the dishes. "Granny, that's not really his thing. His family isn't close like ours, so he doesn't understand the importance of the occasion. I forgot to ask him last night, but when I talk to him again, I will ask him."

She gives me her knowing look—the look that tells me Lizzie has been talking to her. Granny has a way of getting information out of you before you know you even told her.

"Well, it's two weeks from today and I'm going to invite our new neighbors too. They don't have any family around here."

Good, I can change the subject, "Where are they from, Granny?"

"I don't remember her saying, but her son works over in Muscle Shoals."

"That's a long drive."

Granny shrugs. She has never driven a day in her life and always depended on Papa to take her everywhere. Now I take them everywhere. We took Papa's license and keys away from him a couple of years ago. He wasn't very happy about giving up those, but in the end I think he knew it wasn't safe for him to drive anymore.

Once I finish the dishes and get a load of laundry going, Granny takes all of her medicine and hands me Papa's. Here goes World War III. "Papa, it's time for your medicine." I tell him, trying to sound assertive.

He shakes his head and pretends to sleep.

"Come on, don't you want to sit outside on the porch while it's pretty? You can watch the squirrels and birds."

He holds out his hand. I give him a couple of pills and his glass of water. He acts like he puts the medicine in his mouth then smiles up at me like the cat who ate the canary.

"Open your hand, please." I stand here tapping my toe on the floor waiting for this game to be over.

He shakes his head and looks away. "I don't need any medicine, I feel fine."

"I would be glad to take you to go see the doctor. We can talk to him about getting you off some of these pills."

Papa crosses his arms, "All you want to do is keep me drugged up."

"I know you don't like them. I don't like medicine either. Let's make a deal. You go ahead and take these, and we'll talk about getting your dosages cut down on your next visit to his office."

He pops the pills into his mouth then opens so I can see he actually swallowed them. We started this when I caught him spitting them out in the garbage. I give him the last few pills and watch him take them. I wait for him to open his mouth. When he does, he sticks out his tongue.

"Are you wanting to be funny today, Papa?" I say teasingly. I can see by these shenanigans, he is going to give me a hard time today, "Do you want to sit on the porch a while?" If I sit him on the porch, will I be able to keep an eye on him and do the flowers?

He nods to me. Since he isn't speaking, I wonder if he is upset with me. I did lose my patience with him last night. "Papa, I'm sorry I got upset with you last night. I was so tired and hadn't been asleep very long." He looks confused.

"What do you mean?" he asks. "What did we do last night?"

He has already forgotten about last night. "Oh, you beat me at checkers." I turn to Granny, "Do you want to sit outside while it's pleasant?" I hope she will so I'll have an easier time keeping an eye on him.

"I think I will."

She gets her walker while I hand Papa his cane then I help them to the porch. The smell of fresh cut grass tickles my nose and makes me sneeze.

"Bless you, baby," Granny says a little breathlessly.

She has been getting out of breath easily over the last few days.

When they are seated in their rockers, I go back inside to get them glasses of ice water, the baby monitor, and the cordless phone for Granny. She can't miss a call. I keep my phone in my back pocket so Papa doesn't hide it.

CASH

The sun is already high in the sky, and beating down on me, making sweat drip from my nose. With the early start I've gotten though, I'll have the whole afternoon to cool down before I head out tonight.

The Jacksons come out on their front porch and sit in these big white rocking chairs, which swallow them whole. The chairs are placed side by side with little white tables on either side of them. The chairs look as weathered as their owners who slowly rock in unison. Mr. Jackson reaches over and takes his wife's hand. The owners of Hallmark could make a bundle from this view.

Hugh Hefner would probably make the most of the other view, though. The girl coming down the porch steps must be their granddaughter. She would be smokin' if she wasn't jailbait. She can't be over sixteen. Her jeans shorts leave little to the imagination. The denim hugs her ass just right, making those some sweet cheeks to lick. Shit, Cash, she's just a little girl. But that little girl needs to go inside and put some clothes on and quit prancing around out here. It's not right for her tits to be that large, and the rest of her to be so miniature. If she were my little sister, I wouldn't let her out of the house dressed like that.

Sweet Baby Jesus. She bent over. I need to do another lap…for the tractor, so it can cool down before I turn it off. That's logical. No. I need to get my ass across the road before I do something stupid like flirt with a minor. I don't have any time in my life for stupid crap. Just go across the road, Cash.

I pull up beside the little country house to tell the Jacksons I'm done and I'll be over to do it again. So I can catch a peek of their granddaughter again. *Damn it, Cash! What is wrong with you?* I hop off the tractor and onto the porch, and Mrs. Jackson's eyes light up. "Cash, we can't thank you enough for helping us out."

"It wasn't any problem, Mrs. Jackson. Let me know if you guys need anything else done over here. I'm pretty handy."

"I want you to meet my granddaughter, Bailey, if I can ever get her to look this way." She gives me a smile.

"There's always next time, I'll be across the road from here on out." I'm about to leave, but I notice the girl is at the edge of the flowerbed now, and I can't seem to make myself leave. I need to get laid worse than I thought if I'm lusting over an underage chick with big boobs. Maybe she's seventeen? Would that make ogling her any better? Hell, she'd still be jailbait. I need to get my ass out of here.

Bailey

As I come out of the shed, I mentally checklist all my tools. I've got my gloves and all the pruning tools I'll need for the rose bushes. The flowerbed mostly requires a good weeding.

Walking over to the flowerbed, I see why Granny loves her roses. They are beautiful and poetic from the tiniest bud to the fullest bloom. I remember being a little girl and following right behind Granny while she worked in her roses. The thorns never bothered her. I asked her once if they hurt her. She said, "Roses teach us to love with our whole heart, Bailey."

She snipped off the smallest white bud and handed it to me to smell. I loved smelling her roses. I would come out and give each one their own sniff while she laughed at me. I didn't understand why roses taught us to love at all. That was just silly to me, and must have been written on my young face. "Roses teach you that nothing is perfect in this world. To love someone, you love the whole person. The beautiful part of that person and the parts that have the thorns."

I looked at her all serious as I hung on her every word. "Granny, do I have thorns?"

She smiled at me, and scooped me into this big hug. She kissed my nose and shook her head. "Bailey, I believe you are the closest thing to perfect I've ever seen."

I beamed at her. I loved my granny. She always made me feel special, like all grandmothers do, I guess. We made matching bonnets to wear while we worked on the roses, but she helped me with mine. She gave me my own little plastic tools that I made a mess with while she worked.

I look toward the porch to make sure Papa is still in his rocking chair and see someone talking to Papa and Granny. He must be the neighbor's son. I'm a hot mess this morning so I'm going to introduce myself some other time when I'm cleaned up and presentable.

I weed the edge of the flowerbed and hope I'm not noticed. I can't see his face well enough to discern his features, but hot damn, that body! He lifts his shirt to wipe his forehead and I catch a glimpse of a chiseled torso. Bodies like his only exist in the books I read. Good Lord! Who moved across the street, Channing Tatum?

A thought dawns on me. I have the baby monitor so I turn it on.

"The yard looks so nice. You even edged everything and did the weed-eating. I would like to give you something for mowing the yard. Are you sure you won't take any money? Bailey does a good job, but she does so much for us already."

By the way Granny is talking, I think she's in love.

"Would you like some tea or water? Why don't you sit down here a minute and cool off?"

I bet she was a big flirt back in her day.

"Mrs. Jackson, I would love to stay and chat with the two of you but I have my own yard to get to. How about I come over for that glass of tea and sit out here another day?"

That deep voice with its thick drawl probably has panties dropping everywhere. A sexy southern accent laced with charm on a man, um that is hot. Makes me want to butter my butt and give it to him as a biscuit. When he gets on his small John Deere tractor and heads back across the street, I do hate to see him go. He is great eye candy. I guess I'll be spending more time outside from now on so I can let my eyes feast on him. Good thing that kind of candy is fat free.

I work another hour in the flowerbed pruning the dead buds off the bushes. Tonight, I'll turn on the sprinklers to give them a good watering. After I put away all my stuff, I help get Papa into the house then shower before I make them some lunch. I don't have the time for my long luxurious baths much anymore. Between housework, taking care of Papa and Granny and my social life, I barely have time to get my real job done. At least I can work from home, and the pay is enough to make my car payment, pay insurance, and give me a little spending money. Granny is always giving me five or ten dollars here and there for gas when I run

errands for them. I tell her I don't need the cash, but she says she knows how much money I make.

After I make their lunch, we all sit at the table to eat and chat. "I still have a lot of work to do in that flowerbed to get it back in shape for you, Granny."

Granny smiles. She has different smiles. If you know her well enough and you pay attention, they will tell you what she is thinking. This smile says she's about to pull something over on me.

"I invited our new neighbors, the Wilsons, to our picnic. That boy is so sweet, Bailey. Why didn't you come over and say hello?"

She is a sly one, but I'm on to her. "Granny, you know I'm dating Hendrix. Besides, I looked like something the cat drug in. You know I can't meet anybody looking like that."

"Bailey, it shouldn't have mattered how you looked if you weren't interested in him." She quirks an eyebrow and tries not to smile.

To know Granny is to love her.

Her cordless phone rings. *I'm saved.*

"Hello? Why haven't you called me?" She chuckles.

She asks that any time somebody in the family is on the other end. They could have called her just a couple of hours ago, but that would be too long for her. Nothing would please her more than to have all of her kids with her twenty-four seven. Now me, it would drive me crazy.

I load the dishwasher and clean up the mess from lunch. By the time I do the rest of the house cleaning and finish a couple of loads of laundry, I feel dirty again and I'm tired. No one tells you taking care of two little old people is so much work. Since both Papa and Granny are napping, I go for that luxurious bath I've been dreaming about.

With my e-reader and a glass of tea to sip on, I head off to my bathroom. Nothing is more relaxing than reading a good steamy book in a hot steamy tub. Sometimes I gets a little too hot when I read a juicy sex scene and I've got to take care of business. I can't help myself. A girl's gotta do what a girl's gotta do.

I shave all my necessary parts quickly in the shower, wash my hair then relax in the tub, letting the hot water relieve my sore muscles. With Luke Bryan on my iPod, a good story to read, and a glass of sweet tea sitting beside me, I'm in heaven. I fire up my reader. I can't wait to see what this hot country boy is up to next!

My phone dings with a text from Lizzie.

Lizzie: What did you and "A Joke" do last night?

Well, she's not getting the truth on that. She will end up giving me another lecture about how he is just using me so I type back.

Me: Nothing much. In the tub. I'll text when I'm out.

I lay here and let the hot water relax all of my muscles while the book relaxes my mind. Sometimes, I really want to try these things I read, but I don't think Hendrix will do anything that sounds country like reverse cowgirl, no matter how pleasurable it may be. He really isn't into kink. His idea of super kinky is car sex. I suggested a few things when we first slept together and he was appalled when I wanted to use a vibrator. I thought all guys were into the kinky shit. He does really like head. He really loves when I slob his nob, but I'm not really a fan. Blow jobs are something I do for him, because he enjoys them so much. That's just nasty—so thick and salty. How have I gone twenty-one years and not swallowed? Easy. I spit into a napkin afterward. While I'm doing the deed for Hendrix, all I can really think about is still being in position and choking when he comes. I panic that I'll die right there in that situation and they won't be able to get my mouth closed for my funeral. Morbid, I know. But that's my one hang up. Everybody has at least one hang up.

My mind wanders from my reading. I wonder where Hendrix will take me tonight. I still get butterflies when we go out. I never know where we are going or if I have on the right clothes. I love when he picks out what he wants me to wear. My anxiety eases when he says, "Wear the navy dress tonight," or "Wear that skirt and top."

Dressing for a man is fun and sensual. I follow the same ritual every time I get ready to go out with Hendrix. It's all part of the "Impeccable Bailey Plan." I layer on the lotion and powder then spritz the perfume followed by pulling my hair up so my neck looks elegant. Next is selecting the right lingerie to go underneath. Hendrix says there isn't anything sexier than a garter belt and thigh high stockings. They are uncomfortable, and the heat makes me avoid wearing them. I like to keep things simple for the most part, a thong and lacy bra. Plus the color sets the mood for the night. Normally, pastels put me in a romantic mood, but when I want to let out my inner kink goddess to play, I go for something racier like red and barely there! Tonight, I choose pink. If Hendrix were to add candlelight, rose petals, and silk sheets, I would be complete putty in his hands. How do you tell your boyfriend you want him to do that stuff for you? You can hint, leave clues, and mention stuff, but I think the romance gene is missing in some guys.

My phone dings again with another incoming text, pulling me from my wayward thoughts. I carefully lay down my e-reader and pick up my phone. Aww, it's Hendrix!

> *Hendrix: Hey, Sweetheart, how's your day?*

> *Me: Babe! It's great now that I'm talking with you!*

> *Hendrix: Aww, I hate to do this to you then.*

Is he cancelling?

> *Me: What?*

> *Hendrix: I have a function I have to attend with my parents. I won't be able to make our date.*

I haven't met his parents, but I'd be willing to if it means I can be with him.

> *Me: I can go with you as your date!*

> *Hendrix: I'm so sorry. They are making me take an old family friend.*

What? I type fast and furious.

> *Me: Babe, you're a grown man. They can't make you take someone else.*

> *Hendrix: Bay, you don't understand. This function means a lot for my future and they want me to be seen with this woman. Believe me, it won't mean a thing. I might be able to swing by your place but it would be really late.*

> *Me: I guess, I just don't understand why you have to take someone else. That makes me feel like you don't think I'm good enough or something.*

Bailey, he just said his parents are making him take this woman.

> *Hendrix: Love you, Sweetheart.*

> *Me: Yeah, you too, babe.*

Well, that is really disappointing. It's more than disappointing. It downright hurts. Being replaced by another woman is the absolute worst thing. Will I ever measure up to his parents' standards? They haven't even met me yet so they're being unfair by judging me already. I've tried so hard to be exactly what Hendrix wants, but I'm not sure if I will ever be good enough.

I'd wanted to go out dancing with Hendrix, but I'm not going to let this get me down. Instead, tonight will be ladies' night! It's on now! I call Lizzie. A little persuasion will be required to convince her to go to a country bar with me, but she will give in! Lizzie doesn't share my love of country music. She thinks it's too whiney. She jokes around with me saying that if their woman ain't leaving them then their dog is. Then she starts in with the songs about trucks. That girl just ain't got good sense. Doesn't she know how hot all these country singers are?

CASH

Man, today was another grueling day. Hot as hell. With the extra physical labor, my energy is zapped, but I need to get away from working on the house for a while, away from all of the demands of just being me. I want to cut loose and be someone else for a few hours, find a warm body to hold and release a little built up frustration. A hook-up isn't a bad thing, as long as you both know the game beforehand so no one gets hurt. I can't stand to see a woman get hurt over a man doing her wrong, I vow to never be a man like that. When I'm with a woman, I'm loyal to a fault. She knows she's the only one for me. We may not be in love, but I won't be with anyone else. I've seen enough and been through too much to ever cheat. If we aren't serious, then we both agree about that too. Some women have a hard time believing how much time I spend making sure we are on the same page, but treating women with respect is important, end of story. I've watched my mom go through hell, and be hospitalized for depression over my dad cheating on her. I could never do that to a woman. I never want to put anyone through what my mom has been through.

As I head out, I hear my mom call from the kitchen.

"Cash, before you leave will you run this peach cobbler over to the Jacksons' with this thank you note for the jelly?"

That was some good jelly, we had some this morning. "Sure mom, let me get my hat." I have a thing about my cowboy hat when I go out. I don't go out without it. I'm not a cowboy or anything. I just like my hat. "Did you make us some, too?"

"Do you ever think about anything other than food?" She swats my bottom and tells me to get across the street.

If she only knew what has been going through my mind today, she wouldn't be sending me to the Jacksons'. I wonder if I'll get another peek at their granddaughter.

I knock on the Jacksons' door figuring a few seconds will pass before one of them can answer. The door creaks open a tad then opens all the way. I almost drop the cobbler.

"Hey, you must be Cash. Come on in."

I apparently misjudged the Jacksons' granddaughter. She turns and walks to the kitchen shaking her ass a little. This isn't a little girl at all. This is a fine ass woman. I follow her, but not too close because I want a good view. She has on jean shorts which have those shiny things that draw all my attention to her ass, but I don't need any help with that as my eyes are there already. And damn, those boots she's wearing wakes "Johnny" up.

Bailey turns and catches me eyeing her ass. She snaps her fingers in front of my face. "Cash?"

"Uh, yeah, I'm Cash. You're Bailey?"

She smiles.

I swear it lights up the whole freaking room. I try to get control and quit making a fool of myself. "It's really nice to meet you. Uh, here is a cobbler. We wanted to thank y'all for the jelly." I'm going to shut up now, I feel at a loss for words.

"Oh gee, I'm sorry. Did she pawn one of those dreadful jars of jelly off on you?" She laughs.

Behind me, I hear someone else coming through the door.

"Bailey, you were right. He does have the body of…"

Bailey is shooting daggers at the girl behind me.

What? Go ahead and finish. I turn to see a blonde dressed similar to Bailey. She is cute as a button, but doesn't have nearly the same sex appeal as Bailey.

"Excuse me," the blonde says, "where are my manners? I'm Lizzie, Bailey's best friend slash sister. From the description I got, you're Cash."

This girl has a little smirk, and mischief in her eyes. I bet she likes to get Bailey's feathers all ruffled. These two together would be a lot to contend with. Heaven help anyone who tries. I wonder what all was said about me, but I feel a little more confident now.

"Are you ready, Lizzie?" Bailey asks.

"Yeah. Where are Granny and Papa? I wanted to go say "hi" real quick. Who is coming over to stay with them tonight anyway?" Lizzie asks, rocking back and forth on her heels.

I'm just standing here, looking stupid I'm sure. I would really like to get to know them, but I'm at a loss for words. I've never had a problem with small talk before.

"Mom is coming over until they go to bed. I just pray Papa has a good night until I make it back home." Bailey does her mouth in this little half smile while raising her eyebrows.

She is completely adorable. "If you just need someone who can come over if something happens," I say, "Mom is going to be home all night and she would be glad to be on call."

They both look at me wide-eyed. Bailey glances at Lizzie with her eyebrows raised and Lizzie shrugs, then nods.

Did they just have a whole conversation? They are good.

"Are you sure she wouldn't mind just being on standby?" Bailey asks. "I'll leave my number for her to call if there happens to be any problems."

I just want to pick her up and wrap her around myself. "It won't be any problem, I assure you. That's what neighbors do, look out for each other." I would like to look out a little more for this girl. I wonder how old they are. Up close, I can tell she is a little older than I thought, but not by much. I don't want to come right out and ask them. "So what are you two beautiful ladies up to tonight?" Maybe I can get some clues by asking the right questions. Who am I kidding? She is still going to be too young to fool around with.

Lizzie pipes up, "We're going to get our dance on!"

She does a couple of sexy moves, popping out her hips. These two need an escort wherever they're going. "Oh, where is there to dance around here?" I ask.

"We go over to Florence. Whichever country place is hopping the most is where we stay," Bailey says.

"Are you meeting a group or going by yourselves?" I want to keep her talking, in hopes that she might invite me to join them.

"It's ladies' night! No guys allowed." Lizzie leaves in search of her grandparents.

I guess that's my answer. Not invited.

Bailey hands me a couple pieces of paper and a pen. "My cell number is on the fridge. If you give me your home number, I'll give it to Granny. It makes me feel better having someone close by."

I scribble down our home number. "Here you go. I'll let you ladies go get to your dancing. Is there anywhere around here to meet people?" I ask Bailey as I hand her the number.

She scoffs, "No, there isn't anything to do around here but cow tipping and barn parties. Both you would rather be dead than caught doing."

"Don't you like living around here? I think this area is beautiful."

She rolls her eyes. "Oh please, we are out in the sticks!"

Lizzie comes back in the room and Bailey picks up her purse, saying, "Well, we need to leave, Cash. I'm sorry to run you off, but I don't get many of these kind of nights and I plan on making the most of it."

I guess that's my clue to leave.

Bailey

Journal Entry: Lizzie and I had a blast dancing at the club. She danced with everyone that asked. Guys were fine with that. They all loved two girls shaking their butts for them. That's where I drew the line though. Just dancing. If they got all handsy, I'd politely remove their hands, telling them I had a boyfriend. For the most part, guys backed off, but there is always one or two that you have to get serious with. Lizzie normally takes care of them. She can be downright ballsy and has been known to throw a punch or two if she feels like we are threatened.

Hendrix sends me a text about midnight telling me he's on his way, and I sit on the front porch because I don't want anyone waking up when he pulls up. I love that he's taking the time to come over to see me on his way home. It validates his desire to be with me.

When my love pulls up in front of the house, I practically break my neck getting to the car. I don't want him to blow his horn to get my attention. I have my trusty baby monitor, so I can hear if I'm needed.

"Hey, Babe, I'm so glad you came by to see me." I go ahead and climb in his lap because that's where I will end up anyway.

"You are? Let me see how excited you are to see me, Sweetheart."

I kiss him slowly, taking my time to show him he means the world to me, perusing his neck and that little place by his ear.

"That's nice, Bailey. Now show me you are really happy to see me." He unbuttons my shorts and tugs at them.

"Babe, you need help?" I snigger at his attempt. These are a little snug on purpose. Sitting like this doesn't help his efforts either.

"Why aren't you in something I bought you? You look like a redneck dressed like this. You know I like those little skirts. We don't have this kind of problem when you're in those."

I should have changed, I didn't even think about my attire. I was just excited he was coming over. He never sees me dressed like this. I'm sure it's a shock to him.

"Did you go somewhere dressed like this?"

He looks appalled.

I've slipped my shorts off and I'm licking his neck. "I went dancing with Lizzie, but that's all we did." I say between kisses. "We danced a few hours and then came home." I take off my tank top. Distraction is the name of the game right now.

"I don't like you going out with her. She's means to cause trouble."

He sounds so stern. He's jealous. All guys get jealous. I unbutton his shirt so I can drag my nails down his chest.

He takes one of my wrists and bends it back. "Don't fucking go out with Lizzie, especially to clubs."

"Ow! Hendrix, that hurts."

He went to clubs with us in college. That is where the verbal jabs started between the two of them. Lizzie was… Let's say a free spirit. Hendrix liked to vocalize his disgust of how much her spirit gave things away for free.

He bends my wrist a little more. *Shit!* Pain radiates down my arm, and for a split second my wrist feels like it's about to snap. His veins pop out on his hand from gripping so hard. Then he releases my wrist inch by inch, watching for my reaction. When he releases my wrist enough that I can pull away, I clutch it to my chest. I am stunned. He has never laid a hand on me before and I'm no longer in the mood for a visit much less screwing around in a car. "Don't ever fucking do that to me again, Hendrix." I move to get in the passenger seat.

He grabs me by the hips. "Where do you think you're going, little girl?" he says smiling.

He's playful again. More like the Hendrix I know and love. He kisses my neck then runs the tip of his tongue along my collarbone.

"I didn't mean to hurt you, let me make it up to you." He rips off another pair of Victoria Secret's undies and rubs on me.

Instantly, my inner kink goddess says, "Hello, did someone come to play with me?"

"Give me that pussy of yours." He puts two fingers inside of me.

I can't believe he expects me to give him some after all of that, but dear Aunt Margaret, if I don't start to move. I kiss him like I will never get enough.

"See, I knew you would succumb to me, Sweetheart. You need this as much as I do."

I break our kiss and unbutton his pants. He rises up a little so I can pull his pants down. I want him inside of me. I need to ride him, hoping this time will be magical. Maybe, just maybe, he can last long enough for me? Who am I kidding? I need to make this as fast as possible in case I'm needed inside. I reach into his boxers and take out his erection, positioning it so I can slide down. He reaches down and reclines the seat all the way back. He places his hands on my hips to help me move. My mind has shut down. I'm in my zone. Nothing else matters, but getting him to his release. My toes are curling and I dig my fingers in his hair pulling it. I need faster. I need more. Maybe I can have my own. He rubs his thumb in my wetness then circles on my bundle of nerves—those achingly slow circles. I tingle, and he intensifies the pressure of his thumb. My little man in the boat throbs He rows and rows his boat, and my nipples tighten. I'm so close, but my boat doesn't get to finish the race.

Hendrix finds his own release, and I'm squeezing him of every drop he has to offer. I let out a tiny moan of frustration, which he thinks is my release. I let him believe it so he thinks everything is kosher. He tried really hard to help me get to my pleasure point when we first got together. He would get so mad whenever I told him I needed him to push me a little further into my own release. At first, I didn't hide that I didn't orgasm, but I quickly learned revealing that was a problem for him.

Once he comes, he never pursues anything further which leaves me teetering on the edge of ecstasy and absolute frustration. I've never orgasmed with him. So my motto is fake it until you make it. After the first few times we had sex, he bought me the exerciser for doing Kegels and told me that my "twat" was the size of Bolivia, and that was the reason I could never get off with him. When I got mad he said he was just joking, of course. I wanted to tell him if he was the size of a man and not a baby, things would be a lot easier, but I didn't argue. Now, I just fake it. I'll just finish the job inside. I have fresh batteries.

His head's laying on the headrest. He's spent now.

"Bay, seriously," he sighs, "best car fuck ever. I knew you wanted me, you just needed to be reminded."

I give him one more kiss, "Every time with you Hendrix is my best time ever." I keep the disappointment out of my voice. He needs this from me. He likes his ego stroked. Climbing back over into my seat, I take what's left of my lace panties and clean up as much as possible. I take out a plastic baggie and a couple wipes from the glove box. Needless to say, this happens a lot so he's prepared. After I finish, I put everything in the baggie. Heaven help me if I make a mess in this car.

Hendrix treats his BMW M4 convertible better than he does me. I love his car, white with red leather interior. He babies this car, having it hand washed every couple of days. That's why he doesn't want to go down our gravel driveway; he is scared the car will get scratched. It is sexy, but I wish he would treat me as well as he does his car. When I asked to drive it, he totally freaked. Asshat, it's just a car. A very nice expensive sports car!

From the monitor, I hear Papa get up. Duty calls. I slip on my shorts and shirt and hop out of the car. "I'll be right back, babe."

Hendrix cranks his engine, rolls his window down "Fuck it, Bailey, you never have time for me. I'm sick of this shit." He is almost screaming at me.

"All you came over here for was a quick fuck, you got what you want, so go!" I point down the street.

He squeals his tires.

I'm left standing on the side of the road, wondering when I will learn to keep my temper down. As much as I love him, he infuriates me sometimes.

From the monitor, I hear Granny has managed to settle Papa down during our exchange. From across the street, I hear, "Does he always treat you that way?"

With the full moon, I can see Cash's outline sitting on a tailgate. What business is this of his? Temper. Bailey, get your temper under control before you say anything. As I walk across the road, so I can talk to him without raising my voice, I wonder how much of a show he saw.

"We like to joke around," I tell him.

Cash is drinking a beer. He reaches behind him and gets one out, offering it to me.

"No thanks, can't stand the stuff. I do think I need something stronger though." I laugh softly.

He pats the space next to him. "Hop up here and tell me why you need a strong one."

He sounds so sweet. Why can't Hendrix be this sweet? I check the light on the monitor making sure I'm still in range. "No reason other than it would help me get my Z's. Did you have fun tonight? Get into any trouble in this big metropolis?"

"You're right, there isn't much to do here, but I love the peace and quiet out here when my neighbors aren't getting their groove on in a tiny sports car." He chuckles.

I'm glad it's dark out here because I can feel my face flame. "Ooops, sorry about that. I'll try not to scream out my dirty deeds from now on." I'm embarrassed. I'm not used to anyone being over here listening to me or possibly seeing the latest episode of Southern Girls Gone Wild.

"This isn't any of my business, but from the little bit that I know about you, you deserve better than that," he whispers, his head really close to mine. "Is that your boyfriend, or just someone you're seeing?"

Heaven help me, his voice sends shivers down my spine. What voodoo does he possess?

"He's my boyfriend. We've been dating almost a year. He isn't always that way." I pause as I think of what to say next. "Are you seeing anyone?" I tell myself I'm making polite conversation here, not that I need to know or that it even matters.

"Not yet, but I plan on it."

I bet his voice alone has girls throwing themselves at him.

"Oh? Do tell? Did you meet someone tonight?" I could sit here and listen to him all night.

"Yeah, you could say that." He takes a pull of his beer.

"Good, everybody needs somebody." I hop off the tailgate and wipe my hand across my butt to remove any dirt. "I need to get back across the road. My neighbor woke me up early this morning mowing the yard." I smirk. "And Granny will get me up early to take her to church." I yawn. I can't help it.

"Goodnight then, it was great talking to you. Don't be a stranger." He tips back his beer then hops down himself.

"Goodnight, sleep tight, don't let the bed bugs bite." I throw my palm over my face at the childish saying I exchange every night with Granny. "Sorry, it's late, forgive my blabbering." Why do I continue to do this to myself? Open my mouth and spew this kind of crap?

"See you later?" he asks.

"Sure, I'll see you around." As I walk back to the house, my fight with Hendrix is the furthest thing from my mind. Maybe when I get out "Old Faithful" tonight, I won't be thinking of him either. Maybe I'll be thinking of a taller, better-built southern talker. OMG! Did I really just admit to myself Cash is much sexier than Hendrix? No, I didn't!

CASH

I need to stay away from her. How will that be possible living right across the street? She's probably at least five years younger than me. That's a good reason to stay away. That, and she has a boyfriend. I don't mess around with anyone in relationships. I can tell without even meeting him he's a prick. She needs to know the difference between a man and a boy. That prick is a boy because a man would not have screwed her in a car, threw her out, then left. I have plenty of reasons to stay away. So, why can't I stop thinking about her? She seems so sweet and funny. She is drop dead gorgeous on top of all that. I'm pissed off that asshole doesn't realize how lucky he is to have her.

I make my way to bed, but I can't get my mind off the little brunette beauty across the way. I truly want to make her mine although I don't know what about her that makes me feel this way. I can't put my finger on it. I have a sixth sense that being with her would be right. So, as far as I can tell, I have two choices here. Find someone else to occupy my mind, or get to know her better and maybe she will see that guy she is with is a jerk and doesn't deserve her. Mom's words ring in my mind, "One day you are going to meet a girl, and she is going to smile at you or laugh, and you will know she is the one." God, that laugh will forever be in my mind.

I think we need to head to church tomorrow, too. Mom needs guidance and who knows there could be a whole church full of Baileys. Plus, everybody needs more religion, prayer has never hurt anyone. Maybe I will get some clarity from the great one above on what path I should be on.

Bailey

"Bailey, get up or we will be late for church!"

Granny is at the foot of my bed. Heavens to Betsy, is it already time to get up?

"I'm up, Granny, I'm up." I sigh, rolling over to look at the clock. It's already 9:15, and she will want to leave by 9:45. I jump up and head to the bathroom. I hate to be in a rush but it is what it is. After showering and drying my hair, I get dressed. I don't have time for my full makeup routine, but I put on some mascara and lip gloss for good measure. The mascara will at least make me look awake. I don't know why I'm worried about how I'll look anyway. No one will be at church, other than a few family members and people I've grown up with my whole life. Who cares what they think anyway? They have all seen me at my worst, plus I can go without makeup every once in a while.

I wear my navy dress today and my boots. I'm so glad they go with everything. I normally wear sandals with my skirts when I go out with Hendrix because I like him to see my toes all cute, but I really love my boots. Wearing boots is in style around here, for my old crowd anyway. I think it's cute to wear them with dresses.

"Alright, are you guys ready?" I announce, coming out of my room in a blur. Granny is hanging up the phone after talking to someone. She picks up her Bible and gets her walker. Papa has his cane and he looks all dapper in his suit and tie. He loves going to church and talking to other men close to his own age. I'm all for any little amount of pleasure we can give him these days. Sometimes he seems depressed or lonely, and I can't always figure out exactly what will make him happy again.

We get into their older model Buick. I don't like driving their car because it is so big and I can't park as it is, but taking the Buick makes things easier for both of them. When I'm at the end of the driveway, I notice Cash is leaving too.

Granny waves then points in the direction we're going.

That's odd. Why in the world would she be pointing? I pull onto the road and he pulls out behind me.

"Bailey, don't run off and leave him. He is going to follow us to church."

Say what? Why wasn't I told this earlier? I look like shit today. "Why is he following us to church?" I ask.

"Everybody needs a home church. Margie was going to come too, but she is under the weather this morning."

Great. Just great. "I wish you had told me this earlier so I could have looked decent. I look horrible today. Look at these dark circles under my eyes." I flip down my visor and my face is not a pretty sight. Dear Lord, why is he coming to church today of all days? He is going to look so good. Get it together, Bailey! I think I have some powder in my purse, I'm feeling around for the compact while keeping my eyes on the road. I feel it! Thank heavens! I rub the sponge under my eyes. This won't take away all of my flaws, but every little bit of coverage I can get will help.

"Bailey, you're dating Henry. You don't care what other boys think, or that's what you always tell me."

I'm glad she isn't a mind reader. I laugh to myself. "I am dating Hendrix, I just hate for new people seeing me this way, and you know first impressions and all." See, I'm keeping my brain sharp. I'm thinking on my feet.

"If you say so. I thought you would have been more concerned last night when you had on those shorty shorts."

She doesn't try to hide her smirk. What has gotten into her today? I do love to see her so tickled, even if it's at my own expense.

Cash meets us at the entryway of the church and is ever the gentleman by opening the door for us. He's positively hot this morning.

Granny beams at him. "Thank you, Cash. You are such a sweet boy."

He grins back at her.

Oh brother, they are making me wanna puke.

"You're welcome, Mrs. Jackson. You're pretty sweet yourself."

Really? I roll my eyes. He's trying to impress us with manners and a good ol' boy attitude. Get real.

I lean over and whisper, "You're laying on the charm thick this morning aren't ya, Cash?" He has a fine looking ass in those tight Wrangler jeans, and that blue shirt sure brings out the blue in his eyes, not that I'm looking. I don't mean to be, but it's right next to me. I'm not blind, and looking doesn't hurt. I love Hendrix and we are meant to be together, I keep reminding myself.

The church service takes forever. Our pastor is always long winded, but he is really on a roll today. Cash is sitting entirely too close to me. His cologne smells yummy, not that I care, and I can feel the heat radiating off of his body. My own body is betraying me and I have to fan myself to cool down.

After three stanzas of Amazing Grace, we are finally dismissed. Amen. Everyone comes up to meet Cash, especially the single women.

"They smell new blood." I lean in and whisper. I nudge Cash on his arm. *Get a life, ladies.*

He is cordial to everyone, young and old alike. That's life in a small town. Everyone knows you and all of your business. When someone new comes to town, they become all the talk. By dinnertime, everyone will know all there is to know about Cash, even if it's all hearsay.

"Thank y'all for inviting me to come to church with you today. I think mom would love it here. May I take you guys to lunch?" Cash asks.

There is no way I can go to lunch with this guy. He is bad news for me. He *makes* me look into those beautiful eyes, and practically flaunts his ass in front of me. Not that I'm interested, no, I'm dating someone.

"We would love too, but I'm afraid we need to get back home. Papa doesn't do well with changes. Church is about the only place we can get him to go." I'm making this up because Papa could go, but Cash is hot. Plain and simple. If I'm around him with all of his smooth talking, I may give in to temptation, and I'm dating Hendrix.

"Maybe some other time then," he says.

I wish he wouldn't smile at me with that panty-dropping smile. "Yeah maybe." I turn and make a beeline for the door.

CASH

Going to church today was both a blessing and hell. I'm always blessed because between the sermon and the old hymns, I feel balanced. The hell was sitting beside Bailey the whole service. She was distracting me with her every move. The way she kept putting small strands of hair behind her ear. When she crossed her legs and her dress would ride up a little. She would fan herself, and I would get a whiff of her scent. Then her fidgeting and sighing kept me aware she was right beside me. I didn't need to be constantly reminded how much I wanted to touch her.

She looked amazing in this navy dress that was a couple of inches above the knees. I have to say her cowboy boots with that dress is a huge turn on. Sexy as hell. Her hair was pulled up in some sort of bun that showed off her neck, making me want to run my tongue up her neck to watch her shiver. She didn't have a lot of crap on her face today so I got to see her natural, fresh-faced beauty, which made me desire her all the more.

I don't just want her physically though, I want to get to know her better and see more of who she is on the inside. I see the way she takes care of her grandparents—out of love, not obligation. That makes her even more beautiful to me.

That prick she's seeing doesn't deserve her. After how he treated her last night, I want to kick his ass. I saw exactly what happened in that car. He took what he wanted then left her, screaming at her like she was a dog. I don't see how anyone can treat ladies like that. I don't have a bad temper, but with him, I wouldn't be able to control myself. I want to teach him a fucking lesson. But that probably wouldn't get me into her good graces. My best course of action is to be a friend right now—a friend who throws out sexual innuendos and wants to fuck her ten ways to Sunday. No, I need to keep our interactions platonic until she wises up and gets rid of that jerk. Why do the assholes of the world get the best girls? Why are girls attracted to guys who treat them like shit? I'll never understand that. Men are not meant to understand women. Just when you think you have one figured out, she changes her mind.

Bailey

I don't work long in the rose bed because of the heat and I'm tired from last night. Managing the undercurrent of Hendrix's mood is exhausting and I need to relax. I pack it in for the day and come in to get a bath; I have a book to finish. The sexy cowboy of my dreams is waiting for me on my Kindle. I love reading because it takes me to another place and time. I've also learned some new sexual positions, not that it has done me any good.

The bath is warm and cozy and pulls all the tension from my muscles. The cowboy is hot and all alpha male. He is about to put this woman in her place and get busy with her when my phone dings with a message from Hendrix.

Dinner tonight at the club, I'll pick you up.

I ignore his message by escaping back into my book, but a nagging thought keeps me from being able to focus on the words on the screen. I have never been to dinner at the "club." Unable to resist the opportunity, I reply, Sure, what time are you going to pick me up?

There isn't any time to be wasted here. Good thing I've already got everything shaved and my hair washed. I jump out of the tub and wrap the towel around me. I have no idea what to wear and I hate to call Lizzie to ask for her help because she will give me shit, but I need advice.

"Hey, girl, whatcha doing?" I ask once she answers. She starts talking so fast, I can barely make out what she is saying.

"...then she bent over and the whole damn dress split up the back. She turned around to see what happened and lost her balance, fell flat on her ass! It was EPIC, Bailey!"

She is laughing so hard I'm scared she is going to crack a rib. "Who are you talking about, Lizzie?" I inspect my manicure. The color is chipping. Maybe she'll want to go get mani-pedis? My mind is running through my beauty routine at ninety miles per hour.

"Have you not been listening to me? Jesus, Bailey, what has gotten into you?" She giggles. "Hilary!"

Now that is funny.

Lizzie is a bridesmaid in Hilary's cousin's wedding. Unfortunately, Hilary is the maid of honor and has been giving Lizzie hell. Back in high school, Hilary was the kind of girl who thought her shit didn't stink. She had the perfect hair, the perfect body, wore only designer clothes and had every guy in school wrapped around her finger. She knew they all wanted to go out with her to screw her, but she used that to her advantage. She tormented us saying we were trashy, or spreading rumors about us. How we didn't kill her in high school is beyond me. I'm glad Lizzie's dealing with her now and not me.

Funny thing is, Hilary gained the freshmen fifteen twice over and it all ended up in her ass. Baby's got back—ha ha. She has enough to balance a glass of water on her bottom but is oblivious to the fact. This wedding has been a fountain of entertainment for us, and Lizzie calls me after every encounter to update me on the current ass-a-demic.

"Really? What did she have on this time? No, don't tell me, I don't even want to know what the dress looked like." If I laughed any harder, I'd probably pee my pants. We really should stop with all of this childishness, but if you saw how she treated us in high school, you would have prayed for her ass to grow two times its regular size too. Praise the Lord. We really aren't mean girls or anything, at least not too much.

"Hey, what should I wear to the country club for dinner? I mean it's not like it's a special occasion or anything, but I've never been there and I don't know how dressed up I should get." I can picture Lizzie rolling her eyes.

"Don't tell me 'A Joke' is finally introducing you to Mommy and Daddy Dearest. How nice."

"They aren't going to be there, just a cozy little dinner for two." I knew asking her wouldn't be a good idea. She hates him.

She lets out a long sigh. "I've never been either, Bay, I would wear something I felt comfortable in, like a church dress. I don't know what you see in him anyway. He is trying to change you."

I'm tired that every one of our conversations involving Hendrix turns in to her bashing him. "Lizzie, not today okay, I don't have a lot of time. Hey, let's get together tomorrow and get our toes and nails done." I'm the master at changing the subject! "I'll even buy you a Chi Tea Latte. We can have a girls' day. I'll see if mom can stay with Papa and Granny. That way we won't have to rush. Doesn't that sound awesome?" We make plans for tomorrow and say our goodbyes. I still don't know what to wear. I stand in front of my closet with my hair wrapped in one towel and the other towel wrapped around me.

A soft knock sounds at my door, "Who is it?"

Granny is standing in my doorway with her walker, and I laugh that she still thinks of me as a little girl she has to come to check on. Granny will know what I should wear. She is one fashionable little lady, and she may have worked hard her whole life, but she still looks so good. Her skin is plump and almost free of wrinkles. She says it is due to her cold cream. All she wants every Christmas is a jar of that "cold cream." I asked her the name of it last year. She just went and got her jar of Oil of Olay. The cheap pink stuff. I think her good skin must be due to living right and good genes. I'm glad I have those genes too.

"What are you doing, Bailey?"

"Come on in, Granny. I'm trying to figure out what to wear for dinner at the country club."

Granny walks over to my closet, and looks into it with me.

"Lord, I haven't been there since your Papa's retirement party, which was when you were just a little thing. I know, how about that sweet little dress you wore to Sadie's wedding back in the spring? You looked so darling in it." She points at my white dress with all of the lace.

The dress spoke to me as I walked by the sales rack when I was shopping with Granny for her dress to wear to the wedding.

"You think that will be okay for the country club? Sadie's wedding was sort of casual with her wanting all of us cousins to wear boots."

She nods. "You look so beautiful in it, no one will even notice that it is a little casual. Bailey, I want to get to know Hank better. Let's invite him for dinner tomorrow night."

She is too sharp for this name game she is playing, "I'm on to you, I know which one of you has the dementia, remember?" I tap my temple. "I was going to see if Mom can stay the afternoon tomorrow because Lizzie and I want to have a girls' day." I take the dress out and hold it up for inspection. The dress is white lace over a white cotton mini dress. I'm so glad I've gotten some sun the last few weeks because the lace-only sleeves will show off my tan. I pair the dress with the same brown belt I wore to the wedding. I hope it doesn't make it look too casual. Without the belt, the dress just hangs funny.

"That sounds like a fun day, I'll call Kathy Rose to see if she has plans for tomorrow afternoon. That will give me some time with her." She wanders off to make plans with my mom.

I hurry back into the bathroom to get my hair dry and finish applying my makeup. I do a light smoky look tonight because I love how the color makes my mossy green eyes pop. I don't want the shadow too dark though, so I add another swish of mascara. The rest of my makeup is subdued. I want to look classy, not trampy. It's all about the image you portray.

I look at my phone, still nothing back from Hendrix. I check to make certain my text went through. Yep and it has been read, too. I throw my phone back on my bed. Since I probably don't have time to straighten my hair, I throw it up in a messy bun. Lizzie thinks having my hair up makes me look more sophisticated. It does look good up this way, even if I do say so myself.

I am contemplating shoes when I hear the doorbell. Please tell me that isn't Hendrix. I put on my boots. I step back and look at myself in the full-length mirror. The boots really do look best with the dress and belt. I put on some chunky bracelets to keep the accessories simple. I hear Granny calling my name. *Earrings.* I need earrings with my hair up like this. I hear a knock at my door. "Come in."

Granny comes in. "That pretty boy is here to pick you up, I'll tell him you need a couple of minutes."

Granny can hardly contain her laughter. She has been around Lizzie way too much if she is picking up on this name calling business. "Hey, watch it or it will be the old folks' home for you." I wink at her.

Her laughter bounces around the room as she closes the door behind her. I can hear her back in the kitchen now talking to Hendrix. I take one last look in the mirror and grab my purse.

"It's in a couple of weeks, right out here in our own backyard. We do this every year, it's just one huge picnic," Granny says.

No, please tell me she is not inviting Hendrix to the family reunion. No, no, no. I round the corner, putting a smile on my face as Hendrix answers Granny.

"That sounds nice. I will check my schedule and let Bailey know if I can make it."

His eyebrows are lowered like he's frowning, but his lips are curved up, at least on one side. He gives a smug half laugh.

"Bailey, there you are, don't you look pretty, honey." Granny tilts her head.

She gives me a gentle smile, and I look over at Hendrix dressed in dress pants and a jacket. He looks so classy. I feel like a country bumpkin. The very thing I have been trying to get away from over the last couple of years. His hair is the perfect shade of sandy brown, and he wears it short. The front is gelled so it stands up just a little. He is what I think of when someone mentions Prince Charming. His eyes are the color of caramel, and a hint of green is always in his eyes when he looks at me. I love being wanted by him, like he needs me. But that's not the case tonight. He looks repulsed.

"You aren't dressed yet?" he exhales and runs a hand across his mouth as he rocks back on his feet.

"I'm ready, or at least I thought I was ready." I look at my feet. I glance at Granny and her face has gone full on hellfire and brimstone. I feel really queasy. Like I'm going to be sick. I need to get Hendrix out of here before Granny does something I will regret. She looks all sweet and innocent, until you do or say something about one of her kids then all bets are off.

"At least change your shoes, Bailey. We are going to the club not the rodeo."

I grab his hand, pulling him with me to go change my shoes. I bite my lip a little hoping it looks as sexy on me as the authors make it sound in the books. I probably need to practice in the mirror some more because based on his pissed off look it doesn't appear to be working.

"I have some sandals, will that work?" I smile as sweetly as possible.

He glances at his watch, rolls his eyes and looks at my boots again. He lets out a long breath. "Just forget it, Bailey. We are already going to be late."

He smiles showing those perfect white teeth. I look into his eyes that are normally so beautiful, and I get the impression that I'm so inadequate. My heart hitches a tad. I can't believe someone like him even wants to go out with me. I will do everything in my power to keep him. I want out of this life and this town. Being with a man like Hendrix will ensure that I will be able to live a better life.

We step outside. Immediately, he pulls me in for a kiss. I stand on my tiptoes and press my lips to his as I wrap my arms around his waist. My dress rises a couple of inches, and he uses the opportunity to grip my ass beneath my dress. His tongue eagerly peruses my mouth. He is always aggressive when he kisses me, showing me how much he wants me. I shift to move away and he pulls me in tighter. See, he's making up for not liking my boots. Once he has me dazed with lust, he lets me go and walks to the car without another word. I am left standing, aroused and breathing hard.

After he gets into his car, he looks over at me. "Well, come on, Bailey, I told you we were in a hurry."

I go to my side of the car and slide in next to him.

CASH

I've been looking for a good excuse to go over to the Jacksons' all afternoon when I finally come up with offering to refinish those old rocking chairs. I'm ready to walk across the street to present my offer when that prick pulls into the driveway and disappears into the house. I wait, hoping he's only stopping by for a few moments. I pace from the driver side to the passenger seat of my old work truck. I am rolling up the window when Bailey comes out of the house on his arm. I watch as he stops and kisses her long and hard then leaves her standing in the driveway while he climbs his ass into the joke of a car. Good, he is leaving. He calls back to her, and she walks around and gets into the car. He didn't even get her door. I thought every man got the door for his lady, at least during the honeymoon period. I'm not in any hurry now to go over to the Jacksons' so I amuse myself with the thoughts of how I can treat Bailey better, and what I would do if she were mine.

An hour later, I stroll across the street to tell the Jacksons what I have in mind. As I'm about to knock on the door, I hear a crash from inside. Then Mr. Jackson starts hollering something I can't understand, but he sounds panicked. Something is wrong! Instead of knocking, I go on in and see Mrs. Jackson on the floor. Mr. Jackson is bent down beside her. I immediately dial 911, but I'm not one to take chances. I bend down to check Mrs. Jackson's vitals while I talk to the 911 operator. I look over at Mr. Jackson and see tears in his eyes. "Mr. Jackson, what happened?"

He looks at me, his eyes wide. "Who are you?"

I stick out my hand. "I'm Cash Wilson, I just moved in across the street, sir."

He nods and shakes my hand.

"Do you know what happened to your wife, sir?"

He shakes his head. "Will she be okay?"

"Her pulse is weak and she's unconscious, but she is breathing." *Thank God she's breathing.* No need to start CPR. "Is there someone we should call?"

He pauses a few seconds then hands me a notebook. I look inside and see phone numbers written down. I look down the list for Bailey's number, but the names aren't in alphabetical order so I call the number at the top, "Hello, may I speak with Kathy Rose, please?"

"This is Kathy."

The woman answering the phone sounds puzzled.

"What is going on? And are my parents okay? Where is Bailey?"

I hear fear in her voice. "Ma'am, I'm Cash Wilson, I moved in across the street a few days back. I came over a few minutes ago and heard your mom fall. She is unconscious and has a faint heartbeat. I think she might have had a heart attack. I've called for an ambulance and they are on their way." I can hear her telling someone else what I just told her.

"Oh, no! Where's Bailey?" She starts to cry.

"Ma'am, I saw her leave an hour ago and there doesn't appear to be anyone else here but Mr. and Mrs. Jackson. I hear the ambulance now, and we should know more in a few minutes." The paramedics come barreling into the house, and I get shoved against the wall while they take their assessment of Mrs. Jackson's condition. I notice Mr. Jackson's wringing his hands, his eyes wild with fear. The paramedics ask to which hospital to take Mrs. Jackson. I give them Kathy's instructions and they load up Mrs. Jackson.

Kathy asks me if I can bring her dad because he has dementia and can't be left alone. I have to physically lift Mr. Jackson into my truck, but he's not very big, neither one of them are. Mr. Jackson is about five six and he might be one hundred forty pounds. Mrs. Jackson is even smaller than he is. She can't even be five feet tall. I close his door for him and walk to my side of the truck and get in.

"Thank you," he says with a nod. "Are we going to go to the hospital too? She needs me up there with her." He rubs the back of his neck.

"Yes, sir, we'll get there as fast as we can," I say.

On the way to the hospital, I call mom to let her know what is going on. Now that I know Mr. Jackson has dementia, I'll research the condition so I know what to expect when I'm keeping an eye on him. I'll ask Kathy to tell me how to best handle Mr. Jackson's fears when he is struggling. Having the woman you love laid out in the middle of the floor is scary enough, let alone having a stranger bust through the door. "Mr. Jackson, are you okay over there?"

He looks over at me. "You know I used to work at an orange packing company in Florida. And so did my wife. I made the boxes to begin with then I became the boss over the women. Addie worked on the line checking the oranges making sure they were good enough to eat..."

I guess he is lost in his own thoughts.

"You know we have been married over sixty-five years?"

Being married that long is almost unheard of these days and is something to be proud of. "Is that right, Mr. Jackson? You must be doing

something right. Are you going to let me in on your secret?" Maybe getting him talking will ease his mind.

"She is always right, that is all you have to know."

I can't help but laugh.

He grins, too. "Always say 'yes dear' and you will stay married forever. That is the secret."

That's kind of funny. I bet he was a lot of fun before he got sick.

He looks out the window, "Do you think she'll be okay?"

I really don't know what to say. Do I reassure him? If something does transpire, what will happen to him? "I'm sure the doctors will do everything possible for her."

His eyes get glossy with tears, "I don't want to live without her. I won't be able to go on with half a heart."

What do I say to that? This feels too deep and I'm not good at this kind of stuff, but I feel like he needs some kind words right now. "Mr. Jackson, I think you've been very lucky to have someone so special in your life that you feel like you can't live without them. I don't think everyone gets that lucky, sir."

"I am the luckiest man to ever walk the face of this Earth. I've spent my whole life loving the woman of my dreams." He wipes his eyes. "You know what, I think you might have a good head on your shoulders, and I like you. So I'm going to let you in on another little secret."

I glance over at him, and he looks so serious, "Please tell me, I need all the help I can get." I can't wait to hear this. I love the advice the older generation likes to dish out. Some of it is useful and some of it is genuinely funny.

"You need to be with someone who can't stay mad at you for very long, and is a little afraid of losing you. You need to feel that way for them too. When you find that then she is the one you say 'yes dear' to. When you're that way with each other, it makes all the ups and downs in life bearable."

I think this man could be a genius. I laugh lightly. "Is that how is goes, Mr. Jackson? I'll have to remember that."

He gazes at me with sad eyes then looks out the window again. I guess he's returning to his own little world.

I pull up in front of the hospital bay and head around the truck to help him out. I walk into the emergency room to help him find his family. At the nurses' desk when I ask about Mrs. Jackson, I hear someone call out.

"Daddy, we're over here."

I look around and see a younger version of Mrs. Jackson. I help guide Mr. Jackson over there as he is a bit unsteady on his feet.

"Hello, I'm Cash, the Jacksons' neighbor." I offer my hand to the lady.

She shakes my hand and gives me a side hug. "I can't thank you enough for all of your help today. I'm Kathy. Mom calls me Kathy Rose. She told me all about you and your mom the other day. Already, she's very fond of you two. This is my best friend, Kate."

Kate gives me a hug too and says her pleasantries.

"Over there is the rest of our crew, you can meet them later." Kathy gives a small smile.

"It's nice to meet you, Kathy, Kate, but I wish it was under other circumstances. Mr. Jackson seems to be awfully worried," I say.

Kathy turns toward Mr. Jackson and talks to him. I guess I should stay at least a few minutes. I would feel bad dropping him off and running. About thirty minutes later, a nurse comes out to tell us Mrs. Jackson has suffered a heart attack and they are moving her up to surgery.

Everyone gets up to walk upstairs, and Kathy says to Kate, "Lizzie went to get Bailey from the country club and I swear, if that jerk causes problems, I will kill him myself. I don't see what Bailey sees in him, I can't believe she is with someone like him."

"Kathy, she will come to her senses, but if you try to keep her from him she'll only want to be with him more and you'll end up with him as your son-in-law. Lizzie said she's going to talk to Bailey soon." Kate says.

They don't like that prick either. That's the best news I've heard all day. Not that I'm eavesdropping, but they aren't whispering.

Everyone shuffles upstairs with worried looks on their faces, and I can feel the tension radiating off everyone. "Is there anything I can go get for anyone or do for y'all?"

They all shake their heads.

"Thank you for just being here, Cash," Kathy says.

I walk over and sit by Mr. Jackson to see if I can get him to talk to me. "Mr. Jackson, how are you holding up? Do you need a coke?"

He is looking at the floor. "Oh, I need to pay you for bringing me up here." He stands up reaching into the back of his jeans pocket for his wallet. "I don't know where my wallet is, do you know where it is?"

He looks concerned.

"I bet with us rushing to get up here, you forgot it at home. Besides, you don't owe me anything at all. Neighbors are supposed to take care of each other, right?"

He is looking at the floor again, and Kathy and Kate have stopped their conversation to look at me. So have all the other family members. I feel a little out of place.

10

Bailey

I turn on the radio to our local country station, and Hendrix looks over at me like I've killed his puppy. I know all too well, he isn't fond of my taste in music. *Let me see if I can change his mind.* Unbuckling my seatbelt, I reach over and unzip his pants. I see his mood is changing already. I pull him out of his boxers and start stroking him gently. "You don't like country music?" I give him my best pouty voice. "Would you like it better like this?" I lay my head down in his lap and give the tip of his cock a little flick. "Are you liking my music any better now?" I taste him, teasing him. I play around licking the vein hard.

He is enjoying this. He has one hand in my hair and the other on the steering wheel. He urges me to take him in my mouth by pushing my head down. I wrap my lips around him and move down his length. He moans and I feel him pulsing in my mouth. He keeps his hand on my head applying more pressure.

I lick and suck for what seems like forever. I let him get very close to finishing then pull off him with a pop. I'm being mischievous. I know that's not all he wants from me. I've heard what he wants several times. I just can't bring myself to "finish" the job.

"That might work one day if you would ever swallow."

He's agitated after that. Seriously? Will anything other than me swallowing please him?

"I don't like that, Hendrix. I told you that." I say softly as I put him back together. I sit back in my seat and look out the window.

"Just this one time, Bailey, finish what you start for fuck's sake."

I should Google and learn how to give better blowjobs. I want to please him but apparently I don't do a good job. I never had any complaints before, but Hendrix is never satisfied. I look over at him. Should I finish him? I unzip him again. I'm not as playful this time as I take him in my mouth. I'm focused on the task at hand and hope this doesn't take long. I wrap my hand around his shaft and pump to make this quicker. I make little noises so he will feel the vibrations and hopefully lose control sooner rather than later. He doesn't take long. In a few short minutes, he spurts in my mouth. I swallow and gag a tad because it's thick, but it doesn't taste as bad as I thought it would. I sit back up and wipe my lips with my fingers. I look at him expectantly.

"Next time, be more careful with your fucking teeth."

I know he didn't just say that. I buckle my seatbelt then turn off the radio. I no longer feel like listening to music. I know good and well, my teeth didn't as much as graze him. He has to have something to complain about. It just can't be good for him. Next time, I'll make sure I accidentally bite him. Asshole.

The rest of the ride to the club goes by in a blur. I hold onto the "Oh, Shit Bar" for dear life. I do try to make idle chit chat in hopes to get back in the right frame of mind. "Do we have a reservation at seven o'clock?"

"Yes, Mother and Father have a standing reservation every Sunday night at seven." He pulls into the parking lot of the country club.

His parents are out of the country. Where did they go? Somewhere for his sister. *Think Bailey.* "Aren't they in Milan for your sister's show?" His sister is getting started in fashion designing and already had a show in Milan. How does someone get that fortunate, really? Getting my lipstick out of my purse, I flip down the visor to use the mirror. I look over at him and give him a sexy wink.

"No, they flew back in yesterday." He pulls up to the valet. The attendants on each side are dressed better than I am.

Shit, dammit, hell.

They open our doors, and Hendrix walks around the car putting his elbow out for me. Okay, I guess I am lacing my arm through his arm. This feels so formal and strained.

"They must be tired. Did they have a nice time?"

He is looking straight ahead with a fixed smile on his face as he escorts me into the dining room, skipping right past the hostess. I guess you don't have to check-in when your parents have standing reservations. I'm glad we don't have to stop and talk to the hostess anyway because she is giving Hendrix, "I want to fuck you" eyes. I lean closer and whisper, "Do you know her?"

"Really, Bailey, do you want to go there right now?"

I guess that answers my question. He gives me a glare before he returns to that perfect smile. I can't help but wonder if she is someone from his past or someone who wants to be in his future. Something tells me that she is someone in his past. I plaster a smile on my face. I can do this. I'm not going to let something in the past bother me now. Your past is in the past for a reason.

I don't see any empty tables besides the ones which seat six or eight. I wonder if we are that late. He keeps walking like he has a destination in mind, so I keep walking. The dining room is beautiful with real flowers on every table. A gigantic chandelier hangs from the center, casting prisms of color from the sparkling crystals. I wouldn't want to be the person in charge of keeping that fixture clean. Too many little doodads are hanging from the lamp. I wouldn't be able to keep track of what I'd cleaned and what needed to be cleaned.

I am too busy taking in the room to notice where we are headed. We stop and Hendrix gestures where he wants me to sit. He pulls out his chair to sit as the waiter gets mine.

"Hmmumm."

I hear a throat clearing, and I look over to my left at a woman I presume is his mother. No, I am not meeting his mom. Tell me this is not the night. She is dressed impeccably and her hair is the most beautiful shade of blonde. Actually, the strands look like spun silk. She has her arms crossed. Her smile looks as fake I'm sure as her hair color is.

"Hendrix, who is this, dear?"

I snap my gaze to his. I'm sure my eyes are as wide as saucers. This is where I lose my appetite. I like to prepare myself for these kinds of things, give myself a little pep talk.

"This is Bailey. Mother, I told you I was bringing her."

He is seated between the two of us. I suddenly feel very uncomfortable and heat rises in my face. That wasn't a real introduction. She is looking at me with disgust, or what I think is disgust. She has a hard time moving her face. I hear that happens with Botox. All I want to do is crawl under the table. There's enough room for me; no one has to know I'm here. No. I'm confident and sweet. I can meet anyone, anytime. Nothing fazes me. The quick pep talk doesn't help, but what can I do? It's now or never. Show her what you're made of Bailey. I hold my head up and put my shoulders back. I learned that from watching Dirty Dancing. A positive and confident attitude changes everything. I'll show her I'm self-assured and mature.

I smile as sweetly as possible. "Hello Mrs. Livingston, I'm Bailey Reynolds. It is a pleasure to finally meet you." I offer my hand. She looks at my hand with amusement on her face. I'm not sure what I have done to offend her already, but I can tell she isn't very happy. She looks at Hendrix.

"What does she mean by "to finally meet" me, Hendrix?"

She sneers, and I pull my hand away and settle back in my seat. I can tell already that I don't like her. Has he never mentioned me in all of the time we have been dating?

"Can we just eat, Mother? I know how much you dislike tardiness."

I fiddle with the silverware on the table to have something to do with my hands. I get a curious look from Hendrix, so I stop and reach for my glass of water, nearly knocking it over. I decide to place my hands in my lap where they will be safe. I take my cue from Hendrix and Mrs. Livingston and place my napkin in my lap as the waiter places salads in front of us. I haven't even ordered yet. I give Hendrix a puzzled look.

He rolls his eyes. "Bailey, Mother takes the liberty of ordering for her guests." He pats her on her hand.

At least I know which fork to use, so I don't look completely stupid. Looking at my salad, I smile and wait for Mrs. Livingston to start eating. The waiter is back filling wine glasses, "Oh, none for me, thank you. Would you have any sweet tea?" They don't of course have any, and no I don't want to sweeten it myself.

"You can't be serious. Where did you find this one, Hendrix? On a farm?"

She looks very amused with herself, and I can feel my face flush, "I actually went to school with Hendrix. We took Business Law together our junior year," I say in my most satisfied, up your ass, bitch voice. I can't be sweet to someone who is that much of a bitch.

When the waiter brings our next course, he sits a small black metal dish in front of each of us containing shells and green pesto looking stuff. He places a small utensil with two prongs and some funny looking tongs.

He must notice the discomfort on my face because he leans to straighten the tablecloth and whispers in my ear, "Escargot à la Bourguignonne."

I'm not one hundred percent sure exactly what that is, but I seem to recall escargot being snails, and the more I look at the shells, I can tell they are snails. *Lovely.*

Behind us I hear a commotion.

"Miss, miss, you can't go in dressed like that," a stern male voice says.

Everyone turns to see what is happening.

"Like hell I can't. Who is going to stop me?"

I'd know that voice anywhere. I close my eyes and say a silent prayer. I shrink three sizes and turn.

Hendrix grabs my elbow and pulls me to him. "What is Elizabeth doing here?"

He is beyond mad. Lizzie is frantically looking around for me. I cringe when I see her cut-off blue jean shorts, tank top, and flip-flops. I give him a small shrug. His mother is sitting with her mouth wide open. I'm sure she will have a lot to say about this.

Lizzie notices me about the time I stand. Something has to be wrong for her to show up here. She would avoid this place at all cost, otherwise.

"Elizabeth, why are you here? I know you're not an invited guest." He leans in and whispers so only we can hear him, "You skank ass hoe." She

I wouldn't be surprised if Lizzie didn't knock the crap out of him. She doesn't take shit off of anyone, especially when something's going on.

"Shut up, pompous ass or I will cut off your fucking nuts."

She's in his face. I'm hoping no one else can hear her, but that Lizzie has never been known to be quiet. I see that she has been crying because her eyes are all red rimmed.

"Bailey, it's Granny. They think she's had a heart attack. I've been calling you. Why haven't you answered your phone?"

I look at her bewildered. *What?* Granny has had a heart attack? She seemed fine when I left her.

"Never mind why, we have to go, now!" She pulls my arm.

"Young lady, you will settle yourself down this instant," says Mrs. Livingston. "You are not to come into this country club dressed like a vagrant and you are to lower your voice. Only trash uses language like that. Were you not raised any better than that?"

Lizzie looks over at me, and I know what is about to happen. I can't do much to stop it. You can't talk about our raising and not have Lizzie go off on you.

I pull on Lizzie's arm, trying to get her attention. "Come on, Lizzie. Let's go."

"Really, Hendrix, you found a real winner this time," Mrs. Livingston flips her hands in my direction.

She's added fuel to the flame with her nasty comment.

"Like hell I will. Our granny is on her deathbed and you want me to calm down? I see where your son gets his pretentious ass from now. Let me tell you something. The clothes you wear don't make you who you are. It is what you are on the inside that counts. I would much rather have a good heart than all the money in the world. Now, you can take your thumb and stick it up your egotistical ass! You are nothing but an old washed up ninny. Come on, Bailey, we need to go." Lizzie pulls my hand.

"I will text you later, okay?" I tell Hendrix, and I see he looks upset. I glance at Mrs. Livingston. I know I need to say it was nice to meet her, but it wasn't nice to meet her and with the way she treated Lizzie, I can't bring myself to acknowledge her. As we walk away, I hear Hendrix's mom whispering to him. I can't make out what she is saying and I can't summon up any reason to care what she thinks at the moment. I leave without a glance back at them.

We rush out of the country club to Lizzie's VW Beetle, which is waiting for us at the door. The valet doesn't look very happy.

"He should apologize to you for his bitch of a mother. You look adorable, by the way," Lizzie says.

A tear runs down my face, and I try to catch it before she notices. I look in my purse for my phone. *Shit,* "I guess I forgot my phone at home. Thank you for coming to get me. How is Granny? Do we know anything?" I wring my hands.

Lizzie is flying down streets and running lights. She can't drive on a good day, much less in an emergency.

"Did you want me to drive?" I look at her and she cuts her eyes over to me. I know that means not to start on her driving.

"We don't know anything yet. Cash was there and heard her fall. He called 911 and got Papa to the hospital." She whips into the emergency room parking lot nearly taking out another car then looks at me. "Not a word."

No way am I going to say anything. I know how she gets when she is all panicky. As long as she doesn't talk about my parking, I won't say a word about her driving. Plus she's in as much of a hurry to get to the hospital as I am. This is her family, too. She squeals into a parking place, pulls the emergency brake and is out of the car before I can get my seatbelt undone.

"Bailey, are you coming?"

Running across the parking lot, we rush through the emergency room doors. Lizzie heads straight for the nurses' desk, and I look around for our family. I don't recognize anyone. Where the hell is everyone? Lizzie motions for me to follow her, and we head to the elevators.

"They have moved her up to surgery." Lizzie pushes the button several times.

She's already in surgery? How much have I missed? The elevator takes forever. Decatur, Alabama isn't that big. Is everyone in the whole damn city here? Finally, we hear the ding of the elevator. This time, I'm the one pulling on Lizzie. Thankfully, the elevator doesn't seem to take as long getting us to the 3rd floor as it did to arrive at the lobby.

When the door opens across from the OR waiting room, I see Mom, Dad, my younger brother, Jake, and a few cousins who are sitting with Papa. Mom gets up and hugs my neck, and shakes her head and tears well up in her eyes. "We've been worried about you, Bailey. Why didn't you answer your phone, honey?"

"Mom, I accidentally left it at home because we were in a hurry. I'm here now, though. Do we know anything? How's Papa taking all of this?"

"He seems to respond well to Cash, the new neighbor. At least for a few minutes at a time."

Dad and Jake are deep into conversation. I give them each a hug then glance over at Papa. He looks like he could use some cheering up. I walk over and kneel in front of him because there isn't an empty seat next to him.

He gazes at me with an expression I've never seen on him before. He looks scared, defeated and his eyes have changed to a deeper green. This can't be easy for him. I don't know if I will be able to help, but I am going to try. From past experience, I know it's better if we don't let him get too upset.

CASH

The elevator doors open and a beautiful vision in white steps off. Bailey looks like an angel, and I want to be the devil that corrupts her. Her lips are absolutely perfect with a slightly puckered pout. I shouldn't be thinking like that with all of this commotion. She isn't even aware of what is going on around her because she's so focused on Mr. Jackson. She smiles and even if it makes me sound sappy, I would swear her expression takes away my breath.

"Hey, Papa. Everything is going to be okay. Granny is a strong woman and she isn't going to let a little thing like this stop her." Bailey says.

She gently strokes his hand. Tears are in his eyes and his weathered beat-up hands are atop his cane. So much pain is reflected in Bailey's eyes and I can hear the agony in her voice.

"You don't understand. That's my life in there." He looks away.

I can literally feel my heart breaking for him.

"I love her and I'm not whole without her. She is part of my soul. I'm scared to lose her," Mr. Jackson says. "We have been married sixty-five years."

He looks at me. I'm going to lose it because this is some deep emotional shit.

"Yes sir, December eighth, right?" Bailey asks.

He nods and goes off in a daze. I move over and motion for her to take my seat. She gives a nod of thanks and sits. She reaches for Mr. Jackson's hand. Bailey has a huge heart for him and she loves this man with everything she has inside of her. He looks a little bewildered.

"The first time I saw her, I told my brother I was going to marry her. Jack laughed and said I was crazy. That I didn't even know her name." He exhales and lifts his shoulders then looks at the floor. "I hadn't even spoken to her yet."

Bailey switches hands and rubs his back. I bet she has heard this story a million times, but she still lovingly acts as if she's hearing it for the first time. I bet she loves listening to it almost as much as he loves telling it.

"My brothers and I had a band and we were playing at a party. I played the mandolin. Jack, he played the fiddle, and Otis... I can't remember what he played." He shakes his head. "I didn't get to go and play at parties much. They made me stay home with our disabled brother most of the time. They were always mean to him."

He is in deep thought now, his memory crystal clear.

"Anyway, I had brought another girl to the dance. I walked her home and hurried back. That's when I met Addie. She was the most beautiful girl I'd ever laid my eyes on. Dark hair and gray eyes. Do you know what she told her sister about me at that dance?"

Now he has the biggest smile across his face, and she shakes her head.

"She said she was going to take me away from that girl." He chuckles.

I love hearing Mr. Jackson reminiscing like this, and Bailey is so good with him. She hangs on every word like this is the first time she's ever heard this story, asking him the appropriate questions.

"She is still beautiful, and I think you look a lot like her, Bailey."

She wraps her arms around him and kisses him on his cheek.

"Do you really think so? I hope I look as good as she does when I get to be her age. But you know what? I've got your eyes, Papa." She pats his shoulder.

Now I can see why Mrs. Jackson was going on and on about her that night. There is something special about this girl. She's not only beautiful, but she knows how to make you feel like you're the only person in the room. She is very loving and sensitive to how he is feeling. You can never be ugly when you have a good heart like that.

"No, you don't." He grins at her, his eyes twinkling, but only for a second, "I've got my own eyes." He winks at her.

He is such a character that sometimes you forget a disease is running through his body, stealing every other moment from him.

Suddenly, he looks around. "Bailey, have you met Cash? He drove me up here. I need to pay him, but I don't have my wallet."

I'm amazed at how quickly he can change. He peeks around her looking for me.

"Cash, this is my granddaughter Bailey. Bailey, give Cash some money and I will pay you back."

She turns and I meet her vivid green eyes, but I speak to Mr. Jackson. "Mr. Jackson, please sir, you don't owe me anything. It's the neighborly thing to do for each other." I give her the smile that normally has panties melting, and hold out my hand then wink. "It's nice to meet you, Bailey."

"Bailey, are you going to shake his hand?" Mr. Jackson asks her.

"I need to give you a hug. Thank you so much for taking care of Papa and Granny for me." She leans over and puts her arms as far around me as she can. She gives me a full body squeeze. I feel her breasts push into me which makes "Johnny" stand to get some attention. I want to know what she would look like in the bed of my truck, on a dirt road, under the stars, with only those boots on. God Cash, get your dick under control. This is not the time or place for these kinds of thoughts.

The doors open to the operating room and a doctor comes out, "The Jackson family."

Bailey stands then turns to help Mr. Jackson, but I am already helping him up.

"Hello, I'm Doctor Thomas, I've been the one working with Mrs. Jackson. She is a very lucky woman," the doctor says. "She got here quickly and we were able to repair the damage done by the attack by doing Cardiac Cauterization. The longer a heart attack goes on, the more damage it does to the heart. We put in a couple of stents and are avoiding doing Open Heart Surgery."

Mr. Jackson is shaking his head and doesn't look like he understands anything. I feel his grief radiating off him, and my empathy for him is overflowing at the moment.

"She will need someone with her twenty-four hours a day for the next month, have to follow a heart healthy diet and start to get a little exercise. She doesn't need too much exercise though; a little walking will be enough as long as it's not during the heat of the day." Doctor Thomas, looking down at the chart in his hands, finishes by telling us, "We are moving her up to ICU, at least overnight. You guys should go get some rest. You'll have a long few days ahead of you." He places the chart under his arm to shake Mr. Jackson's hand. "Let me know if you have any questions, Mr. Jackson."

"How long will she be in the hospital?" Bailey asks then bites on her nails.

"It depends on how well she recovers and how determined she is to get better. The more she can get up and walk and do her breathing treatments, the faster she will recover. It is really up to her, but normally it's anywhere from three to eight days. With her age, it will probably be closer to eight days."

"Thank you, Doctor Thomas. We all appreciate everything you have done for her." Bailey says. She heads over to Lizzie, "Can you take me home so we can pack some things for her? I think I'll come back up here and sleep in the waiting room."

"Sorry, Bailey, I have a test tomorrow and I haven't even started to study." Lizzie glances at me. "I'm taking some classes at the community college this summer." She focuses on Bailey again. "You do'nt need to come back up here and spend the night. You need your rest because the next few days Granny will need you more. Besides, there isn't anything you can do, and you won't be able to see her until visiting hours tomorrow, Bay."

Everyone has said their goodbyes and is leaving. Kathy is taking Mr. Jackson home with her. I hear her tell Kate, who I find out is Lizzie's mom, that she has a few days of emergency medicine for him at her house so they won't be going out to the Jacksons' house. I think Lizzie is up to something because of the way Bailey is looking at her.

"Maybe Cash can give you a ride home," Lizzie says as we walk out to the parking lot.

Lizzie is my new favorite person. She and I are going to get along just fine.

"No problem, I'm going that way. You know living right across the street and all."

Bailey is looking at me, and Lizzie has a smirk on her face.

"I could even come back up here and stay with you if you would like." I want to be there in case she needs someone. I don't want her to have to go through this alone. She may need someone to talk to, or a shoulder to lay her head on. She wouldn't have to be alone.

"Oh, I know you would take real good care of her, Cash." Lizzie says.

"I guess I'll be needing a ride since everyone is deserting me." She looks up at me through her lashes, but her eyes are so sad.

What is she doing to me? Even when she is in so much pain, she is still beautiful. I wish I could do something to take that hurt away, to make her smile. I know that is a useless wish right now. I guess just being here and being supportive will have to do. "It would be my pleasure, ma'am."

I run my hand through my hair noticing it has started to rain. "If you wait here, I'll pull around so you don't have to get wet." I know how to be a gentleman, unlike that prick she's seeing. Once she sees how much of a prick he is, as I predict will happen, and her Granny is better, I'll be here to be the devil to her angel because she is as hot as hell.

"That's okay, I won't melt." She gives me a little smile.

I'm so glad I could take away some of her sorrow, if only for a moment. I reach out for her hand and we take off running. My black Tundra Crew Cab is only parked three rows back.

I open the door for her. She is reaching for the sidebar to help herself up since the truck is elevated, but I put my hands on her hips and lift her into the truck. She turns to look in my eyes with tenderness. My hand accidentally slides down her leg a fraction and she shivers.

"Thanks, Cash, you are so sweet." She swallows and sounds a little shaky.

I hope she doesn't think that I'm doing all of this to get with her or something. Right now, I know she needs a friend and I want to be that friend. I can't believe her boyfriend isn't here for her. She clearly is upset and on the verge of tears. How could she not be? If the truth be told, I want to spend more time with her and get to know her, too. She draws me in, like a moth to a flame.

Why have I suddenly lost my ability to communicate? "Johnny" sure isn't having any problem. I'm glad my Wranglers are tight and don't give him a whole hella lot of room to make an introduction. The moment she stepped off the elevator in that white dress and boots, she had my attention. I need to calm myself down though because the last thing she needs right now is me making a move on her.

Her stomach lets out a loud growl, and I can't help but laugh at how something that small can make that big of a noise. "Hungry? Why don't we go and get you something to eat? Kathy said you were at dinner when Lizzie went to get you. Did you get the chance to eat?"

"I am starving. Do you mind going through a drive-thru so I can pick up something for the road?"

She needs something that will fill her up and stick with her, not some greasy hamburger. I'd bet my last dollar that food will be the last thing on her mind during the next few days. "I'm hungry too." I say. "I'd love some pancakes."

You can't eat pancakes on the road. Maybe she'll agree. Anyway, who can turn down pancakes? And they are a great alternative to fast food crap.

"Pancakes, this late?" She laughs.

I'm glad I can lift her spirits. She obviously cares deeply for her grandparents. I think if you're lucky enough to still have your grandparents you should cherish them, and she obviously does. She knew just what to do to soothe Mr. Jackson and showed him a kindness that a lot of people lack.

"Okay, pancakes it is then," she says with a smile.

She has the best smile and I hope I can make her smile a few more times tonight. I would do almost anything in my power to lessen her worry.

"Good, I know just the place." Because there is nothing better than a few tunes for background noise, I turn on the radio low.

"I like your choice in music."

I figured she would. She has country girl written all over her. My mind goes to what she would look like in the bed of my truck with just those boots on, but I try to get my mind on something else as I pull into IHOP's parking lot. Their service is slow this time of night, which will give us time to talk. I've found that sometimes just talking about what's on your mind makes you feel better. That's what I want to do. Encourage her to talk about what she is going through. Perhaps, help her understand her feelings. She's probably a little bit scared too. To take her mind off of everything that is going on until she gets some food in her stomach, I say, "So, you like country music. Let me guess, you like Eric Church, Dierks Bentley, Luke Bryan, and Miranda Lambert... Am I getting close?" There is that smile again. It lights up her whole face.

I park then walk around to open her door and help her down.

"Like that would be hard to guess since I like country music," she laughs.

After we're seated in the restaurant, she says, "So tell me about Cash?"

I don't like to talk about myself, not about my real self. It's too depressing to give someone those kinds of details when you're just getting to know them. "There isn't a lot to know about me. I bought the land over by you guys a while back, I work all the time and take pretty ladies to eat pancakes at midnight."

"Don't forget that you help your elderly neighbors." She looks down and whispers, "You saved my Granny's life tonight. I don't know how to thank you."

She looks up and her eyes are glistening with tears. I love her beautiful eyes. They are one of my weaknesses; but right now they are filled with such sorrow, and their sadness lets me see right into her heart. I'd give anything to be able to take that pain away. "I'm so glad I was there at the right time. Your grandparents are great people."

"Not to be rude, but can we talk about something other than my grandparents?"

I get it. She isn't ready to talk about her pain yet so I smile and say, "Sure. Now it's your turn, tell me about the world according to Bailey."

"I like that. The World According To Bailey sounds like a good book. For starters, I'm twenty-one, but my birthday is at the end of the summer. How old are you, Cash?"

Our food comes and she digs into her pancakes. I love to see that she wastes no time and isn't embarrassed to eat in front of me.

"I turned twenty-six last month, but this is your turn, remember." I want to sit here and talk to her all night.

"You really didn't tell me much. I'm willing to bet there is more to you. Let's see, you're twenty-six, you're a workaholic, great neighbor, and like to eat pancakes. That's all there is to know about you?"

I like a woman who is determined and has a playful side. "I'm a Computer Systems Analysis, so that makes me a nerd, I guess. I started working for my company as a junior in high school, paid my way through college and bought the company when I graduated."

"Oh, you make that sound so exciting." She fakes a yawn. "I've taken all of my basics and I'm a few classes short of taking my C.P.A. exam. See how this works." She lifts her eyebrows and forms an O shape with her mouth.

Yep, she is teasing, proof positive that just sitting here talking is helping her.

"You tell me something then I tell you something."

"Is that how this game is played, a little tit for tat?" I smile at her, encouraging her lighthearted nature. Talking with Bailey is easy. She isn't trying to impress me, and from what I can tell and from what I know about her, she is just being who she is. And I like that she ordered sweet tea. She is southern to the core. Before I know it, we've finished eating and I'm on my third cup of coffee.

She looks at her watch, "I really need to go home and get my Jeep." She looks around for the waitress. "This is on me by the way, as my thank you. You've helped me more than you can possibly know. I'm not talking about just with what happened tonight. You also lifted my spirits."

We'll see about her picking up the check. I motion to our waitress, and she heads our way. When she places the check on the table, we both reach for it. The touch of Bailey's hand sends sparks to my dick. "Johnny" is awake and wondering what in the hell is going on.

"Sweet Cheeks, a real man never lets a lady pay, and in case you haven't noticed, I'm a real man." Shit, did I really call her sweet cheeks out loud?

"Sweet Cheeks?" She lifts both eyebrows, smiling a big grin. "That's a new one, are you trying to say I have fat cheeks?"

Her grin tells me she must not be mad about me calling her "Sweet Cheeks." I grin in return and realize I have smiled more tonight than I have in my whole life. I'm not giving her the fake smiles I give to everyone else because my life hasn't given me much to smile about. These have been genuine and I can't seem to stop them. They feel good and I want to make her smile and feel good too, and she does. She gives me her million-dollar smile and still, I want more.

"Bailey, it would be my honor to pay for your meal tonight. So, please allow me this, okay?"

"Okay, but next time it's on me, capisce?"

After I pay the bill, I place my hand in the small of her back and escort her to the truck. I have never been more thankful for my old four by four lifted truck than I am tonight. Having to pick Bailey up gives me the perfect view of her sweet ass. I'm only looking because she is feeling better, otherwise I would have closed my eyes. *Right!* I would like to take a bite because her ass reminds me of a peach. Hell, I want to see all of her naked, but there is a five-year age difference between us that is something to be considered. *Is five years really that big of a difference?* Probably not in the grand scheme of things, but it's something to consider. I can't lie, though; I like the flirty conversation we have on our drive out to Mt. Hope.

12

Bailey

When we pull up to Papa and Granny's, Cash jumps out of the truck and comes around to help me down.

He walks me to the door, and I reach up and give him a kiss on the cheek. "Goodnight, Cash."

There's nothing wrong with kissing him on the cheek as a thank you because he was so sweet tonight. He took my mind off of my circumstances, and even made me laugh. That has to be a talent, to make me smile when I feel like my world has been turned upside down. He asks for my cell number then types it in his phone as I reel off the digits.

"I'm right across the street if you need me. I sent you a message so you'll have my phone number."

Can he get any more supportive? Seriously, he has to be a knight in shining armor. His white horse has to hiding around here somewhere.

"Goodnight, Bailey, sweet dreams." He gives me a longing look then stuffs his hands in his pockets as he takes a step back. "Will you please go inside before I leave? I need to know you're safe."

He needs to know I'm inside safe? Maybe chivalry isn't dead. He's worried for me.

"Bye, Cash, thank you for the ride and the pancakes. Those were probably the best pancakes I've ever had." I smile, looking up at him because he's so tall. His dark hair is a tad long, a length you can run your fingers through and really grab onto. His eyes are blue with a darker blue rim, and in them I see genuine concern for me. Granny was right. He is a good guy. Too bad I like my guys a little bit naughty. Even if he is so great to look at, I can't be with a good guy. I need naughtiness. Someone who pushes me a little, infuriates me at times. "You're a great neighbor, Cash. Really. Thank you so much for what you did for Granny and Papa because they mean everything to me."

He puts his arm up on the doorframe, and leans in much closer. "I would like to be much more than neighborly, but I know now isn't the right time, Bailey. You're going through one of the most emotional times of your life and you need me more as a friend, but I wanted to let you know my intentions after things with your grandparents are back to normal."

"You're right. I can use a friend right now, but while I'm flattered about your intentions, I'm dating someone."

He comes closer, and I feel his breath on my face. Sensations ripple through me merely from him standing close. I hear the phone ringing inside. *Thank the Lord!* I turn and open the door, and Cash follows.

As I pick up the phone, I see it's Hendrix. Awe, he's checking in to see how everything's going. "Hey, babe."

"Bailey, I need to talk to you. I'm sorry to do this over the phone. I was going to talk to you after dinner, but you really left me no other choice." His matter of fact tone tells me he means business.

"What is it, Hendrix? Just tell me." It can't be that bad because my spidery senses aren't tingling.

"Until you get done with your babysitting detail, we need to take a break," he says. "You don't ever have time for me anymore, and I have needs and obligations to fill."

I'm not believing this. He has reached into my chest and twisted my heart, making me feel even worse than I thought possible. I feel a tear run down my face, and I quickly wipe it away. "What do you mean when I finally have time for you? I'm with you all the time, babe, I just can't stay the night."

"Bailey, while you get all of your shit figured out, let's date other people. I'm not going to be stuck babysitting every damn weekend."

I guess my spidery senses were off tonight. I am on emotional overload after all. He can't really be breaking up with me because I'm taking care of my grandparents. I am about to come unglued. I've got to remain calm. Deep cleansing breath, Bailey. Don't go all bat shit crazy. "Honey, don't be that way. We have been together close to a year. We can't let a little bump in the road get in the way of a good thing." There. That's all I'm saying, I'm not going to beg him to stay with me. That's not me.

"We can still date. We just won't be exclusive like we are now."

"Whatever!" I'm close to turning my bitch side loose on his ass. "The more I think about it, Hendrix, the more I think you're right. We do need to date other people." I really want to slam the phone down and scream at the top of my lungs, but I close my eyes and take a minute before I say, "Bye, Hendrix, I'll talk to you later."

"We're not over, Sweetheart," he says soothingly. "We're just taking a break until you get out of that hellhole."

He did not just say that. I take a deep breath holding back the bitch side, and say, "Sure babe, talk to you later?" I hope that sounded sweeter than I feel. I hang up. He better keep his fucking little sports car away from me for a few a days or I'll have to jack it up. I can't lie, though. My heart is broken. I feel the tears building. Who is that pecker head wanting to date? I can't decide if I'm mad or if I'm sad. I feel arms go around my waist from behind and I nearly jump out of my own skin. *What the hell?*

"Cash! Oh my goodness, I forgot you were even here. I'm so sorry. That was so rude of me to act that way in front of you." My face heats up. I'm sure it is as red as a lobster.

"Shh, Bailey, it's okay. He is only a boy who has no idea of the good thing he has."

With that, I can't hold back the waterworks. My breakdown isn't a few tears running down my face. No, this is the makeup ruining kind. It's not a pretty sight and I always end up with a snotty nose. He turns me and holds me close.

"Do you want to talk about it?" he asks.

"Cash, thank you for the ride home and the sweet words, but I really don't want to talk about all of this right now. I need time to wrap my brain around it." I push out of his hold, but I really wish I hadn't. His arms felt good around me. His whole body felt wonderful pressed up against mine. I just can't go there. It has been such a stressful day and I can't let my emotions make me do something I might regret later. "Cash, there isn't any doubt that I'm attracted to you."

"I can be your friend for now." He reaches out and strokes my cheek.

I feel the tenderness in his touch, and I lean into his caress. He might be able to keep things between us as friends only, but will I be able to? He steps closer. I do need comforting, or I would at least like some. Having someone to lean on after a day like I've had sounds nice. He has taken the time to listen and make me feel better.

"Can you stay for a while so we can talk? I really don't want to be alone right now." I look up at him, hoping he will agree to stay. I can't bear the thought of having to sit in this dark house and dwell on everything that's happened tonight.

"Sure, I can stay. Whatever helps you cope with everything that's happened to your grandparents, with whatever happened just now between you and your boyfriend."

I heave a deep breath of relief. "I'm going to get out of this dress, and into something comfortable." Ugh! That didn't sound cliché. Why am I even worrying about this kind of stuff?

When I return to the living room, I'm barefooted and wearing my comfy sleep pants and an old t-shirt. Cash is sitting in the middle of the couch. One point for him for allowing me to only put minimal distance between us. I sit on the couch, but not too close to him.

"So, what all do you have planned for tomorrow?" he asks.

"I need to take some stuff to the hospital for Granny and make sure she gets up and walks around. She'll have to have some good coffee in the morning too," I laugh. I touch his bicep. He works out. You can't have a body like his and not work on it. *Oh, good Lord, help me now, don't let me touch anything else on him.* "Do you want some tea or a coke?" I get up to fix some tea.

"Yeah, I'll take some tea." He follows me into the kitchen.

"We could go outside and sit on the picnic table since it's a nice night." I try not to notice his tight ass Wrangler jeans as I fix our tea. Or the button up shirt with the sleeves rolled way up above his elbow.

"Sitting outside looking up at the stars is my second favorite past-time." He gives me a wink and that damn smile, which isn't shadowed by the cowboy hat he was wearing earlier.

He looks good with his cowboy hat, but without it I just want to put my hands in his hair. He doesn't wear any styling products like Hendrix does. His hair is just naturally gorgeous, and most girls would love to have hair they didn't have to do anything with.

I don't need to be alone with him because I'm still in a relationship with Hendrix. I think. He did say we were seeing other people, but I don't see how that will work.

We sit outside on the picnic table with our glasses of tea. The view of the stars is brilliant here in the country without the streetlights dulling their twinkling. The crickets are chirping, as always, but you don't hear much of anything else, except for a passing car now and then. It is so peaceful out here at night.

I lean back on my hands to get a better view of the stars. "Do you ever wish on a star, Cash?" I want to see a deeper side of him. I want a peek into his head.

"I stopped wishing on stars a long time ago."

He looks serious.

"I've learned to quit thinking about the 'what ifs' and live in the 'right now,'" he says. "Let's live in this moment and enjoy it together. We don't have to worry about wishing for anything else. If something is meant to be, it will happen one way or another. What do you say, Sweet Cheeks?"

I say he isn't playing fair. I wasn't expecting that answer from him. All he has been so far is kind or funny, sweet and charming. He may be deeper than any guy I've ever known.

"Okay. I say 'yes' to living in the moment." I hold up my glass for a toast, and he lifts his to touch mine, and we laugh a little. "Are you always so deep and philosophical?" I raise one of my eyebrows then lean back on my elbows and so does he.

"That's not deep or philosophical. That's just me living life for a few more years than you."

We both turn onto our sides facing each other.

That is the most ridiculous thing I ever heard. "I'm not that much younger than you, Cash. We're really only four years apart." He is crazy.

"What I mean is if you'd experienced a little more of life, you wouldn't even be dating a prick who makes you cry instead of doing whatever he can to support you tonight. You would know that you're worth so much more and you wouldn't let him disrespect you."

I've got to set this shit straight. This is just too much. He and I are about to have a coming to Jesus meeting. I don't let anyone disrespect me!

CASH

"Cash, I'm not as innocent as you think I am. I'm sure I could even teach you and thing or two."

I have to hold back my laughter. She still has this all wrong. There are different levels of being grown. Knowing what you want out of life is one of them. Knowing when to let people go when they continue to hurt and disappoint you is another.

"Bailey, you haven't even been kissed." I intend to show her she hasn't had a relationship that is worthy of her. I want her to understand she is so much more than that prick has led her to believe. "Let me show you, if you don't believe me."

"You are awfully full of yourself." She jumps off the picnic table putting her hands on those perfect little hips.

I get up from the picnic table, take her by the hand and pull her into me. She smells like honeysuckles and I wonder if she will taste like them too. I want to kiss her ten different ways and take my time to and explore her body, but tonight isn't about that. Tonight is about making her feel like a lady and a woman. The way she'd be kissed if she was in a mature relationship. With me. I take her face in my hands and look into those eyes that make my heart skip a beat every time I see them. I kiss her gently, just a brush of my lips.

She moves her hands around my neck, giving my skin feather light caresses Those little wisps of touches awaken things in me that need attention, but not right now. She deserves to be worshiped and I'm going to show her I'm the man who can take care of her. I move next to her eyelids, and place a tender kiss on each one of them.

She sighs.

There isn't any need to rush kissing. It's the first step to falling in love. I go back to her mouth giving her the slightest nibbles. She is opening her mouth for more. I don't think she has ever been loved this way. Her neck, right behind her ear, is where I land next. I get a little taste there with my tongue. She tastes damn good. She presses her hips against my leg. My dick is on full alert, but this isn't about him. It's about this first kiss with her. This might be my last chance to show her she has been kissed.

I go back to her lips and give them a little lick then seal my lips to hers. I take her tongue and give it a little suck. She moans, clearly enjoying this. I have my hands in her hair playing. I give her lips another little nip and

follow that up with more hunger in my kiss. I end with a few gentle touches then look into her eyes, which are hooded and dazed.

"Now, you've been kissed." I walk away before "Johnny" takes over. "Goodnight, Sweet Cheeks, sleep well," I call back to her.

"You can't give someone a kiss like that and leave them, Cash."

I stop and look over my shoulder. "You're not ready for this," I say then I get my ass across the street before I change my mind.

Bailey

Journal Entry: I'm done with being sad over Hendrix. He has hurt me for the last time. I thought he loved me. I thought we were meant to be together, but he's hit me with this landslide, and I'm finally able to see him as everyone else does. He wants to see other people, and he wants to screw me then he wants to have some high society girl on his arm. I guess he wants to keep me as his dirty little secret. I feel so used, and I'm tired of stroking his ego. I don't need anyone in my life that needs my apologies when I haven't done anything wrong. I thought he was making me a better person, but in reality he has made me feel worthless. He has finally opened my eyes to the kind of person he really is. From this point on, I'm no longer a doormat. I won't be used as anyone's come disposal system. If a guy can't return the favor, they no longer get to party in my hoo-ha. I've had it with all of the egotistical bastards in this world. I want a guy to worship me as much as I do him.

Maybe that will be Cash? He's sweet and he's certainly hot. That kiss set me on fire, and if a kiss can do that to me, I can only imagine how he can rock my world in other ways. His body is hard and when I ran my hand down his chest, I felt him tremble just a little. We have an intense sexual tension. The way he looks at me, so passionate with those deep blue penetrating eyes.

I put away my journal and get out 'old faithful' again to release all the tension Cash built up. This, of course, isn't a replacement for the real thing, but I can lay here and think about Cash. In my fantasy, he has his shirt off, and his body is ripped. I picture all of those well placed hard muscles wet. Drops of water are running down his chest, and he is heaving. His nipples are pebbled, and I lick away the water. I look up at him through my eyelashes and he is watching me. I run my hands down his torso, into his jeans and pull out his rock hard cock. It glistens, begging to be taken into my mouth. He pushes me down on the bed and licks my pussy with a passion and hunger of a starving man. Then he takes me hard, pumping and grinding into me making me come again and again. He turns me over and takes me from behind holding me up with his hands. The images push me over the edge and I've blissfully made my own magic.

Now I can sleep without a care in the world. All the stress of the day is gone. All thoughts of fighting with Hendrix have disappeared. I can breathe deeply and drift off to slumber land. I won't need any alcohol assistance to get my zees tonight. I'm sure my dreams will be pornographic. I know my thoughts are. I snuggle down under my covers and glide into my dreams of Cash.

I wake up to my alarm at six and hop into the shower. After getting dressed, I pack Granny's essentials and grab a breakfast bar on my way out the door. I call the hospital and find out Granny has already been moved to a private room. The operator connects me to her room, and Granny picks up on the first ring.

"Hello."

She sounds chipper today. "Hey Granny, how are you feeling?" I am relieved to hear a little pep in her voice.

"I'm fine, Baby. Why haven't you called me?"

You've got to love her, not even twelve hours out of surgery and she is up to her shenanigans. I laugh, "What am I doing right now, Granny? I'm on my way with your nightgown and housecoat. Is there anything else you need? Can I stop by and get you a book or a magazine?"

"Did you get my cold cream, I've got to have my cold cream. You can bring me one of the books you like to read, but I would rather have your company."

She sounds hopeful, but she doesn't have to hint around. I will be there for her.

"Yes, ma'am, I've got your cold cream packed, right along with your other toiletries. I don't have any of my books with me now, so my company will have to do."

"That sounds like a good plan to me. How long will it be before you get here? Will you stop and get me a cup of coffee at McDonalds?"

"We had the same idea. I'm almost at McDonalds now because you know I can't go long without my sweet tea. I should be there in another ten minutes or so. I'll see you then. Bye, love you."

"Love you too, Baby."

I can hear the smile in her voice.

I grab the coffee, and my tea then I'm on my way. I stop by and pick up some roses in the gift shop. I spend the next few hours visiting as I walk her around the hall as much as she's able. What she lacks in strength, she makes up for in willpower by walking for a short distance then sitting in the seat of her walker to catch her breath. I tell her she is pushing herself too much, but she is stubborn and won't listen to me, and I end up pushing her back to her room the last trip out before lunch.

"So tell me something now we're not out in that hallway where everyone can hear us."

She grins with naughtiness in her blue gray eyes.

"I want to know what you think about Cash's butt. Don't you think he has a good butt?"

She is being a stinker at the moment and I'm going to fix her. "Why Granny, I did notice that he had a nice butt. That's why Lizzie hog tied him and I spanked him."

She laughs until tears roll down her face. She loves for me to tease her like that.

"Bailey, I don't put anything past you and Lizzie, not one thing." She is still laughing and shaking her head. She pats the side of her bed for me to take a seat.

I walk over and gently lower onto the bed. I don't want to pull on any of the wires she has hooked up to the monitors, or hurt her. I reach for her hand and kiss it. I love this woman. I hope one day that I turn out just like her.

"Baby, I want to talk to you for a minute."

She takes on a serious tone.

"Now, please keep an open mind. You know I've never steered you wrong before, right?"

This must be important because Granny is determined that I listen.

"No, ma'am, you've always given me the best advice. I can always count on your words of wisdom, Granny," I tell her, smiling.

"Good, I'm glad you feel that way because what I have to say might not be what you want to hear."

Her eyes crinkle up in concern and I pat her hand, "What is it, Granny? Goodness knows, I need all the help I can get!"

"I want to talk about your relationship with Hendrix. Bailey, never let anyone talk down to you like he did last night when he came to pick you up. He doesn't treat you with respect. A man's job is to treat you with respect, Baby. Didn't you know that? It's the woman's job to give the man a reason to respect her. When God created Eve, what part of Adam did he take out to make her?"

"Uh, the rib?" Where is she going with this?

"That's right, close to the heart to be loved. He didn't take from the feet, so we could be walked all over. So, don't allow any man do that to you. If you don't accept being treated that way, then they won't treat you that way. You have to show them how you want them to treat you. If they really love you, they will want to treat you with respect."

"How did learn all of this, Granny? I mean, I know how you learned the biblical stuff. You're always reading your Bible."

"It's nothing I've learned. It's more common sense. I guess when you get to be my age things just get to be clearer and you see things differently than you do when you're in your twenties." She smiles and turns her head a little.

"You really are the best granny a girl could ask for, ya know that?" I ask.

"So you're not upset with me about this whole conversation?"

"How can I be upset when I know it's the truth, whether I want to acknowledge it or not? Granny, I see what you're saying and I'll give it some thought, okay?"

"Fair enough."

She looks delighted.

After lunch, Granny settles down for a nap. "Thank you, baby, for spending the morning with me, Bailey, but I'm going to rest for a while now because I know everyone else will be up here this afternoon." She yawns.

While she sleeps, I go to Mom's to see if there is anything I can do to help out with Papa and hopefully grab a catnap.

I walk into a dark and quiet house. Mom must have taken Papa to the hospital. The air is turned down low. Ah, my utopia. I'm taking this opportunity to spend time in La La Land because I need a siesta to get me through the rest of the day. Soon, I'm sawing logs.

After I wake up, I wipe the drool from my mouth and clear the sleep from my eyes. What Granny said to me in the hospital this afternoon has me thinking. I need to take control of my life and quit living to please someone else. Constantly pleasing Hendrix has only led to me feeling rejected. I want to be me again. I think I'm pretty damn likeable just the

way I am, and if anyone doesn't like me this way…screw them. They weren't my true friends anyway. People who matter will always be there for you. You can take that to the bank.

I decide to call Hendrix because I want to get this whole mess straightened out between us. I still can't believe he was rude last night. He must have been out of his mind.

Once I hear him answer, I ask, "Hey, can we talk?"

"I was getting ready to head out to the beach for the week, can this wait until I get back?"

The beach? When did he decide to go to the beach? He doesn't start his internship with his daddy's law firm until next week, but the last we discussed it, we were going the Fourth of July, not before then. "No, this can't wait. I really need to talk with you. I didn't know you were going to the beach this week. When did you plan this?" He hadn't mentioned the change in plans when we were together last night.

"Last night at the club. Hilary came over after you left, and I made plans with her."

What the fucking hell did he just say? "What? Wait a minute. Hilary who and why the fuck are you taking her to the beach, Hendrix?" Breathe, Bailey. There has to be some mistake. I've heard this wrong. "This is why you wanted to date other people? Because you wanted to take some other girl to the beach?"

"Bailey, you know we are not exclusive. I told you that last night. Hilary Madison and I are old friends. We dated back in high school. Our families are friends as well, remember, Sweetheart?"

See, this is where the issue of him not respecting me comes in. We're not exclusive now, but he made those plans with Hilary before he broke up with me. He expects me to simply accept his relationship with Hilary. And don't even get me started on ass-ademic Hilary Madison. Doesn't he realize how big her ass is now? "Hendrix, I didn't know you knew Hilary. You guys didn't go to high school together because she went to high school with me." I'm done with this pig-headed, uppity, prick! "This relationship is no longer working for me, Hendrix. For one thing, you treated me like shit last night, and I gave you a fucking blowjob in your car. You want to talk about family being uncouth? Well, your mom is a bitch, and she made sure to let me know how low class she thought I was. You get mad at me for leaving after my granny had a heart attack. Then you turn around and invite another fucking girl to Destin? You still do not understand that I had to leave, Hendrix. My family comes first."

"Cool your tits. It's not like I said I wouldn't see you anymore. Get your shit together while I'm gone to Destin, Bailey, and I'll talk to you when I get back." He hangs up.

He fucking hangs up the phone on me. Who does he think he is? I'm about to come unglued. I pour myself a glass of tea and sit at the kitchen table to calm down. I get ready to send Lizzie a 911 text when I notice Cash has texted me.

> *Cash: Will you be at hospital tonight? I'm bringing mom to see your granny. She wants to meet you, too.*

Holy crap. He wants me to meet his mother? That is too awkward.

Cash: Before you start psychoanalyzing that last text, she's heard so much about you from your granny. That's why she wants to meet you.

He is worried about what I will think? How cute is that? But he's right.

> *Bailey: Lol! I was about to say creepy! I am going up there now. What time are y'all going?*

> *Cash: It will be a few hours for us. I have a few things to finish up for work. Can we meet you around 6?*

> *Bailey: That will be fine, I plan on staying until visiting hours are over. I will see you guys then.*

I put my phone down. I'm in a better mood now. Cash is sweet and he certainly sends tingles all over my body with just a kiss, but I'm still agitated at Hendrix. I need to let this go for now though because no good comes from worrying about something you can't change. Maybe Lizzie was right, and I need to let Hendrix go all together. Once she hears about all of this, she will advise me to dump his ass. Instead of sending her that 911, I'm going to sit on this and weigh my options on my own. Hell, what am I thinking? This isn't how I want to be treated, how I deserve to be treated. This isn't me. I'm not a doormat. I'm calling Hendrix back and giving him a piece of my mind.

"What, Bailey? I told you I was getting ready to leave."

He has a pissed off tone to his voice. That's okay. I'm pretty pissed off myself. "Hendrix, I would like to see you, if for only a few minutes, before you leave." I'm trying to remain calm because if he knows I'm this irate he will never agree to meet with me.

"You didn't have time for me last night, and I don't have time for you today." This is all about a wounded ego? I left him last night and he can't get over it? If he wants to act childish, he will get this over the phone then. "Is that what this is about? Me leaving you last night when my grandmother had a heart attack? Listen, I don't want to see you any more on any level. You've never treated me with respect, and I have enough respect for myself to know it's time I walk away from you. I can't make you respect me, and care for me, but I care enough for myself to not let you hurt me. I've tried and tried to be the person you wanted, but I'm done. I thought you were different. Your wealth and status don't make you any better of a person than anyone else. Showing kindness toward others, caring for your neighbors or people in general make you a better person, but you suck at all of those. I deserve to be happy and treated with respect. Don't call me anymore, Hendrix." I say all of that in what feels like one big breath.

"Fuck you, Bailey and your backwoods redneck family, too. You *will* come crawling back to me. Don't go all self-righteous on me because you love my wealth and status." He lets out a long breath. "Look, Sweetheart, I will be back in a few days. Let's not make decisions until then. I love you, Bailey. Hilary doesn't mean anything to me. It's you. It will always be you. You put a spark in my life, Bailey. We're going to make a life together. I'm sorry I got all upset. Can you forgive me? We'll start over when I get back."

He is out of his mind. This is over. All the sweet talking in the world can't change my mind. "Are you still taking her to the beach?"

"Bailey, it's not what I led you to believe before, Sweetheart. Hilary is going to be with her family, and my family will be there as well."

"Hendrix, it's over. Leave me alone or I'll let Lizzie to cut off your balls." See, I had to get childish with him. I hang up on him, and I feel like the weight of the world is off of my shoulders now, or at least I think I do. I send Lizzie a text because I know she will be happy.

Bailey: It's over with Hendrix :-P!

Lizzie: YAY!!! I want details!

Bailey: Later. When are you going to the hospital?

Lizzie: I was going after class tonight about 7. Are you really going to tell me in front of everyone, lol?

She has a point. I call her and fill her in. She didn't say I told you so. She says she was sorry I had to go through it.

I get to the hospital later than I intended, but I stop by the bookstore anyway to pick Granny up a couple of magazines and a book. I can't let her read one of my books. She'd have another heart attack then turn me over her knee.

Granny is sitting in her bed, basking in the attention she's getting from a few of my cousins. No wonder she is so loved. She gives so much love. They finish their visit and I sit on the edge of her bed.

"You just missed your Papa. He was getting tired, and your mom took him back home," Granny says. She's the one in the hospital, yet she is still taking care of him. Granny and Papa share an incredible love for each other. I want someone to love me like that one day. A love that stands the test of time, the kind that gets down in your core. You feel the love running through every vein and living in every cell of your body. The kind of love in which you can't live without the other person because you're not whole.

Granny told me the first time Papa kissed her, she knew he was the one that she wanted to be kissing him for the rest of her life. When Cash kissed me last night, I didn't want him to stop. I'm not sure if that is the same thing. If love like that still exists, I hope it is in my stars. I've decided I'm not going to settle for any half-ass romance. Not anymore. If I can't be loved liked that, I don't want to be loved at all. I'm ready to live for myself and adopt a little of Lizzie's attitude of "take no shit"!

"How is Papa taking you being in the hospital and not at home with him?"

She does her hand back and forth in a so-so motion.

"How are you feeling?" I lean over and give her a kiss on the cheek.

"I feel like a million bucks. Doctor Thomas told me I could go home tomorrow night, if I continue to improve, so cross your fingers."

She crosses her fingers on both hands, and I do too.

"What all did you do today?" she asks. "Did you bring me some coffee?"

Oops. "Granny, I didn't even think about it. I can text Cash or Lizzie to get you some." She has the biggest smile on her face.

"Are you and Cash doing that texting stuff now?"

I laugh. I can't help it. "He gave me his number last night in case I needed anything." I say, hoping she gets rid of whatever crazy notion she has in her head. I can get my own dates. I don't want help.

"Don't bother them. I'll be fine drinking water. I won't sleep a wink tonight if I drink anymore coffee today anyway. What did you bring me?"

She is like a little kid at Christmas. She can't wait to see what is in the bag.

After we sit and chat for a couple of hours, we hear a knock at the door.

"That's probably Cash and Margie." I say.

"Oh, good. I'm glad she's coming to visit me. Come in," she calls out.

Cash walks in behind a lady a few years older than my own mom.

"Hi, Margie, Cash, y'all come in," Granny says.

Granny is always the hostess, making everyone feel welcome. "Margie, this is my granddaughter, Bailey. Bailey, this is our neighbor and my new friend, Margie Wilson."

I extend my hand, but Margie envelops me in a hug instead. She leans back and looks at me with kind eyes and a warm smile. Normally, I would have been uncomfortable being hugged by a complete stranger, but her hug made me feel all cozy inside.

"Hello, Bailey, I feel like I already know you." Margie smiles at Granny. "How are you feeling, Addie? Are they taking good care of you up here?"

I like Margie, instantly, and I get the impression she doesn't meet a stranger.

They chat, and I go stand by Cash at the window. He smells delicious, with hints of citrus and wood. I want to merely stand here and inhale him. He is intoxicating. My body goes wild with want. I want to bury my face in his neck. I want his scent all over me. I want to suck on his lips. Last night, they were so soft and felt so good on mine. Get it together, Bailey. You haven't even been broken up with your boyfriend for twenty-four hours yet.

"Have you had a good day, Sweet Cheeks?" he asks, leaning toward me.

"It was okay, it could have been better. What about yours?" I look up into his eyes and lay my hand on his arm. I can't help myself. I want to feel that muscle. I squeeze then I feel him flex. Why in the hell am I gripping his bicep? I don't know what kind of spell he has over me, but I feel like he has me locked under it.

He has some stubble tonight which makes him look even better, if that's possible. He also has that cowboy hat on again which makes him look a little rugged with the scruff.

The door to Granny's room swings open and Lizzie bounces inside. She is grinning from ear to ear. I wonder what she is up to. She gives me a small wave then goes over to talk to Granny.

"Do you have any plans after visiting hours?" Cash asks.

He has thoughtful eyes, I think.

"I'm sure Lizzie and I will go out and do something, I'm not sure what that may be. With Lizzie you never know."

He looks at me questioningly, and I shrug.

Time flies by and before we know it visiting hours are over.

Margie tells Cash she is ready to go, and we all say our goodbyes.

Cash looks over to us and says. "I'm going to take mom home, but do the two of you want to get some dinner?"

Lizzie answers for us. "Cash, we would love to go to dinner. Why don't we just follow you out to Mt. Hope and eat out there?"

I smile because that's all I can do.

"That sounds like fun," says Granny. "I'll just get dressed and we will all go. How does that sound?" She smiles.

"You, young lady, are grounded until further notice." I tell her.

Everyone laughs.

"Granny, I will be back in the morning with a cup of coffee for you. Is there anything else you need?" I bend down and give her a kiss. She holds onto my arm so she can whisper in my ear.

"Baby, don't underestimate yourself. Remember it has to rain for there to be a rainbow." She pats my shoulder. "Love you, baby."

It's like she can read my mind. I haven't told what's going on between me and Cash, but she knows. "Love you too, Granny. Be good and don't go chasing any cute doctors around the hospital tonight." I wag my finger. I don't know what I would do without her in my life to guide me.

Lizzie and I take separate cars out to Mt. Hope, but we talk all the way there.

"I saw that look you were giving Cash, Bay. You want him."

She sounds triumphant.

"I just ended things with Hendrix. Don't you think I need to let the dust settle a while before I conquer Mt. Steamy?" She wants me to hop out of bed with one guy and straight into another. No thank you. I mean he has a body to die for, and I can't seem to keep my hands off of him. I did promise him that I would live in the now, live for this moment. He did almost make me hyperventilate with a mere kiss and I practically begged for more, but my head is on straight now.

"Don't give me that bullshit. Have you forgotten who you're talking to? Need I remind you of our freshman and sophomore year at college?"

She is laughing at me. I don't need reminding of my indiscretions.

"Lizzie, one day you'll have to remind me why I put up with you. You never let me get away with shit. You were right there with me every step of the way, sister." Sigh, those were the days, not a care in the world. Then I started dating Hendrix.

"That's the reason why you love me, I'm the only one who calls you on your shit. You have everyone else fooled by this good girl act, which is quite funny."

She's right again. My moral compass didn't always point north, well my sexually active moral compass.

I pull into the restaurant parking lot. "Bye bitch!" I say and hang up before she can come up with a retort.

CASH

I thought I really screwed up and scared the shit out of Bailey when I texted her that mom wanted to meet her. I didn't think that through very well. I wanted an excuse to see her and Mom did want to check on Mrs. Jackson. The kiss I gave her last night made me come alive. I've never believed in love at first sight, and I'm still not saying that's what's between us, but there is certainly something about this girl. She has a magnetism, and I want to see where our attraction goes. This could be a turning point.

If I ever have a daughter, I wouldn't want her going out with a guy like me because I know the kind of thoughts running through my mind. I woke up this morning from a dream about her that would put any porn flick to shame. It gave me some ideas that I really want to try with Bailey. But that's not all I want with her.

I drop mom off and head over to the only restaurant there is here in Mt. Hope, The Steakhouse. The name is as good as any other. The food is excellent and that's all that matters. The place is family owned and the staff is friendly. The atmosphere is comfortable and laid back. The décor is antique theme and some of the walls have corrugated steel on them, while others have wooden planks, and the salad bar looks like an old chuck wagon. The entrance is made from a silo and has wooden benches with wagon wheels on the end. This place gets crowded on the weekends and Sundays after church.

I walk in and look around to see where Bailey and Lizzie are seated. I see Lizzie over at the salad bar. I walk over to ask where we are seated.

"Just follow me, I'm on my way there," Lizzie says.

She gives me an amused look. She always looks amused. I think she is always up to something. She will make a great friend.

At our table, she takes the booth opposite of Bailey. I slide in beside Bailey, brushing her thigh with my hand accidentally on purpose. I just want to touch her, to caress that smooth golden skin and suck on those lips....*baseball, football, Chandler Bing*. Shit, I need to think about something else. I need to get my mind into the conversation they're having and off of wanting to show her the difference between a boy and a man.

"What have you ladies been up to today? Do you have a big week planned?" I ask.

Lizzie gives me a big smile before answering, "I was trying to get Bailey to go out Friday night with me since she is all free and single now. Why don't we at least catch a movie or something? We could even catch a movie tomorrow night."

"Oh, what movie are you going to see? My friend wants to see the new Quentin Tarantino film." I say.

"I can't go tomorrow night," Bailey says.

No excuse or reason. Bailey leaves me questioning if I've read her body language wrong. She is running hot and cold. Last night she was all into me, and now she acts like she doesn't want to be seen with me. Have I lost my swagger? She was all over me last night, and now she's not sure. Maybe I can coerce her into going. "What about you, Lizzie? Do you want to go with me and my friend, Dylan?"

Lizzie looks a tad confused, but she catches on quick. She is a sharp girl.

"That does sound like fun. Bailey, what do you have to do anyway? I will help you get whatever it is done. Don't leave me alone to go out with two boys. Bay, you owe me, remember?" Lizzie says.

Lizzie gives Bailey a pointed look. They are having some kind of telepathic exchange again. All I can do is look back and forth between them. I don't have a chance of deciphering their code.

"It's not that I don't want to go out with you, Cash. This isn't a good time for me right now. I hope you understand that I can't make it tomorrow night, maybe some other time."

Her demeanor has changed from resolute to apologetic. What is this about? Does her moodiness have something to do with her and that prick? I'm changing the subject to get her mind onto other things. I don't want to piss her off. "Hey, no problem." I say lightly, with a smile that I hope doesn't look fake. I'm not sure what is going on here, but I'm backing off for now.

Our food comes to the table and we dig in.

"This is the best steak I've had in a long time." So lame, but I'm at a loss.

"They do have the best steaks, don't they?" Lizzie pipes up.

Her voice is always happy.

"I am working in Granny's rose garden tomorrow and getting the house ready for when she comes home," Bailey says.

"I saw a few little things that needed repairing while I was mowing. I thought I could do those tomorrow."

Bailey looks surprised and I add, "I noticed how bad your grandfather's health is. He can barely get around with that cane, and no one should be out in this humidity. If you need any help with the roses after I'm done, I'd be glad to help. Your granny told me how much she loves her roses." I hope to spend time with her this way.

"I'm not working on the roses until early evening because of the heat. I'm cleaning the house and doing the laundry first. She doesn't like for you to mess with her roses in the heat of the day."

Everyone laughs. Mrs. Jackson must be a lot like mom. They get you to do exactly what they want done, the way they want it done, and don't even ask for it to be done.

We finish up our meal with idle conversation, nothing too deep. The waitress brings us our ticket and I pick it up to pay.

"Oh no you don't, Cash, you paid last night, tonight it is on me," Bailey says.

She's sounding all authoritative, but she should know from last night that this isn't going to work. Still, she looks so damn cute trying to be in charge.

"Do you not remember our conversation from last night? I told you that I pay for meals of pretty ladies. Besides, it's the gentlemanly thing to do since I was the one who did the inviting." I stand up with the bill in my hand.

She slides out of the booth, too, then looks up at me sweetly as she pats my arm. With the other hand, she snatches the bill, and turns toward Lizzie. "One point for the pretty lady, zero for the incredibility sweet man!"

Oh, she is hot when she goes sassy like that. Her attitude makes me want to spank her bottom then make it feel all better, but that's not appropriate behavior for a public place. I do know a suitable way to even this score, though. Let's see what little miss sassy does then.

We walk up to the cashier. Bailey is smiling big, and she thinks she has gotten one over on me. She lays the bill down on the counter and reaches into her purse for her wallet.

I lay my credit card on top of the bill then say to the older gentleman running the cash register, "I don't know what to think about a lady not letting you buy her dinner, do you?" He gives me an all knowing grin.

"I'm glad to see you were brought up right, that's how we used to do it back in my day," says the older gentleman. "These days, you never know who is going to pay. I don't like it, I think the man should pay, that's just the respectable thing to do."

I like him. I nod in thanks for backing me up then I leave a good tip on my card.

We walk outside. Lizzie heads on to her car and waves goodbye. I walk Bailey to her Jeep.

"Lizzie is something to be reckoned with, isn't she?" I say.

Bailey smiles. "Lizzie thinks she can always fix everything. Even when there isn't anything to fix."

So, she is accustomed to Lizzie messing in her business.

"I really want to take you out, I want to get to know you better." I kiss her softly then put my arms around her and hug her. When I let her go, I see she has a tear running down her cheek. I wipe it away with my thumb. "What's wrong, Bailey? Why are you crying, Sweet Cheeks?"

I get upset when women cry and I want to correct the wrong. Bailey is a kind-hearted woman who doesn't deserve to be hurt.

"It's nothing, Cash, really."

I wish she would open up to me, but we are still basically strangers. She doesn't know if she can trust me or not.

"Are you ready to call it a night or would you like to go for a ride? Find a dirt road to get lost on?" Her face brightens a little.

"That sounds nice, I could go for a ride," she says.

We drop her Jeep off at her house and head on out from there.

Sometimes taking a drive on back roads is all you need to make everything right in the world. Some of my best memories come from country roads. Maybe I can change this night into a better one for her.

I turn the radio on low.

"I love riding out here in the country. It's relaxing and helps leave all of your worries behind," she tells me. "I ended things with Hendrix today. I finally realized he wasn't treating me with respect. I decided to say goodbye to that chapter in my life, and you know what they say. If God closes one door, he'll open another."

She smiles meekly.

"It takes a lot of courage to stand up for yourself like that. It takes some people their whole life to see that they deserve respect. This is your journey in life and you're the only one who should decide what path to take," I say.

"What I think really attracted me to him, and this is going to sound horrible, is that I thought he could take me away and give me a better life. I wanted more than this simple life."

She looks so sad.

"Not to disagree with you but, truthfully, I've found living as simple as possible can make you unbelievably happy."

"I guess it's really all about who you're with and not about where you are anyway. I don't think I'd be very happy too far away from my family."

I lean my head toward her, "I like to come out here and watch the sun go down, and dance under the stars. Have you ever danced under the stars? Just pulled over on a whim and been held close while swaying to whatever song happens to be on the radio?" This is probably the sappiest shit I've ever spouted.

"I can't say I have, but that sounds sweet."

I pull over and turn up the radio. She looks puzzled. I get out and walk around to her side of the truck then open the door and help her down. I lead her to the front of the truck and take her in my arms, holding her close. George Strait is on the radio, making my job easier. We sway to the music and I sing along. George is singing the perfect song: "Give It All We Got Tonight."

Her eyes are glistening with tears and she lays her head on my chest.

She just looks too damn sweet for tears.

"You know, I'm a really good listener. Just lay it all on me. It always helps me when I talk about things with friends."

She looks up and I brush her lips with mine.

"There isn't anything to talk about, Cash." She sighs and shakes her head. "Why can't all guys be as sweet as you are? I've been hurt so many times, Cash, and I don't think I can start anything else right now. I don't think my heart can take anymore."

I really like kissing her, every kiss with her makes me want more. I want to kiss away all the hurt I see in her.

"I need to get back to being me. Have you ever lost who you were so much that you don't even recognize yourself anymore? Do you know what I mean? I'm tired of being the one who gets damaged and trampled on." Bailey's eyes burn and her jaw is set.

I hug her tight. "I know all about being hurt. It's been my life. I promise you, though, I'm not out to hurt you. I never want to hurt you." I rub her back, then I cradle the back of her head. "I don't think we are meant to stay the same after intimate connections. If our bonds with other people don't make us grow and change who we are a little, were they really worth our time? You should always learn and grow and then move on. I get that you just got out of a relationship, but painful endings are really just disguises for new beginning. Bailey, I dare you to take a chance on us."

She is shaking her head before I'm even finished.

"Who are you? Guys don't say things like that. They don't act the way you do. Who pulls over and dances on the side of the road? Cash, I've read way too many romance novels, and stuff like this only happens in books."

She is scared.

"You're right, not all guys say the things that I do. They don't treat women like ladies, but I am different, Bailey. Let me be the one who catches those tears for you. I can mend your broken heart because I know this kind of heartbreak. I've lived it. When someone has been hurt greatly, it just means they know how to love greatly."

She lets out a long sigh. "Romance book guys are every woman's fantasy and the fantasy is exciting, but when the covers are pulled back, what's left? Show me something real, something tangible. I've had the faux fantasy with Hendrix and I know now that isn't real. Real is more than pretty words. I don't want someone who has to tell me they love me for me to know it. I want to know they love me because they show me. I want the real. Not the kind that is bought because the real is priceless. I want the ridiculous, the all-consuming. I need the 'I can't live without you' kind of guy. That's my real."

"I'll be your real," I say then I kiss her, deeply and tenderly. She is hurt and doesn't need me going all caveman. I intend to be her everything. She will be the first and the last thing I think about every day. She will be mine, and I'll be her real. My job—my privilege—will be to give her moments like this and keep that beautiful smile on her face.

Bailey

Journal Entry: He wants to be my real. I poured my heart out to Cash. It was crazy for me to tell him all of that stuff, but it did feel good to finally admit it all aloud. Hendrix wasn't my real, and I see that now. I would have never had the kind of commitment from him that I want. I'm really pissed off that I wasted so much of my time on a person who only wanted to change me. I was never good enough. He always wanted to enhance this or change that. He only loved me for what I was pretending to be. When my life changed and I could no longer be the fictitious person he was grooming me to become, he stopped loving me. Actually, he never loved me because when you love someone, you accept them for who they are, flaws and all. I feel free, I'm free from struggling to be something I am not. Love isn't blind. Lust and infatuation is blind. That is what I had with Hendrix, infatuation. I was so obsessed with getting out of my life situation that I allowed him to shatter my self-esteem. His never realizing my worth as a person still hurts all the same, though.

Can Cash really be all the things that he's portraying? I want to believe him. I want it all to be true.

Lizzie has always been my go-to girl. No matter what life may throw at me, Lizzie is there. We don't always agree on everything, but this girl would go to war for me. I trust her with my life. She gives me courage to open my heart and take risks. She mother hens me to death and puts her two cents in on my life. The things I keep hidden from the rest of the world, she knows by heart. She is my footprint friend. Some friends are in your life for only a season; they come and go. Then you have those friends that leave a footprint on your heart, and you're never the same. That's how things are with Lizzie and me. She has her footprint on my heart. Even when she is calling me on my shit and I don't want to hear it, I still love her. I still trust her with everything in my life.

Cash took my breath away with all of the sweet nothings he was whispering to me. My head feels all jumbled up. I need to talk through this. Too much has happened, and I have to sort it all out. My head tells me one thing, and my heart tells me something else. Then my lady parts are screaming at me, and I'm hearing them loud and clear. I think I need professional help, but instead I call Lizzie. I know it's late, but I need her to come over. Besides, she must be dying to know what all happened. Between breaking up with Hendrix, and Cash wanting to be my real, I can't focus. Be my real? Pfft. Guys aren't really like that. Not since my Papa's day, anyway. Is Cash just a bunch of sweet talk or is he a real deal? I'm not sure if I can allow my heart to take another hit, but it's telling me to try. I want to know if Cash can be everything he's talked about. I desire to have the kind of love that stands the test of time. I have so much to give someone, I have an abundant of love to share. Can I trust he won't break me down? I want to find out.

Lizzie arrives with what we affectionately refer to as our weapons of destruction, Blue Bell's Tin Roof Ice Cream, kettle corn microwave popcorn, my favorite chocolate and caramel candy and a bottle of Riesling. I have Frito's and pickles for salty snacks. Things we would bring out when one of us got a broken heart or failed a test in high school, all but the wine anyway. We just added the wine since turning twenty-one, before that we always had sweet tea. Now we are set for my "figuring shit out" party.

I've seen Lizzie through a major ordeal and these snacks have powerful healing properties. That's what we tell ourselves. My Lizzie girl has been through a heartache as epic as any catastrophe written. Since she isn't a stranger to anguish, she will be my rock. Lizzie is the queen of "not allowing yourself to get hurt again". Not only is she in the anti-love club, she is the founding president. But that is her demon to fight. She refuses to talk about her own misfortune anymore and has built up walls so high, I wonder if anyone will ever break through. But tonight is about me, and my go-to girl is here for me.

"Hey, Bay, how are ya?" Lizzie gives me a hug after she empties her arms.

This has been one crazy messed up day. I tell her everything that happened with Cash. She is literally swooning over how sweet and romantic he treated me tonight. This surprises me. She isn't one for the hearts and roses. She is more keep that romantic bullshit to yourself and doesn't fall for any sweet talking crap. She likes to keep things casual. I can't blame her though, not with the shit storm relationship she had in the past. The one that keeps her from commitment.

"Lizzie, I haven't a clue of how I should feel," I say. "I feel broken and I'm soaring at the same time."

We are sitting in the middle of the floor, in our pjs. Just like when we were teenagers. Sometimes it seems as time has stood still because we still go back to our roots when things get serious.

"Tell me what it is you're really worried about? Are you holding out for another chance with Hendrix?" Lizzie asks.

"No, you were right, Liz. He's just an asshole that wants sex from me. But when I told him we were over, he didn't accept it. He changed his tune and became Prince Charming." That is only a little of the confusing part.

"Do you feel like things are moving too fast? I need to understand what has you all tied up in knots over this."

"Lizzie, I refuse to settle for any ol' country boy just because he has a great ass and beautiful eyes. Even when I feel live wires are coursing through my body with just a kiss. I'm not going to get stuck here without a pot to piss in, struggling to raise my kids. I can't do this…" I motion around me, "forever Lizzie. Not the taking care of Granny and Papa part, I will gladly take care of them. I'm talking about the whole country girl life."

She nods for me to go on as she eats another chip.

"So, Hendrix isn't perfect. No one is Lizzie, but maybe he's as perfect as I will get. He isn't the same when we are alone as he is when we are around everyone else. He treats me good then, Lizzie. He makes me feel loved, and I want to be loved by him. I know what you see. You see him demanding my attention. That is because he's so in love with me and he can't stand the thought of someone else even in my thoughts. He wants all of me, Lizzie. He even wants my thoughts. At least that was what I thought until he told me he was taking Hilary to the beach. Now I'm not sure what to think when it comes to him." I can feel tears getting ready to pour like rain.

"Have you ever thought that you're settling by choosing Hendrix? Yes, he does want to consume your thoughts and he also wants to control who you see. Mark my words, Bailey. If you stay with him, he'll tear you away from your family. I just want you to be happy, and I don't think Hendrix is the guy to make you happy." Lizzie strokes my back.

Maybe Lizzie has a point. Why does this stuff have to be so hard?

"You can't choose someone based on money and their ability to get you out of this little town. When they treat you like a piece of shit—"

She pauses as if reconsidering her words.

"Bailey, you already know the solution with Hendrix. You're too afraid to admit it to yourself."

She is right. I know she is right.

"At one time, you were a strong confident woman. I miss that woman. All I see now, Bay, is a shell of that woman because she has been beaten down by someone who doesn't give a fuck about her. You have on these rose colored glasses when it comes to Hendrix."

She has pulled off the gloves tonight, and all I can do is nod as I feel the tears spring free.

"Oh, Love, don't cry." Lizzie wraps her arms around me and pulls me in to her. "Shh, it's okay, Bailey, I love you. I just can't stand by any longer and watch you be hurt by a jackass. You are too precious to me for that."

Now we are both crying, "I kn...." I sniffle. "I know, Lizzie, I know. I've got a lot to think about." We sway together. "I love you too. You know that, right?" I am trying to quit my crying.

Lizzie wipes her eyes and, always the strong sensible one, says. "Now, on to dilemma number two, Cash." She sips her wine. "This tastes like shit with pickles and corn chips."

I laugh. Lizzie always knows how to lighten the mood. "You're right. Give me that glass." I get up to make us some tea.

She holds onto my arm, keeping me beside her. "I want to talk about Cash. He did *not* really pull over and dance with you out of the blue. Then sing to you on top of that. Where do I sign up for one of those?" She fans herself. "I'll take him, Bailey, if you don't want him."

She isn't really impressed, because I know she thinks all of that stuff is stupid. I give her a small smile. "Yeah, he did." Hold on a minute. I'm not ready to give him up, am I? "Lizzie, he is really sweet, but is he too sweet for me?"

She gives me an "Are you serious?" look.

"No one said you had to marry the guy to go out with him, Bailey. Take it slow on the relationship front and just have fun with him." She gives me a wink. "Besides, it can't be as bad as "Vanilla Only" Hendrix. You have nothing to lose going forward. It's just backward that you don't need to go. Plus, I know you love all the hearts and romance crap. You are one romance book away from being in a perpetual state of 'swoon'. You don't know the difference between fantasy and reality anymore. You make that

stuff your second religion, so don't give me that 'He may be too sweet' crap."

Why did I ever tell her about him being so sweet?

"Let's Google some new kinky shit for you to try when you find a new hook up," Lizzie says, her eyes glowing.

Did I mention that I love this girl? She has completely changed the mood of our whole conversation. I get my tablet, and we look up different positions and toys. Then we come across a video about grapefruit blowjobs. We laugh so hard tears are rolling down our face. This is where I quit looking things up. If I really want to know something about kinky sex, I'll go to the mistress herself.

We worked for **Hedrovibes by Kissin' Karen** for the past three and a half years. It is the most fun I have ever had working. Karen is such a great boss, and she knows everything you could ever want to know about sex. A customer could walk in the shop, and Karen could tell them about every product in the shop. Working there has been the education of a lifetime. I came out of my shy eighteen-year-old shell to awaken my inner sex goddess. She gave me my first vibrator which helped unleash my kinky side. I'll call her in the morning after she opens up the shop for business.

All of this talk about kinky sex makes me think of Cash. How kinky he would be? I get worked up thinking about the possibility and before I lose my nerve, I grab my phone and text Cash.

> *Bailey: Hey, are you still up? I want to talk. Can you come over?*
>
> *Cash: Yeah, I'm still up... I'll be over in a few minutes.*
>
> *Bailey: Just come around back to the picnic table.*
>
> *Cash: See you in a few.*

"I'm going outside to talk to Cash," I say. "I'll talk to you in the morning."

She gives me a smug smile.

"Just don't give your heart away and you'll be fine."

I get a blanket and head out back. I plan on using that picnic table. Cash makes it around the house about the time I put the blanket over the scarred piece of wood.

"Hey." He walks over and sits beside me on the table.

"I've been thinking about everything you said tonight." I turn and wrap my arms around him. "If you're willing to take the relationship part slow, I want to take that chance with you. First thing you need to know, I'm not a vanilla kind of girl." I release him and take off my shirt. "In fact, I want to show you right now what exactly you're getting yourself into." I shimmy out of my shorts and I get in his lap. "The second thing is I'm not afraid to get a little dirty. Now, what I really want to know," I say as I unbutton his shirt, "are you going to be able to handle a little spice in your life?" I push his shirt off of his shoulders and run my hands down his rippled chest. I feel every well-defined muscle as I go. I look at him before bending to lick the side of his neck. He tastes slightly salty.

He takes his shirt off and puts his hands on my hips, "Ah Sweet Cheeks, you want to play? Is that what you like? I can show you more than a little spice. I can set you on fire."

Good, I need it! I'm ready for a rough and rowdy happy finish. I push him back, setting my knees on each side of him. His long legs are hanging off the end of the table. I lower my head at his waist and slowly lick my way up, looking at him through my eyelashes.

Then he surprises me by flipping us.

"Let me tell you what to expect with me." He moves my panties to the side, licks a couple of his fingers and strokes my folds. "One, you may not be afraid to get dirty, darlin', but I am dirty." He draws small lazy circles around my belly button. "Two, I don't think you have been properly introduced to any real flavors, yet."

I want whatever flavor he is willing to give me right now.

He pulls my panties off then licks those small circles at my belly button now. Around and around.

I'm about to come off these planks of wood, and this blanket will be torn up when I'm finished.

He dips his tongue in and out while he caresses his hand downward.

I am breathing heavily and still he is very calm. How can he be so freaking calm right now? Who knew the belly button could be sensual. He runs his finger down my inner thigh and up to the apex.

"Now, darlin', do you really want our first time to be on a rickety old table? I see things much different for the first time. After that, I'll take you anywhere and everywhere, and you will be more than satisfied when I'm finished with you." He whispers this right over my center folds and takes a little lick.

I can feel his breath and it fires up my body. I don't care where we are. I want him now. He licks the apex of my thigh now, and I start to lose control. He takes one of his fingers and circles my opening on the inside edge. I push myself against his finger to induce the orgasm I'm on the verge of. He replaces his finger with his mouth.

"We'll pick this up right here, Sweet Cheeks. We just need a bed and how about a first date too?" He gives my little man in a boat a few more flicks and sticks a couple of fingers inside, pressing upward.

The pressure hits that delightful spot and my release is explosive, leaving me moaning Cash's name in a blissful haze.

He picks up my panties and slips them on me.

My entire body is limp. *What the hell?* He seriously can't be done. "What the hell, Cash? You can't just stop like that. Let me return the favor."

He picks up my shirt and pulls it over my head. He hands me my shorts and picks up his shirt, slipping it on.

I look at him completely stunned. He isn't taking anything for his own gratification? He gave it all to me and didn't take anything for himself?

He reaches for my face, and kisses me.

Another one of his Earth shattering kisses. He sucks on my tongue and I can taste myself which makes me want him more. I feel sprinkles of rain, but he doesn't stop. I wrap my legs around his as I try to crawl up his body. I have never wanted another guy like I want him right now. He is just as worked up as I am because his cock is hard and he is breathing a little faster than normal. "Tomorrow, I want to go out tomorrow night for that movie," I tell him, panting.

He smirks.

He is actually smirking.

"Is that right? Are you telling me when we'll go out?"

He looks amused. I'm coming unglued, undone and he is teasing me now.

"I'll pick you up at seven, Sweet Cheeks. Now go inside before you get sick and we have to delay this outing."

I see he is hard in his tight jeans, and I know under the cool exterior, he desires me too.

"That sounds like fun, Cash, almost as much fun as the cold shower I know you'll be taking tonight. Come in with me, let me take care of you." I sound pathetic, but I want to tie him up, and make him beg for more. He has me wanting more. I bet he can coax gushing orgasms out of me.

He gives me one last kiss, "Lock the doors behind yourself, and call me if you get scared." He leaves.

He fucking leaves me, again. I don't know what man gives up a free opportunity for sex, but this shit has to stop.

CASH

A bitterly cold shower has benefits. Besides strengthening blood circulation, it improves mood and decreases testosterone levels. My testosterone has undergone acceleration at a colossal rate since meeting Bailey. Why am I torturing myself? Hell if I know.

She is a firecracker begging to be set on fire, but I don't want her as another notch on my bedpost. She is too special for that. What I do know is Bailey is a woman to be cherished, and she needs to know how it feels to be adored. I plan on showing her how she should be respected and then I will validate that kinky side of hers.

For this cold shower to work, though, I have to quit thinking about her body. She is fun sized, I've always liked short girls. They seem more feminine to me. I have this urge to pick them up off their feet and hold them. She has the largest breasts, small waist, and the most delectable hips that I keep dreaming about holding on to while I thrust inside of her. I have to quit entertaining what it would be like to explore her kinky side. I've determined that the cold shower didn't work. Masturbation will help, but my appetite won't be quenched without the real thing.

It took steadfast determination and sheer willpower to not throw Bailey on that rickety lumber and take her up on her proposition. I'm elated that she takes the initiative, but tonight wasn't the time for her to be in control. Her little dominatrix act was above and beyond arousing. An animalistic thirst came over me that I had trouble tapping down, and I couldn't let her stay in command. I had to change the ascendancy. Not only has this woman stolen my heart but she has ignited something in me that I didn't know existed.

I rub one out to release this buildup of carnal lust. I've never been able to come so quickly with the mere image of a woman. Not without some fantasy of a sexual act, but with Bailey all I need is the vision of those perfect attributes. My release isn't nearly satisfactory. Tomorrow night won't get here soon enough. I need her, all of her. This isn't about a fucking craving. No, it's an actual need for survival now.

I need her in the most innocent of ways. I need to be the one protecting her. I need to be the one she holds on to when all hope is lost. I need to be the one who kisses her forehead, and wakes up with her. To tell her she is special, and she's adored. I need to be her whipping boy because I'm fucking pussy whipped without even meeting her pussy. I feel like everything in my life has led me to her, every heartache, every decision, and every breath I've taken. When I finally do fuck her, I can die a happy man because I will have loved her as she should have been loved.

She may not be over that boy she was dating, but sometimes life is about risk. Women need to go through bad relationships to know when they have a good man to take care of them. I've never been obsessed with a woman. Dammit, if I don't get my mind off of her, I'll stay stiff the rest of the night. I've got to watch some NASCAR, baseball or go fishing and let my mind go numb, so maybe my dick will go limp.

Sleep bypasses me. I've watched three episodes of Friends, and I still can't unwind. I switch to infomercials. If those can't put me to sleep, I don't think anything can. After another hour, I've almost given up on sleep. I turn off the TV and I toss and turn. I look at the clock and it's 4 am.

I give up on sleep and go into my home office to get some paperwork done. I sit behind the massive desk which belonged to Mom's grandfather. I'm the fourth generation to use it and I take pride in keeping it clear of clutter. It is solid cherry wood and the heaviest bitch I've ever had to move.

I catch up on my paperwork and pay a few bills then I take another shower, and brew some coffee. I will need a few shots of espresso this afternoon to keep going. I end up cooking breakfast. Mom has been cooking most of our meals, but I know how to cook somewhat, and I have good knife skills. I know bacon and eggs anyway. The smell of coffee and bacon wake up mom an hour earlier than normal. I pop some bread in the toaster, and she sits down to eat with me.

"Mornin', baby boy. Did I hear you leave again last night?" She peeks over her coffee mug at me. She is still half asleep, but I made the coffee

strong today, so she'll be "wide eyed and bushy tailed" soon. Those are her words not mine.

"Yes, ma'am, I went across the street and checked on Bailey and Lizzie." I keep eating. If I look at her, I'm sure my true intention from last night will be written all over my face.

"That was nice of you, baby. Did something go bump?" she snickers.

I'm glad she thinks this is funny, but I refuse to discuss my sex life with my mother. She'd probably love more details, but she's out of luck. Although, I should straight up tell her one time and embarrass the hell out of her. I couldn't ever bring myself to do that because I have more respect for her than that.

As we eat, we talk about what we want to accomplish on the house this week and the normal small talk we do every morning. She doesn't ask why I'm up early, but she's pretty sharp. I've never been able to get anything past her.

After I finish eating, I put my dishes in the sink then kiss her on the cheek and tell her I will be home early but won't be eating dinner. She smiles knowingly then sips on her coffee.

"So, you'll be checking on the girls across the road again tonight?"

"I'll just be checking on one of them tonight, if that's alright with you." I give her a wink. "Bye, mom." I head out the door.

I ride to work with my windows down. Nothing like the cool breeze to get you going in the morning. I enjoy the drive to and from work. The drive in gives me time to get my plan for the day all set in my head and the drive home helps me unwind.

Once I'm at work, I find nothing alleviates my uncontrollable desire to fuck Bailey. I find myself thinking up new and inventive ways to make her all breathy again. She makes me want to sin hard and fast. But she is more than a sexual temptation. She has a softness and vulnerability I want to explore, too.

A new perspective is in order. I need to think of ways to Bailey's heart. That will be my direction today. I recline in my chair and put my feet on my desk while I contemplate the best course of action. She adores her grandparents. I pick up the phone and order Mrs. Jackson flowers. I text Bailey. She needs to know she is on my mind.

Cash: Good morning, beautiful.

I've got this shit. Romeo hasn't got crap on me. Casanova was an amateur, and that Darcy fella was a joke. Cash Wilson has made up his mind and he will conquer. I get out a legal pad so I can make a to-do list.

Yes, a list always helps get things done. Things get accomplished when you take inventory of what needs to be accomplished.

Bailey: Morning, handsome, are you working today?

My plan is in the works, she will be falling at my feet after tonight. I just have to play my cards right, I'll go all in, and win the jackpot. Maybe it's just a lot of little things to show her I care. There doesn't have to be a grand romantic gesture, right? Tapping my ballpoint pen on the tablet, romantic gesture.... Damn, this is harder than it looks.

Cash: I'm hardly working, what about you?

She will be putty in the master's hands. I will mold her to my will. Confidence. Add that to my list.

TEXT LIZZIE TO SEE HER LIKES / DISLIKES

PICNIC, BLANKET & STARS

HOLD HER HAND

SEND HER TEXT TO LET HER KNOW I'M THINKING OF HER,

CHIVALRY...

Bailey: I was about to go to the hospital, but they aren't letting Granny out yet.

Cash: I hope she isn't worse. Is there anything I can do to help? Do you need anything? Are you scared to stay alone?

Bailey: You had your chance last night, big boy. You snooze, you lose.

I laugh. I love me some sassy Bailey.

Cash: Ow now, don't be like that, Sweet Cheeks. I'll make it all good tonight. You deserve more than splinters in your ass.

Bailey: Lol! Would you pick them out for me?

Shit. So much for not thinking about her perfect attributes.

Cash: With my teeth! If that is what you want.

See, it's all going to work out. She is all flirty today, but I need to move this along. What time will you be done?

> *Cash: Can I pick you up at seven for dinner and then we'll go to that movie, or we can go wish on some stars?*
>
> *Bailey: Wishing on stars? Is that your code word for sex because I thought you didn't wish on stars. But I do like the sound of wishing on stars. I think I can swing 7. I'll see you then, handsome.*

Checkmate. I text Lizzie asking about Bailey's favorite things. This woman is going to be swept off her feet before she realizes what hit her. She can't know I'm trying so hard. It has to seem like a piece of cake.

My office phone rings. My secretary, Dawn, passes the call through to me, alerting me it's my mom. I answer, "Hey Mom, what's up?" She is in tears, and I can't make out a word she is saying. "Mom, I'm on my way home. I'll be right there."

Mom has been through hell and back. She has even been hospitalized for depression, so whatever is happening could be a volatile situation for her. I wish there was someone who could go stay with her until I get there. I rush out, telling Dawn I won't be back until tomorrow. I waste no time getting to my truck and flooring the gas hoping to make it to Mt. Hope in record time.

I hope this is just something minor, but I know she wouldn't be this upset over something minor. I go eighty down Highway 24, passing everyone with my hazard lights flashing. On the bright side, if there can even be one, is there isn't any traffic this time of the day. I pull into my driveway and slam on the brakes, sure I've broken a dozen traffic laws, but who the fuck cares about that. I notice a strange motorcycle parked by mom's car. Who the hell could that be? They will have hell to pay if they've messed with my momma. I run inside my house, worried as to what I may find.

Mom is laying on the couch curled into herself. A guy a couple of years younger than me is kneeling beside her.

"Who the hell are you and what did you do to my momma?" I'm fighting mad, and this guy has some explaining to do. I bend down to check on mom, "Hey, are you okay? What happened, Momma?" I stroke her back. I stand up getting ready to kick some ass when he stands and turns to look at me. I feel like I should know him from somewhere, but I can't place him.

"Hello, you must be Cash." He extends his hand.

He looks friendly and a little worried too, given the mess my mom is in, but looks can be deceiving.

"Yes, I'm Cash, and you are?" I don't know if I trust this guy yet or not.

"My name is Clayton, you can call me Clay." His smile droops. He rubs the back of his neck and says, "I'm your half-brother."

My mom sobs louder, and that's when I punch him right in the chin. Shaking out my hand, I stand here fuming, ready for this guy to get the hell out of my house. My dad has always been good at hurting her and this must be one of his sick jokes.

"Can we talk before you start trying to kick my ass, please?" he asks, rubbing his chin.

"No, you need to get the fu— You need to leave. You're upsetting my mom." Pointing at the door, I grab him by the arm. He's a skinny twig of a guy so I can easily maneuver him. I half drag him to the front door.

"I think you are going to want to talk to me."

He is fucking wrong about that, "Get out of here, and don't come back!" I push him through the door I left open on the way in.

"Cash, our dad died last night in an accidental shooting."

He stands there looking at me, waiting expectantly, and I stand here looking at a younger version of myself. We share the same intense gaze. Other than our size, the only major difference is his eyes are a dark chocolate brown. I plop down on the edge of the porch and motion for him to take a seat beside me. This little runt has some explaining to do, and he better start talking.

"Why don't you start from the beginning and I'll decide if I want to talk to you or not."

Again, he rubs his chin where I hit him. Good, it still hurts. He knows I mean business and I'm not someone who you want to screw over.

Bailey

Journal Entry: Granny isn't getting better. She has developed pneumonia. Either her breathing exercises didn't work or she didn't do them. The doctor told us that she is still retaining fluid on her lungs. They are giving her medicine through her IV to help draw off the fluid. All of this is terrifying.

Mom said Papa is getting worse by not being with Granny. I'm worried to death about them both. I feel so helpless, I want to do something to fix it, make it better. I've been in Granny's hospital room all day. I'm torn with wanting to be here for her and wanting to take Papa home so he can get back on his schedule somewhat.

If Mom could take care of him in his own home, he would be so much more comfortable, and he wouldn't be irate with her. But having him at her house makes things easier on her because she can take him to work with her. If I could just split myself in half, I could help them both, but the truth is, I can't help Granny. And Papa would still be going to be upset in his own home without Granny. I'm scared at the hard road ahead that lies ahead of them.

I put my journal back in my purse, and I pace around the room. The air is suffocating, and smells of Clorox and the medicine burns my nostrils. Granny has been sleeping for a while now. Her snores remind me of a freight train. At home, the sound drives me crazy but here it is almost reassuring.

I've been trying to keep myself busy, but there is only so much you can do at the hospital. Cash sent Granny a dozen roses. He might just be a keeper. I guess time will tell. As Granny says, you've got to let the crazy out a little at a time. So, I'm waiting for his crazy, but how long are you supposed to wait for that shoe to fall? When do you know they aren't going to turn bat shit crazy on you?

Lizzie and I have been texting on and off all day. She has class and will be here later, but I feel the need to cancel my date with Cash. My heart is telling me to stay with her. I hope he will understand, but if he doesn't, at least I'll find out what kind of person he is early on.

Bailey: Hey, I have bad news. I need to reschedule our date.

Cash: That's fine, Bailey, I have things to take care of anyway. Can I talk with you later?

Bailey: Sure, that will be alright. I hope you have a good night.

Cash: Yeah, you too.

He was so short with me so maybe he isn't Prince Charming after all. I don't have time for all of that anyway, so why are tears rolling down my face? I'm freaking stressed out, and I guess I was hoping he could take my mind off of this mess.

"You're going to wear a hole in the floor if you keep up that pacing." says Cindy, the nurse who comes into the room to check on Granny's stats.

She has been the friendliest one so far, and Granny has enjoyed getting to know her.

"Doctor Thomas is moving her back up to ICU. With pneumonia and now low potassium, she is in a more serious condition."

My heart falls to the pit of my stomach. I need to call my family and let them know. "What should I do?" I ask Cindy.

She walks over and puts her arm around my shoulder. "All you can do is pray for her, honey."

The tears are flowing freely down my face now, I wipe them away, but I can't stop them. "I do know you won't be able to see her again today after they get her set up. Doctor Thomas wants her to rest."

I nod.

Granny is waking up with the orderly who's preparing to move her.

I walk over and kiss the side of her forehead. "I love you, Granny, and I will be back for visiting hours tomorrow."

She takes my hand and squeezes it. "Baby, you need to get some rest too. Why don't you go home early and get you some dreamtime for me? Dry those tears up, I'm fine, I'm too mean for anything bad to happen." She gives a weak smile.

"Yes, ma'am, that's exactly what I will do." I reach down and give her one last kiss before Cindy and an orderly whisk her off to the ICU. I take the flowers with me since she can't have flowers in the ICU. I text my family to let them all know about Granny's deteriorating condition on my way to the parking lot.

I make it to my Jeep and my phone dings with an incoming text.

Hendrix: I'm sorry, Babe. I came back from the beach early. I couldn't be away from you. I made a mistake, please come talk to me.

Me: I told you it was over. Besides, I'm kind of seeing someone, Hendrix.

Hendrix: We need to talk this out. I have something for you and something to help your grandparents too.

He has something to help my grandparents out? Well, he has my interest piqued. I guess it wouldn't hurt to hear what he has to say.

Me: Okay, I'll come over, but only to talk.

Hendrix: Good, Sweetheart, I'll see you soon.

I give Lizzie a call while I drive over to his house. She isn't impressed with me going to see him. She instructs me to call her as soon as I leave. I want to see what he has up his sleeve this time, although it won't change my mind. I pull into the driveway of his apartment and set my emergency brake.

He meets me at the door and envelops me in a hug. "I missed you, Baby. I'm sorry. I was wrong."

Who is this guy? Where is the real Hendrix?

"I'm so sorry about your grandmother. I just heard how sick she is, Bailey. Come in." He releases me.

I go inside and have a seat on his sofa. "Sorry to rush you, Hendrix, but what do you have to help Granny and Papa?"

He walks in to his bedroom then returns. "Here, I bought you a couple of dresses and shoes for the next time we go to the club."

He hands over two beautiful dresses. The labels say Valentino. They must have cost a fortune. He hands me two boxes and two handbags, and I stare at them. One purse is Louis Vuitton and the other is Prada. I feel like I could catch flies in my mouth. He has bought me things in the past. Hell, he paid for my breast implants, but he can't buy me now. "I told you we are over, I don't want to see you anymore. I'm done with you."

He smirks. "I've also hired around the clock care for your grandparents and I have set up to get their driveway paved. I see the error of my ways, and I want to make it up to you. The team of health care providers I've hired, Bailey, are the best money can buy." He sits beside me and wraps his arms around me.

I don't return the hug. *He did that for me?* Helping take care of my Granny and Papa is more than I could ask for. From anyone. "I don't know what to say. You wanted to see other people and you took Hilary to Destin, but now you are giving me gifts and taking care of my Granny and Papa." I'm in shock. Anyone who wants to help me with them has to be an angel. This has to be a dream. "Who told you about Granny? That she's worse?"

"My family has always been a major benefactor of the hospital. We can find out anything that goes on in the hospital. I want to help you, Bailey. I know how much you love them." He gets up and paces.

He wants to help me now? "Hendrix, thank you for your help with my grandparents, but we are still going to see other people, right? I've met someone that I'm seeing."

He comes to sit beside me again. "Bailey, I know it will take some time to build your trust back, but I love you and I can't live without you. Besides, with around the clock nurses, you can move in here with me. I don't want you seeing anyone else. You are mine. We can work through this, Bailey. We have been together so long."

He rubs my leg soothingly and all I can do is sit here. This day has been too much, and he's taken away my breath with this change in behavior and his generous offer. "I've got to think about all of this, Hendrix. I've opened my eyes to how you treated me like shit our whole relationship. A few presents aren't going to change that, but paying for my grandparents' healthcare gives me something to think about."

He pulls me to him and tries to kiss me.

I pull away from him. I need to leave so I can think. Him kissing and hugging me is clouding my judgment. It always does. "Let me go so I can think about this." I stand up.

"I'm apologizing for all of that, Bailey. Give me another chance. At least promise me you won't see anyone else until you decide."

"I can't make promises like that."

"Why?" Hendrix pops up from the sofa. "Who are you seeing? Who did you meet?"

"His name is Cash. He's our new neighbor."

He bends over laughing. "Oh, that's a good one, Bailey. A redneck. No, really, who are you seeing?"

See, him looking down on people is what has gotten us into this mess in the first place. "I have to go," I pick up my Target purse and leave the gifts. "I'll call you tomorrow about your offer, but I'm going to see Cash. I owe him for getting my Granny to the hospital."

I move to walk away and Hendrix pulls me back into his embrace. He isn't happy about this decision.

"Bailey, maybe you don't understand. I love you and I want to make a life with you."

My emotions are on overload.

"Now kiss me, Baby, before you leave me. I will have someone out paving your drive tomorrow, and I will have a full staff ready for your grandfather in the morning. It's time for us now, Bailey. Our future will be perfect. I can provide for you and take care of your grandparents."

He is talking to me so sweetly and running his hand softy over my hair. I turn and give him the tiniest smile ever then let him kiss me.

"That's better. That's my girl. You can't replace me with a redneck. How can he take care of you like I can? We belong together, Babe. You know this, right?"

I nod and kiss him back.

He pushes me against the wall and presses his body hard into mine.

"You're right, Hendrix. We have been together for a long time."

I kiss him hard.

"I knew you would come around to my way of thinking, Baby. This is our destiny." He insists on walking me to my Jeep, buckling my seatbelt for me. "I think we need to get you something decent to drive too. Pick out anything you want. It's yours. Whatever you want, Bailey. I can give you the world."

I give him a little nod. "Bye, Hendrix, I will call you later. You are so kind for helping out my family. I love you, but this is all a little sudden and I need time to think." I close my door and back out of his driveway. He stands there with his arms crossed. What the shit am I going to do now? I need his help more than I need anything else in this world, but something tells me he isn't being genuine.

I need help from a higher power. Why does life have to be so complicated? My mind whirls a hundred miles an hour. What would Granny tell me to do? If I were to ask my dad, he would say make a pro's and con's list. Mom would probably tell me to follow my heart. But I really want to know what Granny would say, and she is the one person who I can't bother with this. Oh brother, what am I going to do now? Decisions... Decisions.

CASH

Today has been a crazy day. I have a lot to process. My mental state has gone haywire. Mom has finally calmed down with a call into her psychiatrist who she's seeing first thing in the morning. We knew my dad had cheated on my mom occasionally, but with Clay's arrival we discovered my dad had been a cheater their whole marriage. He has a whole other family. We hadn't a clue about Clay or his seventeen-year-old sister, Oakley. Mom is devastated over the news of dad's death more than the news of this additional family.

Apparently, dad was a lot better at hiding his cheating ways from wife number two than he was from mom because when Ann, Clay and Oakley's mom, found out about us, things got ugly. That is why he filed for divorce from Mom, although Ann still wasn't happy about all his years of deceit.

Even though Ann and Dad had been arguing non-stop since she found out about us, they made things work for a few months. Dad was away on a gig for a week, but when he returned, Ann was suspicious of every move he made. Clay said that things escalated quickly, that Dad was trying to get a gun away from Ann when he was accidentally shot. The mess the impact of the bullet made sent them all into shock. Ann couldn't live with herself over what happened and ended up turning the gun on herself. All of this happened in front of Clay and Oakley.

Oakley is having a difficult time dealing with the death of both of her parents, and Clay, who is only twenty himself, has no idea what to do for Oakley. He came here to inform us about dad, but if the truth be told, he is here for some guidance. Both sets of his grandparents have passed away. Overnight, he is the legal guardian of his younger sister. Heck, I wouldn't know how to raise a teenager either.

When mom finally calms down and comes to her senses somewhat, she wants to meet Oakley and get to know her and Clayton. Mom has always had a big heart, and she hates they are now parentless. She insists Clay and I go pick Oakley up from the hotel.

We pick up Oakley, who looks nothing like me or Clay. She must be the spitting image of her mother. We bring her back to the house, and when Mom sees her in so much pain, something inside of her must click because she pulls Oakley in for a big hug. That's when the poor girl breaks down.

Mom says, "Look at me, Oakley. I know nothing I will say or do will make you feel any better, but I know you will feel better after you talk about it. I'm here for that, and for both of you boys too. Why don't we sit down and express our feelings."

I love that woman. She is hurting herself, probably dying on the inside, but her motherly instincts have taken over.

Oakley nods, and mom leads her to the sofa then sits beside her. Clay and I follow suit.

"The best thing we can do is talk about our loved ones. That will help us get over our grief and keep them alive in our hearts," Mom says, kicking off the conversation.

"I'm going to miss them so much, I can't believe they're gone." Oakley cries.

"There, there, baby girl. You cry as much as you want. Tears help heal your heart. It's okay to cry," Mom says.

As I watch Mom comfort Oakley, I wonder how she puts her own grief aside to attend to ours?

"Oakley, remember when Mom played that April Fool's joke on Dad last year telling him I got a girl preggers?" Clay asks.

He looks deep in thought.

"She kept him going for days until he started coming down on you and wouldn't let you go out. He was going to protect your virtue from guys like me."

Clay gives a half-hearted laugh.

"Yeah, I had got invited to prom and he wasn't going to let me go. Then he relented, but made me get a dress that looked like it was for a nun." She wipes her eyes.

"Sounds like Dad was playful with you guys," I say. "I wish he'd been more playful here. I hate to even say it, but he only brought misery to us."

"Cash, you don't remember but when you were younger, we went out on the road with him," Mom says. "He was so proud of you, showing you off. He would bring you on stage and get you to sing a little song that he taught you."

"Really?" I don't remember that, but I do remember him asking me to go out with him some as a teenager. I was dead set against doing anything with him by that time.

"Clay, will you take me back to the hotel? I'm tired," Oakley says.

"There's no reason for you guys to stay in that hotel. You're family, and you'll be staying with us. We have an extra room for Oakley, and Clay, we have a cot you can put anywhere you like. I'll even sleep on the couch, and you can have my bed." Mom says, holding onto Oakley and soothing her.

"Mrs. Wilson…" Clay says.

"Margie." Mom shakes a finger at him. "There won't be any of that formal stuff, and I won't take no for an answer." She has said her piece.

"Yes, ma'am, but there won't be any of this you sleeping on the couch business and I'll be picking up dinner for everyone. I insist on that. Deal?" Clay extends his hand to confirm the agreement.

"You drive a hard bargain, Clay, but it's a fair one. Deal." Mom shakes Clay's hand. Mom has a way of making you feel better even in horrible circumstances.

Clay and Oakley leave to check out of the hotel and grab their stuff. I try to wrap my head around having siblings. I reckon I need to get to know them, too. Our father being a fucking asshole is not their fault. They were in the dark as much as we were. They both seem like good people, and if mom can come to terms with all of this, I can too.

They return and Mom helps Oakley get settled in the guest bedroom then let's her have some alone time. Mom probably needs her own time to process all of this too, so I motion for Clay to follow me outside.

"Man, I'm sorry about hitting you like that." I look at the ground, a little embarrassed at the way I reacted. "All I could see was my momma hurting."

"No hard feelings, Cash, it would have been the same way with my mom. The way I look at it, if we grew up together as brothers, we would have been throwing punches for years."

He gets quiet on me, in his own thoughts, I guess.

"So, he did it to you too, huh?" Clay asks.

Am I missing something? "Excuse me?" He has lost me.

"I'm assuming you are named after Johnny Cash, am I right?"

Well that isn't hard to figure out. "Yeah, so he named you after Clay Walker?" That would be just like my dad to do something like that. He thought he was God's gift to country music and wanted me to have the name of one of his idols.

"No, I'm named after Clayton Moore."

I guess he can see I'm still confused.

"The Lone Ranger," he says. "Clayton was the original Lone Ranger."

I bust out laughing. This is even better than being named after Johnny Cash. I hum the theme song, "I bet you never get that. Wait, don't tell me. Your bike is named Silver."

I hop off the porch, and we walk over to his bike.

"I didn't even think about that when I bought my bike." He says, running a hand along the leather of the seat. "I just fell in love with it and dude, it's a Harley, who wouldn't love it."

"You know this is cause for endless harassment from me, right?" Hey, isn't that what a big brother is for? Giving the little brother hell? "I do agree it is a badass bike. I like how you've got it all chromed out."

"Yeah, but it's hell to keep it all polished. My bars are custom drags, but they're the easiest to keep up. My wheels are a pain in my ass to keep clean. When I bought them, all those intricate details were the deal. Now, they are the bane of my existence. They don't call them the Reaper for nothing. See all those sharp edges, yeah, they get me every time." He examines his hands.

"What kind of Harley is this? Soft-tail, Roadster?" I bend down to take a closer look at the motor.

"It's a Fat-boy Soft-tail custom. Definitely a piece of art, if I do say so myself. Yeah, you go right ahead, Johnny. At least I'm Moore Wilson than you."

I'm glad he can joke around with me. Maybe I can help him forget this hell for a few minutes. "At least Oakley has a cool name." I tell her before it hits me that dad wasn't very original on names.

"She is glad it's not Annie." He leans up against the post on the porch.

"Is she good with a gun?" He shakes his head and grimaces.

Me and my big mouth. I need to start thinking before I speak. Guns are a touchy subject right now. "I'm sorry, I didn't even think about it."

He stares across the street. I follow his gaze, which reminds me I need to call Bailey and explain things to her. I can't believe I blew her off like I did. I should have taken a couple of minutes and at least texted her. I hope she isn't too pissed.

I go and grab us a couple of beers, and we talk for a while. I notice Lizzie's little bug pulls into the Jacksons' driveway. That girl is a trip, but she is sweet. Not five seconds later, Bailey pulls in behind her. I need to just go over there, and let her know what's going on.

"Who are the fine ass chicks?" Clay points with his beer bottle.

"One is the girl of my dreams and the other is her friend or cousin, I think."

"Which one is the dream girl? Please don't say the blonde."

My eyes are glued on Bailey. "Come on, I'll introduce you. The blonde is Lizzie, and Bailey is mine, so don't get any ideas."

I push off the side of the house. Now that things have settled down, I can focus on Bailey again. A little TLC might be in order, but I want to give her more than a little. Clay follows me across the street. We step up on the porch and knock on the door. Lizzie opens it.

"Hey, Cash." She pulls me in by my arm, "I'm glad you came over. I think I'm going to need your help in a big way. She has lost her mind and you're the only one who can fix it right now," Lizzie says in a hushed tone.

Bailey is sitting on the couch with her legs drawn to her chest. She has her right cheek resting on her knee. Tears stream down her face and I can hear the soft sounds of her breath catching from all the crying. Her beautiful face is reflecting all the anguish she is feeling inside, and I would do anything to take this heartache away from her.

I don't bother introducing Clay. I go straight to my girl. I hear Clay talking.

"Do you know what this shirt is made of? Boyfriend material." Clay tells Lizzie.

Please tell me he isn't that cheesy.

My girl is upset, and she needs me. "What's wrong with my Sweet Cheeks? Is it your Granny? Is she okay?" I sit on the couch with her and she crawls into my lap and curls into a little ball. I kiss her hair and just hold her. She isn't crying, now, but something is weighing heavy on her mind. "What can I do to make everything all better?"

She lifts her head and looks at me then she nips at my lips hungrily. She puts her hands in my hair and kisses me with full on passion.

We need to take this somewhere else. I look over to tell Clay, signaling I will be back. I stand back up with Bailey wrapped all around me. "Let's go talk, Sweetheart." I carry her outside to our picnic table. I sit her on the end and stand between her legs, still hugging her. I pull her chin up to look at me, "Tell me, what has you troubled? Please? I can't help you if I don't know." A fear washes over me, something tells me this isn't going to be good.

"Cash, I don't think you can help me."

I wipe away a tear that runs down her cheek. "Why don't you let me be the judge of that?"

"Granny's not getting any better and she is going to need a lot of experienced medical care. Even with her insurance and Medicare, I don't see how I can afford it. Their Social Security checks aren't that much and it takes most of my current income to pay my car payment and insurance. My family will help out some, but they really can't afford it all either." Her cheeks redden.

I see the shame in her eyes and she ducks her head. She has nothing to be ashamed about. Everybody struggles from time to time. "Hey, you will make it through this, I promise. I won't let you suffer. I'm here for you, all of this. We can handle it, one step at a time. You have me to lean on now."

"Hendrix has offered to take care of Granny with around the clock medical care," she blurts out.

Is she telling me our relationship is over before it's even began?

"I don't want to take his help, Cash, I really don't. I don't want to be with him, but he's promised he's changed and Granny needs the care."

She is bawling now. She is torn up over this.

"What exactly does she need, Bailey? Is she really going to need around the clock care? What has the doctor suggested that you guys do? Have you looked into that?"

She shakes her head. "I don't even know what she needs. They put her back into the ICU with pneumonia. She has a long road ahead of her."

She proceeds to tell me a very interesting conversation between her and this prick. She is clearly wanting to do what she can for her grandparents because she has a devotion to them which is real. But she told me last night all of the reasons she wanted out of the relationship.

"Why don't you call and make an appointment to talk to the doctor? Find out what your granny is going to need before you make any kind of decision like that." She isn't thinking logically right now. She can't see through her pain that the prick is trying to manipulate her. I can't allow that to happen, but is she going to listen to reason?

"I don't know, Cash."

What in the hell is there not to know? Her eyes are all puffy and her face is blotchy, but she is still the most beautiful woman in the world to me. How am I going to make her see this? "What is that you don't know, Bailey? You tell me you don't want to accept Hendrix's help. I offer my

help and you won't accept it either? Are you too proud for a man to help you? Is that it?"

"Noooo," she wails. "Cash, he is offering financial help, don't you see how hard that is for me to pass up? This will not only help them get better, but have a better quality of life, too. How do I turn that down?"

I can't help it. I'm pissed off that she is even considering going back to that prick. She is putting her own needs and happiness last because of money. I really get that she wants to take care of her grandparents. I do, but I don't want to lose her before we even get started. I am infuriated that prick is using his wealth to control her.

"The way I see it, Bailey, is that you can go through your life and let people like Hendrix manipulate you this way, or you can grow the fuck up and start living for yourself. Do you really think your grandparents would want you to sacrifice your own happiness for them to have a better quality of life? Does money mean that much to you?"

She looks at me like I just slapped the shit out of her, but it's the truth. Yes, I'm infuriated that he is manipulating her, but I'm beyond infuriated that she is allowing him. She is too bright not to see this for herself.

"Please leave, Cash, I need to be alone."

She is going to be shallow and stay with Hendrix because he can make her life easier? "So this is it? You're picking him because of his money, even when he treats you like shit?"

"I'm not picking anyone or doing anything, Cash. I just can't deal with you doing the same thing he has been doing. He was trying his best to make me want to come back to him by offering me all the things I ever wanted in life. What have you been doing? Aren't you doing the same?"

"No, Bailey, I was offering help. I wasn't offering to fix everything for you. I think you're capable of taking care of things yourself, but apparently you aren't as mature as I thought. When you grow the fuck up, and decide to handle your own problems, why don't you give me a call." I turn and go back into the house.

Clay has moved in closer to Lizzie. That boy doesn't waste any time. I'm glad that he can get his mind off the fucked up shit that is going on in his life right now. "Take your time, Clay, but I'm outta here." I'm out the door and I'm not looking back.

I want Bailey, and I still think she is the woman of my dreams, but she needs to grow up. I thought the age difference wasn't going to matter, but I guess I was wrong. Why the hell do I feel so bad for leaving her this way? Why can't she see that prick for what he is? I should have never opened myself up, never let down my guard like this.

All I want to do is go back over there and take her in my arms and tell her I'll take care of all of it. I have more than enough money to do that. She just made me so fucking mad with her thinking his money was the solution to her problem. I already regret my actions, but I need to cool down, and she needs to come to her senses. If she does choose that prick in the meantime, I'll deal with my broken heart then.

19

Bailey

Journal Entry: I've spent the last couple of days in a fog, going back and forth to the hospital and talking to doctors and healthcare providers. I have enough information I could start my own clinic now. Cash telling me to grow the fuck up infuriated me as much as it tore my heart out. At first my attitude was, who the hell does he think he is? He doesn't know who I am and what I've been through. I've been taking care of my grandparents almost by myself and doing a damn awesome job of it. The hell with him! I don't need him. And fuck Hendrix too. I can do all of this by myself. I am Bailey Grace Reynolds, and I don't need a man to fix anything for me.

Then I realize that was exactly what he was trying to tell me. I'm a strong confident woman. Look at who raised me. Granny taught me to take care of my family and myself. The Jackson family has always bonded and taken care of our own and hell if I'm going to let that change now.

Though a man to take care of my internal plumbing would be nice. I could use one for sex. Guys do it all the time. Why not me? Hell yeah! Ha! Ha! I hope I haven't blown my chance with Cash because I do want things to work out with him. I'll talk to him and offer him the "friends with benefits package" in hopes he is an all or nothing type of guy. I need to play this out to see where his head is.

First, I need to wash my hands of Hendrix so I can move forward in my life and not look back. I text him.

Me: Don't bother doing anything for me or my family, Hendrix, I said we are over and I meant every word. I can handle everything myself.

Surprise, surprise. He texts back immediately.

Hendrix: Let's still be friends at least. I want to rebuild your trust in me.

Me: I don't even want to be your friend. You couldn't treat me with respect before. Why would I think you would now? It's over, that's it—end of story.

Hendrix: Oh, Babe, you will come around. I still want to help and you can't stop me if I pay for things on my own.

Me: Whatever. Just stay the hell away from me.

I refuse to respond any more to him, I block his number. I don't know what I ever saw in him.

I haven't worked on my real job or done any housework in several days, so I get busy. This will take my mind off of men. I put on my headphone so I can zone out while I do the books for the church. There is nothing as boring as mindless data entry. I can knock this stuff out in about an hour and move on to some housework.

I wish it were that easy to keep my mind off of Cash. I don't need him to fix my problems for me, but I was really getting into him. Damn him. I want him to fill my sexual needs, but I also really like him. If I can't have all of him, I'll take just his body for my pleasure. He can be my boy toy. I shall call him Man Candy! Is that so bad? Guys do that kind of shit all of the time and no one ever says a word.

I haven't been sexually satisfied by a guy until he got me off with his fingers. I mean never—ever! If his fingers can work that kind of magic, I bet his cock will rock my world—hard. I'm going to seduce the shit out of him, and he isn't going to know what hit him. Time for this girl to take control of her needs and get what she wants. If I have to, I'll tie him to the bed. I'm not above a little bondage. It can be fun with the right partner. Oh, I haven't called Karen. I've been scatterbrained with everything going on.

Now to text Cash and move on to the next, and hopefully the best, phase of my life.

Bailey: I AM GROWN THE FUCK UP!

Cash: Typing me in all caps proves that.

Bailey: Come over here please, and let's talk. I'm not going to let Hendrix help me. I told him we were done and I mean it.

Cash: I don't play games. I'm too old for that shit. We can talk. I'll be over there in a little while. How about an hour?

Bailey: An hour is good.

I want to shower before Cash comes over, but of course as always my phone rings. "Hey, girl!" I say to Lizzie.

"You sound like you're in a better mood," She says, giggling into the phone.

"I am. You sound pretty chipper yourself. Does Clay have anything to do with that?" She gives a loud audible ugh. I had thought they were getting along well, but with Lizzie, you can never tell.

"He is full of shit and as cheesy as hell. I don't see how he is related to Cash."

Well, I guess that won't be a match made in heaven. She will find someone that can handle all of that attitude and big heart she hides from everyone. When she finds them, Lord help them, they are in for a crazy ride.

"So, I know you want to know what's going on, Lizzie, what I've decided to do about Hendrix's offer." She goes eerily quiet. There is a first time for everything. "I love Granny and Papa with all of my heart, they have sacrificed their whole lives for us, Lizzie." I pause to take a breath.

She jumps in. "Bailey. You. Can. Not. Do. This."

She won't even let me reply because she is in full-on rant now.

"If I need to quit school too and take on two full time jobs to help with their bills and medical expenses, I will do it, Bailey."

God, I love this girl. "Wait a minute, Lizzie. Cool your tits. If you will let me get a breath in, I will tell you what I've decided. Even though I love them, I can't go back to Hendrix, even if they would get top of the line health care. Is that selfish? Probably, but Lizzie, I want a love like theirs. I want their kind of love or nothing at all."

I think my take no shit friend is crying.

"Bailey, I want that kind of love too, but I just don't think it's possible for me."

I hate that she feels this way. "Lizzie, there is someone out there for everyone, even you. I truly believe that. I've asked Cash to come over to talk because I want to clear the air with him. I feel this connection with him, Lizzie. I can't explain it, but it's like kismet."

She sniffs a little. "I think he is your prince charming, Bailey. You need to go get him and if he says it's too late, call me and we will hog tie him just like you told Granny."

We both end up laughing. I'm so glad we could turn this around on a happier note.

"Right now, I'm scared that I don't have time for a real relationship, Lizzie. I have too much going on. I have to devote my time to getting Papa and Granny taken care of. I have to put them first." I hope she can understand.

"You know I'm here to help. You're not in this alone, and you've never been alone in this."

I know she is right, but I can only focus on them right now.

I hear a knock at the door, so we say our goodbyes. Only a few minutes have passed, but I open the door and hold my arm out wide to Cash. "Hey, I want to apologize for my behavior. You were right, I do need to grow the fuck up."

He walks into the house. "Bailey, I shouldn't have said that to you. It was uncalled for. I think you are worth so much more than Hendrix is willing to give you." He reaches over and touches my face, running his thumb over my cheekbone.

He has beautiful eyes that I almost get lost in every time he looks at me. I need to turn away or close my eyes to get through with what I have to say or I will cave. "I've come to realize I don't need a man to take care of me or my grandparents, I can do all of that myself."

"Bailey, has that prick got you thinking, if you're grown up you don't need anyone? Or was it me that made you feel that way? If so, I'm sorry. Growing up isn't about not needing someone. We all need someone. It's about taking care of your own shit."

He looks at me sadly.

"The point was not to go back to him just for his money. I can help you with money."

"Cash, I don't need or want your money. However, I need you...want you for a few other reasons." Yeah, that last part was corny, but I need him to know I want him for sex, or at least for him to know only sex is an option.

He looks skeptical. *What the fuck is wrong with him?* "I was wondering if you would be interested in a mutually beneficial relationship."

He pulls me close. "Bailey, I want more than that with you. Don't you know that you deserve more than being someone's fuck buddy?"

I stare into those baby blues. "What if that's all I have time for, Cash?" The tear running down my cheek doesn't help my case for being grownup. "Doing all of this shit on my own is going to take all of my time. My choice is to put my responsibilities first, but I will have to get my sexual desires met whenever possible."

"I still think you are worth more than this. I'm willing to give you all the time you need. I will come sit over here with you and play checkers, if that is all you can give me, because I want all of you, Bailey. I want your kind, loving heart, your sass and attitude, your beautiful smile, and I'll take whatever you're willing to give me now, but I'll wait for the rest because nothing else in this world would feel right."

He has made my day. He's spoken all the words I didn't even know I wanted to hear.

"It's over between Hendrix and me. I don't want anything else to do with him, I told him that. He also knows that I don't even want to remain friends with him. There isn't anyone else I want to have a relationship with. Only you." I reach up on my tippy toes and kiss him. I can feel the moment he gives in to the idea because his body relaxes, and his kiss becomes passionate.

He picks me up and I wrap my legs around his waist, "Which way to your room?"

He is kissing me like these will be our last kisses.

"Tha..." Even kissing this man feels erotic. "Over." I point as I continue kissing him.

He opens my door and sets me down as he lets out a long-winded breath. "Sweet Cheeks, you seem like you want things rough and hard."

I nod eagerly. He is so in tune with me.

"But I want to show you how a man worships a woman. When I'm finished with you, you will know how it feels to be a woman. I want to take my time and enjoy every inch of you." He slowly unbuttons my top.

"What if I just want hard? Not all the sweet stuff, Cash? I've never been able to come with the slow sex. I need fast. I'm a grown ass woman after all. That's what you want. Not some kind of little princess you have to treat with kid gloves."

He pulls me to him hard and kisses me with more desire than I ever thought was possible with kissing alone. He has my shirt all undone and sees I'm not wearing a bra. I push him down on the bed.

"Bailey, I never said I intend to treat you like you were made of glass." He does that little flip thing again, and takes my nipple in his mouth and bites down on it.

"Augh." That's more than a nip.

He licks it and sucks on it then journeys downward, kissing, licking, and nipping along the way. He burns me, making me ache everywhere he touches. He moves to my core, murmuring about me tasting like honey. The vibrations of his words make me tingle. He slides a finger inside of me, twisting it, and I'm completely drenched. He takes his time kissing and licking me.

He pushes both of my legs up with one hand, rather high in the air and grips my ass. Then he moves his head down and gives one of my cheeks a bite, "I've wanted to bite this ass for a while now. It's a perfect ass. It fits in my palms. I just want to lick it and make it mine." He licks from my ass to my bundle of nerves, sending sparks down my legs.

Hendrix had always refused to go down on me because he thought it was unhygienic. He said anything that smells that bad when it bleeds can't taste good. I always thought maybe I had an odor that repelled him.

Cash seems to like my smell. He is licking, biting, and sucking on me. He has taken ownership. He has his fingers in me while sucking and nipping. Then he moves his tongue down a little further while moving his thumb on my nub.

I'm coming up off the bed, pressing my hips harder into his face. My legs tremble. I can't lie still and I feel myself tighten. "Cash, oh Cash, you need to, oh I'm about to, oh I can't..." Then I do. I come on his face. This is our first time and I exploded on his face.

He looks at me with his face all moistened then takes his hand and wipes off the wetness. "What was it you were trying to say, Sweet Cheeks?" He crawls up my body.

I'm tearing at his clothes. He has on way too many things. They have to go, now. "I was saying that you need to take your clothes off, too!"

He laughs. No one laughs during sex, at least not in my experience. I finally get him undressed and see his entire body for the first time. He is beautiful. He has been chiseled by masterful hands. That using him for sex idea I had was awesome. I need to do more brainstorming while I'm pissed off.

I rub my hands over the contours of his body then I leisurely run the tips of my fingers over his pecs and follow by licking them.

I look into his eyes and they have gone hooded. He can't keep his hands off of me either. Between kisses, touches and exploring each other's bodies, I make my way down his body. He is twice the size of Hendrix. I never realized how big those things can get. Hell, he is bigger than anyone I have ever been with, and his cock is beautiful. I never knew they could be beautiful, but his is a work of art. I want to take him in my mouth and taste him, but now that it is my turn to give him pleasure, I want to savor the moment. I kiss him from his hips downward until I get to his inner thighs where I lick and gently cup his balls, rolling them around just a tad in my hand. I lick on each side of the base of his shaft, and he twitches, so I look at him. Desire is all over his face. His lips are parted and I see a flush on his cheeks.

He reaches down and plays in my hair. He doesn't push me toward his cock or ram himself at me. He runs his fingers through my hair.

His touch is gentle. It feels tender. I've never had tender. It's nice and makes me want him more. I lick the tip of his erection with little butterfly flicks.

He moans my name.

His hips twitch.

He holds his breath.

I swirl my tongue around the tip watching for his reactions. I flatten my tongue against the surface at the bottom, swirling it as I go back up to the tip.

He blows out a long, soulful, deep exhale.

Then I take him in, a little at a time, twirling my tongue and making humming noises. I want to see if the vibrations feel as good for him as they did for me.

He whispers something about heaven.

I move one of my hands to his shaft now that it's good and wet, pumping rhythmically.

He takes one of his hands out of my hair and pinches my nipple.

Chills race down my spine. I increase the pressure and the pace of my pumping.

He is getting more vocal, and his eyes are closed now with his mouth open. He pulsates, he is getting close.

I don't stop because I want him to explode in my mouth then afterward I want to lick every drop off of him.

He grips my comforter, his fingers holding on tight.

I can see his veins popping out on his forearm. Then just like that, he comes in my mouth and I swallow down every last ounce he provides for me. I can't help but smile at him. He is smoldering.

Cash pulls me up and kisses me fervently. We both want more, and I want him inside of me now. "I have condoms in my nightstand."

He reaches over and pulls open the drawer. Looking inside, his face breaks into a grin. "Sweet Cheeks, you do like to play!" He gets a condom but leaves the drawer open. "We can get to your toys later, but right now, it's just you and me."

CASH

She isn't supposed to feel this good. She isn't a virgin, but she is so tight around my cock she fucking feels like one. Sinking into her is heaven. Anyone can have sex, but I want to make love to her. I'm watching her. A pure carnal lust comes over her face and her teeth sink down into her bottom lip. I'm slowly learning her body, and I want to take my time and make this good for her. There isn't any reason to rush this.

"Cash, more," she pleads. "Mmmm."

I increase my rhythmic thrust, just enough to give her a sweet ache. Not too much yet.

Her body arches.

I thrust in a little further, pump a little faster. I have to remain in control, somewhat, because I don't want to hurt her.

"Cash." She says a little breathy—almost panting. "You feel so good, Cash. Ahh!"

She'll make me lose my control with all these little moans, and I don't want this over too quickly so I kiss her neck and nibble at her collarbone. She is getting louder with her acknowledgments of pleasure. She moves her hips, meeting me thrust for thrust.

"Oh my gawd, Cash."

She turns into a wildcat. She can't stay in sync.

"On top," she lets out in a small cry, "top, top, let me on top!"

I flip us over without pulling out of that hot tight pussy. She is riding me with reckless abandon, and I hold on to her hips, keeping pace with her.

Her inner walls tighten around me and I know it won't be long now. "Let go, Sweet Cheeks. Just let go."

She throws her head back.

I add my thumb to her clit.

Then she lets go, trembling all over. I pump a few more times for my own release then I pull her down and hold her to me, kissing the side of her face. We are both breathless. I give us time to enjoy the high. She is perfect, and I love seeing her lose control. It is the sexiest thing I have ever seen in my life. I go dispose of the condom and come back to hold her in my arms.

She raises up a little. "My throat is a little sore now," she says hoarsely.

She was so vocal, I'll be surprised if my mom didn't hear her. "Baby Doll, let me get you some water and something to clean you up a little."

She stares at me and nods.

"Lay right here, and I'll be right back." I quickly get her a glass of water from the kitchen. After I take it to her, I get a warm wet washcloth. I wash between her legs, gently cleaning her.

A tear runs down her face.

"Oh, Baby Doll, are you okay? Did I hurt you?"

She cries harder.

"Shh, it's okay, tell me, Baby Doll." I sit down on the bed, pulling her into my arms.

She wraps herself around me, "Cash, no one has ever taken care of me afterward. You are so different than the other guys I've been with. No one ever even made sure I climaxed first."

I feel a sense of pride. "Baby Doll, you've never been with a man. You've only been with boys. I wasn't born a gentleman either, but I was raised to be one." I wipe her tears away. "No more crying now. Let me hold you and kiss you."

She holds on to me tightly, and I cradle her, stroking her hair. She falls asleep, and I contemplate on how to keep her in my arms forever.

She has buried herself in my heart. If she leaves me now, there will be a hole. I want to be her all, her everything. She already is mine, but if I let her know, will it scare her off? How did she do it? How did she wrap herself around me and get so tightly wound into my emotions?

21

Bailey

I wake up still wrapped up in Cash's arms. The love and care he showed last night was amazing. This is how I've always imagined making love could be. I want to show him my appreciation. I want to show him how good things can be, too. I'll make a little breakfast to serve in bed and he'll reap all the benefits.

I get a quick shower and put on the sexiest lingerie that I have. I grab my computer to Google that video on the grapefruit blowjobs again. This woman is epic, just sayin'. I hate grapefruit, but I remember she said something about using another kind of fruit, so I look up that. I plan on knocking his socks off. If this works, I could go down in Alabama history.

The phone rings. Of course, it's Lizzie.

"What are you doing?" she asks.

"I'm preparing an orange." I snicker.

"Preparing an orange? Like peeling an orange for your breakfast? What are you talking about, Bailey?"

I'm still snickering. "I'm getting it ready for Cash. Instead of a grapefruit."

She lets out a full gut-busting laugh.

"Oh mi gawd. You have to let me know how that turns out. I knew it had to be for Cash." She can't stop laughing. "You would have to use a kumquat for Hendrix."

I almost choke on the water I'm drinking. I hear Cash stirring in my bedroom. "On that note, I've got to go, Lizzie. Bye!"

When I return to my bedroom, I see Cash propped on an elbow.

Cash says, "Good morning, beautiful, did you shower without me?" He fakes a pout. "I do like what you're wearing. Come here and let me take it off of you," he growls.

I love his voice. "Mornin', handsome. I have a little surprise for you, if you're man enough for it."

He pops up, grabs me and turns us at the same time, "Man enough, Sweet Cheeks? I think last night you were singing how much of a man I am. Do you need reminding?" He kisses me and nips at my neck between every couple of words. He moves down my body licking me.

I need to stop him while I can. I wiggle out from under him. "Right now, I would like to show you a little something I've learned. This will be about your pleasure." I straddle him and his eyes have gone from the normal brilliant blue to one that is hazier. "Are you up for something a little new?"

He puts his hands on my hips, "We were in this position last night, but hey, you'll never hear me complaining."

He gives me that sexy, "I know how to get in your panties" smile.

"I need to blindfold you with my lucky bandanna." I dangle the well-worn red square of cloth in front of him. I hide a laugh at how fast the look on his face changes from excited to worried.

"Blindfolded? Why do I need to be blindfolded? I don't know about this."

Isn't he the sweetest? This is going to be a delight. "Trust me on this one thing, Cash. If this isn't the experience of your life, I will be at your mercy. Deal? The only thing is you have to be blindfolded for this to work. Are you afraid I will take advantage of you?"

He gives me that smile again, and my panties are wet now.

"That almost sounds like a challenge to me. What are you wanting to do? I'll wear the blindfold, but I want to give you the experience of a lifetime next. Do I get to blindfold you next?"

He really likes to be in control, but he needs to learn to share it.

"After I blindfold you, you need to lay back, and comply. If you want to blindfold me next, you can. Now, be a good boy and do as you are told."

He gives little sigh.

I tie my bandanna around his head and make sure he can't see anything. "I want you to leave this on until I tell you to take it off. Is that clear?"

He is smiling, "Is this how we are going to start things out, Sweet Cheeks? Blindfolded? I promise not to peek, but you know it will be my turn next to do things as I see fit." He barely contains his laughter.

I check one more time to make sure the well-worn bandanna is secure around his eyes. "Now stay here, and I will be right back." I hurry to the kitchen to get the orange. I'm excited to see how all of this turns out myself. When I walk back into my bedroom, I see he is laying on the bed with his hands behind his head. He has a semi already. The idea of the unknown must be a turn on to him.

"Are you ready?"

"Sweet Cheeks, do with me as you please."

He sounds so amused. I'm glad he thinks this is funny. He needs to prepare for more pleasure than he has ever felt before in his life.

CASH

I don't know what Bailey is up to, but who can say no to her? She looks so excited and happier than I've seen her over the last few days. I'm thankful she decided not to take that prick up on his offer. My mind is alive with anticipation of what she has planned. Isn't anticipation half of the pleasure anyway?

She has a wildcat in her. I could tell that from the night she texted me to come over. I'm not going to lie. I'm feeling a little vulnerable right now, but I can't resist some kinky sex.

She's on the bed now, and I get a whiff of something citrus. "What do you have with you?"

"Are you scared, Cash? Are you worried a little five foot girl is going to hurt the big man?"

She is taunting me. My heart rate is accelerating. "Johnny" is at half-mast and she hasn't even touched me.

"Don't worry about anything, but the pleasure you're about to receive."

She licks my torso, and my hands instinctively go to her hair. Then she gets to business, licking my cock like it's her lollypop. Shit, that feels good. She is amazing at this. She takes me into her mouth, and I instantly go hard. She does her tongue swirl thing again and massages my balls at the same time. Being blindfolded does makes this kind of erotic. She pulls off, but then she slides something warm and wet down over my cock.

Holy Mother of God. What the fuck is it?

Now, she has her mouth on me, and this warm, wet fleshy feeling… What is she doing to me? She is twisting and turning the thing while she sucks with her mouth.

Oh sweet baby Jesus! "Bailey, *fuck*! I've never felt anything like this before in my life." This is ecstasy. I'm completely overwhelmed by elated bliss. I feel like I'm getting fucked and sucked at the same time. "Baby Doll, this is the best of both worlds." I feel liquid running down my balls. "Is this something citrus?" I have to know what she's doing. I take the fucking blindfold off and she does have a fucking orange on my cock, but shit it feels fan-fucking-tastic. I come harder and faster than I have ever before. "You are a little kinky freak, aren't you? I like that. I see a trip to the Farmers Market in our near future."

She puts the plate and orange on her nightstand and laughs.

"That even tastes good so I take it you liked that just a little bit."

She puts her thumb and her pointer finger close together to show how much.

My whole body feels like jelly. I don't think I can move. She snuggles into my side and I pull her close, kissing her sweetly.

Once I've recovered, I say, "Let's get in the shower, and I will give my kinky girl a run for her money." I pick her up and carry her to the shower, and things progress in there until the hot water runs cold. We get out and I dry her off first, but I need to hurry because I've got to get to work. But I do take a little time to remind her she is mine and I will be thinking about her all day. As much as I would like to stay in bed all day, people are counting on me. I might own the company, but I still have work to do.

"Sweet Cheeks, what all do you have to do today?" I ask her as I put my clothes back on from yesterday.

"I work from home for a few companies, doing their accounting. So I have a couple of hours of work I need to get done. I'm also going to the hospital. I've been talking to them about options for Granny's and Papa's health care."

She has on a little sundress and her cowboy boots looking hotter than ever.

"What about you, do you have a lot to do today?"

"Not a lot. Then I'll be back home fixing up some things. Do you need me to help you to talk to anyone? I would like to help you, Bailey. I'm sure if we put our heads together, we can figure something out to help them."

She smiles. "That's really sweet of you, Cash, but I've got this. Now, you get across the street and get dressed so you can get to work and back home. I'll have you some things over here that need fixing."

She gives me an evil grin.

"Besides, when Granny and Papa get home, I won't be as free anymore, and I won't be having any overnight guests." She stands on her tippy toes and gives me a kiss.

I think I'm falling in love, fast and hard.

23

Bailey

Three Months Later

Journal Entry: Granny and Papa came home last week. Granny went to the best rehabilitation center after she was released from the hospital. The money was donated anonymously for her care, but Hendrix can't fool me. I know he's the benefactor, and I called and thanked him.

Hendrix and I are back to being friends, but only friends. He is still taking care of Granny and Papa anonymously. I just laugh and say thank you. Cash doesn't like Hendrix being the good guy for once, but what can he say. Hendrix's generosity takes a huge burden off of my family and me.

Cash's mom sits with Granny and Papa a couple of nights a week. She is having a hard time dealing with her husband's death. They were not officially divorced yet, and he had a nice chunk of change in the bank, so she no longer has to live with Cash. She is still there for the time being because she says there isn't any reason to rush moving out. Cash is building his own house on the property and he wants her to stay in the current house. The house is so cute, I'd live there and I hate the country.

Cash's half- sister Oakley lives with Clay on a horse ranch and is having a really hard time adjusting after her parents' death. I'd have a hard time in the same situation, too, so I take her out when I can and she is warming up to me.

I turned twenty-two last week, and we had a small intimate party. Cash gave me the perfect gift—a bracelet with an orange charm and a sweet tea charm on it. Hendrix gave me two-carat diamond earrings which I promptly gave them back to him. They weren't an appropriate gift to receive from an ex-boyfriend, and I would never disrespect or hurt Cash by accepting them. However at this time last year, I would have been jumping for joy. Funny how things change. What was he even thinking giving me any gift? I wouldn't accept anything from him now as a gift, I wish I didn't have to accept his generosity toward my grandparents.

Cash and I are going strong. We are exclusive and I couldn't be happier. He treats me like I'm his princess, and he treats his momma like a queen. Granny is always telling Lizzie and me to watch how boys treat their mommas and that's how they will treat their wives one day. We are a long way from marriage, but I like the way he treats her. She is the sweetest person, too.

I hear a car pulling up in the driveway. The house will be all abuzz over the next few weeks with people wishing Granny well and bringing casseroles. I open the door to find Hendrix with two-dozen long stem pink roses. "Hi, Hendrix. Come in."

He comes around a lot more than he ever did when we were dating. He seems genuinely interested in Granny and Papa's welfare and I want to encourage his caring side, but I've told him in no uncertain terms we're only friends so he doesn't get the wrong idea. I will never go there again. Never.

"Hey, Bailey. I brought these to welcome Mrs. Jackson home. She told me pink roses were her favorite."

He smiles and comes in, looking back over his shoulder at Cash coming up the stairs.

"She's in the living room, go on in." He hands me the flowers, kisses me on the cheek, and goes on in to talk to Granny.

CASH

I don't know what that prick is doing bringing my girl flowers and kissing her on the cheek. But if I've learned anything in my life, it is not to overreact. The less you act like something bothers you, the more it bothers them. Things with Bailey have been so good. Besides, she can't stand the prick anymore.

"Hey, Sweet Cheeks."

She wraps herself around me as well as she can with roses in her hand.

"Hey, Handsome. I've been missing our nights. I need my Man Candy."

We have spent every night together for the last three months. Mom loves Bailey, and has volunteered to stay with the Jacksons a few nights a week so we can have some time together. Someone has been hired to come twice a week to do the laundry and clean the house for them. Someone else is coming three times a week to help the Jacksons with their baths. They both deteriorated significantly while Mrs. Jackson was in the hospital for so long. She will never be back one hundred percent and will always need assistance now.

Bailey thinks Hendrix is a saint now because she believes he is behind the anonymous payments for the Jacksons' care. He is full of shit and taking credit for something he didn't do. Once a prick, always a prick. Lizzie isn't falling for his shit either. She rolls her eyes every time he comes around. I'm glad at least she can see through him. He just needs to stay the hell away from all of them.

We go inside, and Bailey goes to put the roses in water. I visit with the Jacksons for a little bit. Mrs. Jackson has insisted that I call them Granny and Papa now that Bailey and I are dating. I give Mrs. Jackson a hug. "Granny, how are you feeling today? I saw Bailey had you and Papa out walking at the crack of dawn."

She laughs at me. "Do you mean Sarg? I think we are in boot camp. She makes me lift these little weights a couple of times a day while I watch TV, too, and cooks turkey bacon. That stuff is nasty. I'm not eating it. You'll get me the real stuff, won't you, Cash?"

Bailey is right. Granny is sly.

"I can hear you, ya know." Bailey walks in and plops down beside me. "You better watch out, or I will make you live with Mom and she won't let you have ANYTHING fried."

Granny rolls her eyes, which makes us all laugh.

"Granny, what can I get for you? There must be something to make you more comfortable," Hendrix asks.

He doesn't like to be left out of the conversation very long.

"Henry, I'm not your Granny. I'm being very well taken care of already. If there is anything I need, my family provides for me. I don't like to take help from others, but thank you for your generosity. That is very nice of you to offer."

Hendrix's cheeks turn a nice shade of crimson, and I love it.

"Bailey, I know you and Cash have some plans, and I'm feeling a little tired. Would you mind helping me to bed? Henry, thank you for stopping by. Please do visit us again."

She is a lady, but she just told him to get the hell out of her house

"Sure, Granny. Cash will show Hendrix out while I help you to bed so you can rest."

Bailey goes to help Granny up. Hendrix walks over to give Granny a hug, but she turns away before he gets there. She really doesn't like him, and I think that is funny as shit. I love it.

"I guess we will be seeing you around, Henry," I say. He hates for anyone to call him anything but Hendrix but he can't say anything.

He snarls.

I just smile at him.

Papa grabs his cane because he doesn't like to be too far away from Granny since her heart attack. Hendrix goes over to him to help him, but pulls Papa a little too forcefully and Papa loses his balance. I try my best to catch him, but Hendrix, who is standing right beside him, just lets him fall.

"What the hell, man?" I shout as I help Papa up.

"What happened?" Bailey comes running into the room with Granny following behind.

As I steady Papa, I realize he can't put any weight on his foot, and he is clearly in pain. I put his arm around my neck and help him to the recliner as I hear Hendrix flat out lying to Bailey.

"I was helping him up and he fell. I tried to catch him, Bailey, but he slipped through my hands."

"Thank you, Hendrix. I appreciate you trying to help him."

I do not believe this. This prick needs to learn a lesson, and I would love to be the one to teach him.

"Let me know if there is anything I can do to help you guys, Bailey. I still love you and I would do anything for you and your family."

Okay! I've. Had. It. Hendrix isn't going to profess his love for her where I can hear and get away with it.

"Don't worry about him, Cash." Granny says. "He isn't worth it, and Bailey knows when someone really loves you they don't have to say it because they show it."

This little lady has class, and her advice is some of the best I've ever received. I could have knocked Hendrix into the middle of next week, but what would that prove? Nothing. Granny is right. Words are cheap when compared to actions. Actions speak so much louder.

Bailey comes back from the kitchen with a bag of ice for Papa's leg.

"Mom will be over here in a few minutes, Bailey. Are you almost ready?" I ask, letting the prick know it's time for him to leave. I walk to the door and open it, "We'll see you later, Henry." I give Hendrix an "I'll fuck you up" look. He looks at Bailey for help.

"Bye, Hendrix. See you later." She arranges the ice pack on Papa's ankle.

Hendrix struts over to the door.

I whisper in his ear as he's about to step outside, "I saw what you did and if you try that shit again, I'll fucking end you."

He smirks.

I want to punch him, but I remember what Granny said to me.

"I will get her back, redneck, and when I do those two old bastards in there will be in a state run institution." He walks off the porch and doesn't look back.

Bailey

I'm not sure what just passed between Cash and Hendrix, but that macho garbage needs to stop. I don't have time for that shit in my life. I peek at Papa's ankle beneath the ice pack. It's swelling. I'll ask Margie what we should do when she gets over here. Granny is sitting in a chair reading, "I thought you were tired."

She grins and nods, but never looks up from her book. "Margie is coming over?" she asks.

She knows Margie is coming because she and Margie have become great friends. She is trying to change the subject. I learned from the master, after all.

"Yes, ma'am, she should be here any minute. But I'm not sure we should go with Papa's ankle swelling."

Granny puts her book away. "Bailey, don't be silly. Margie can handle everything and if he gets worse, she can call you."

"Can I ask you a question, Granny?"

"Of course, baby, you can always ask me anything." She gives me a sweet smile.

"Why were you being so mean to Hendrix? He brought you flowers. And you know he is paying for all this stuff for you guys, too. I think he has changed or at the very least he is trying."

"Bailey, have you lost your mind? That boy isn't paying for anything but that goop he puts in his hair. You need to stay away from him. He is up to no good. I can see it in his eyes."

"Granny, who else would be paying for all of this? No one we know has that kind of money. None of us suddenly won Publisher's Clearing House. You're holding a grudge against him because of how he was before. Besides, we're only friends now. It won't hurt to cut him a little slack."

"Hey," Margie calls out.

Since Margie is here, I drop the subject.

"How are you, Granny? Papa?" Margie asks, looking between the two.

If Granny likes you, she wants you to call her Granny. Papa doesn't care. Whatever makes Granny happy has always made him happy.

"My goodness, what happened to your foot?" Margie goes over to Papa.

"That boy jerked me down."

Papa's dementia has been bad since Granny's heart attack. He makes up stories about things happening to him, he is losing control of his bodily functions, and his memory is getting worse. Margie looks over at me in horror. I shake my head a little to let her know it's not true.

"Do you need something for pain? Does it hurt?" She lifts the ice pack to examine it and he nods.

I get him some ibuprofen and water while she pets him like he is her baby.

He eats it up.

"Bailey, y'all have fun," Granny says. "Don't worry, Margie will take care of us."

If I didn't know better, I would think she was trying to get rid of me. I give them all a hug and tell them when they can expect us back.

Cash and I have a wonderful day, and I love spending time with him. We laugh and joke around with each other. He has become my best friend and the love of my life. I feel true intensity every time I'm with him. Even when he kisses me on my forehead, I feel love from him. I never knew love until Cash, I only thought I was in love.

Then when we make love, he fucking rocks my world. He is constantly coming up with new stuff for us to try. He lets my kink flag fly and loves it. We have been to Hedrovibes By Kissin' Karen several times and Karen loves him. He thinks we need to open our own store up around here. He's crazy. My family would die of embarrassment. Maybe if we opened one up over by where he owned his business and didn't tell anyone, that might work. Though, I don't have time for a job away from home right now.

He is the most understanding guy I've ever met. He will come over and watch TV with us until Granny and Papa go to bed. He refuses to have sex with me when they are in the house. Believe me, I've tried.

Cash is everything to me. I no longer want to leave this little town. I want to stay here. I want to raise a family and work hard. He has changed my way of thinking. Money makes very little difference in the grand scheme of things. And why should I be any different than my grandparents? They are the best, most loving people I know, and if I turn out to be half the woman Granny is, I'll be happy.

CASH

Bailey and I had a late night last night because Mom called about two hours into our date and told us Papa's ankle was the size of a cantaloupe and he wouldn't stay off of it.

We took him to the emergency room. The doctor said it was a bad sprain and he needed to stay off of it. With his dementia, he didn't understand any of this and became agitated. He didn't like being told he had to sit down. At times, he would push Bailey out of his way so he could get up.

Over the last three months he has gone downhill. Bailey thinks his deterioration happened because he wasn't around Granny all during her sickness. I think we're close to needing someone here to help full time. I can stay overnight, and Mom said she would stay during the day, but Bailey won't admit she needs help. She is determined to take care of them by herself.

She has grown up a lot in the past three months and has quit letting people run over her. I wish she could see through Hendrix, though. She thinks he has changed, has had some kind of spiritual awakening. I think he is full of shit. She and I had a conversation with him, letting him know that all they ever would be is friends. He seemed to take it all in stride, but I know how guys like him operate. He will use every play in the book to get her back. I should personally thank him for being such an ass because Bailey now knows a good man when she sees one.

He called this morning to see if he could do anything for her, and she is letting him pick up the Jacksons' prescriptions. I would have done that, but she said that would give us an extra hour together before I leave for work. Maybe I can head him off at the door and get the medicines so he can be on his way.

Hendrix arrives with balloons, an oxygen tank, and a huge bag of medicine. He looks prissy with his pressed khakis and button down long sleeved shirt.

"Hello, Henry, thank you for bringing the medicine, I can take it from here. You have a good day." I reach for the bag, and he uses his arm to push past me.

"Get out of my way, redneck." He glares at me.

I'm not sure what the oxygen tank is for. Neither one of the Jacksons have been prescribed one as far as I know.

"Bailey, I have everything you needed," he calls out.

She walks out of the bedroom where she was changing Papa. He is in adult diapers now.

"Thanks, Hendrix, how much was it? I can write you a check. Who is getting the oxygen? I don't remember any of the doctors telling me anything about either one of them needing oxygen."

He gives her a smile and tries to hug her, but she shrugs away from him.

"You don't owe me anything, Bailey. Really, I would do anything for them. There is a new study for dementia patients that is top secret, that more oxygen to the brain is linked to calming situations," he says. "I've been researching alternative treatments for dementia."

This is a lie if I have ever heard one in my life. I'm not sure what his angle is on this one, but he isn't going to get away with this. "That's the biggest load of crap, Bailey, you're not falling for this are you?" This guy's a piece of work.

"It couldn't hurt, could it? I mean, it's just oxygen, right? I'll call his doctor in a little bit to make sure though. Thank you, Hendrix, for being so thoughtful."

You have to be fucking kidding me right now.

"Are those balloons for Papa?"

She gives him a sweet look. I hate this prick.

"Yes, I thought maybe they would cheer him up." he says.

He's a little too gleeful for my taste.

"Can I take them in to him?" he asks.

"Please, go on in. I need to go help Granny out of the shower," she says.

I wait right outside the door so I can hear what is being said between Papa and Hendrix. I decide I don't like Hendrix being left alone with him so I go on in, and I find Hendrix leaning over the bed with his face down close to Papa's ear and a snarl on his face. He starts to raise up when I walk in, and Papa reaches up and knocks the shit out of him. I bust out laughing and Hendrix covers his nose which is gushing blood. His fancy button down shirt with a guy on a horse now has blood droplets on it. I hope it's ruined.

"You fucking bastard, I'll kill you," he tells Papa.

That's it. He's out of here. I grab him by his collar. I'm dragging his ass toward the bedroom door, and Bailey comes running in.

"What's going on in here?" she asks.

Hendrix looks at me and shakes his head. "Bailey, I'm not sure what is wrong with Cash today, but he just hit me for no reason."

Now it is on. We have a serious problem. "He is lying to you, Sweet Cheeks. I came in and he was leaning over Papa whispering in his ear. When he raised up, Papa hit him in his nose."

Her mouth drops open and she looks at Papa, then back to me. "How dare you blame this on a poor defenseless man, Cash."

"Bailey, I'll leave." Hendrix raises his hands. "I don't want to upset your grandfather any more than he has already been upset."

Hendrix looks over at me with a sneer on his face.

"You better be glad I respect the Jacksons or I'd kick your ass."

I act like I'm about to hit him and he jumps three feet in the air. Kick my ass, I bet. "Yeah, you need to leave, pretty boy. You're not fooling anyone with your lies. Bailey sees through you, don't you, Sweet Cheeks?" I reach for her, and she shrugs away from me this time.

"Both of you need to leave, I don't need any drama in my life. I have real problems." She points toward the door.

He has had it now. Little fucker. He leaves the bedroom and I take a few moments with her. She needs to understand what happened. "Bailey, I didn't do anything. That really was Papa that knocked the shit out of him."

We both look over at Papa and he nods his head. He is more lucid than she gives him credit sometime.

"Cash, when I came in the room you were the one with your hands on Hendrix and he was the one with a bloody nose. All I know is what I saw with my own two eyes."

She believes him over me? This hurts me, tears at me.

"I guess that is what you would see, Bailey." I leave the bedroom and walk out of the house. Good thing that little fucker is already gone because I would have lost my self-control and beat him until he was nothing but a bloody mess.

I keep replaying everything in my mind to see where it went wrong. No wonder the little fucker is going to be a lawyer. He is good at lying. How can he look Bailey in the eye and flat out lie?

Something bothers me about that oxygen tank. I want to do my own research. I'm going to figure out what that fucking prick is up to and then I'm going to shut him down, but right now I have to cool down. I don't want to do something while I'm angry, something I'll end up regretting. Being angry doesn't solve anything, and could potentially ruin everything that Bailey and I have built together. These are the things I have to keep telling myself. I keep my mantra going and start doing pull ups.

26

Bailey

Granny makes it to the bedroom. "What was all of that about?"

I'm rubbing my forehead, wishing I knew what happened. I want to believe Cash. I don't think he would lie to me. The scene I walked in on was convincing though. Hendrix was about ready to shit a brick. Hendrix hasn't always been forth coming. I've seen him lie, if it benefits himself, at frat parties. He's lied to get out of tickets, but who hasn't.

"I guess it depends on who you believe. Hendrix said Cash hit him for no reason. Cash said Papa hit Hendrix." I shrug my shoulders. "So who do you believe?"

"Did you ask Papa?" She looks over at him.

"Well, he nodded but I didn't know if he knew what he was nodding about," I say. He has been getting mean here lately. My normally sweetheart of a papa has changed so much. Would he even know what he was saying?

"What happened in here? Did you hit Hendrix?" Granny asks.

We both look at him expectantly. He is silent for a few seconds then sighs. He has a puzzled look on his face and is concentrating, trying to think of what to say.

Finally he asks, "Are you going to make me leave too?"

Make him leave? "What are you talking about, Papa?"

"You made both of them other two fellers leave because of this and I wanna know if I have to leave too. I hit that boy because he said he was gonna take my woman. Then after I hit him, he said he was gonna kill me. That other fella grabbed him. Now, do I have to go or not?"

This is funny but it's not, I have no doubt that is what he thought he heard from Hendrix. Did he really hit Hendrix? Why would Hendrix lie about that? Hendrix has changed, and maybe Papa just remembers him back when he was being a jerk.

"You don't ever have to leave, okay. I won't let those guys come back over here and upset you anymore," I say. "I'm going to get your medicine ready." I walk into the kitchen, and Granny is coming after me just as fast as she can. I look at the bottles of medicine. There are more than normal.

"Bailey, Hendrix was clearly doing something. We need to talk to Cash and figure this out."

She regards me with concern. I know how much animosity she has toward Hendrix, and Cash left here furious with me. I don't know what to do. I tell her the exchange between Cash and myself. She thinks Cash is more hurt than mad, and I need to go and make it right.

"I'll go talk to him as soon as I make heads or tails of this medicine."

"What's wrong with the medicine?"

"There is a lot of it here. Where did we put your release paperwork? I want to check the medicine off and make sure they didn't mix something up." I find the papers and thumb through them trying to find what new prescriptions she is on. Half an hour later, I finally have all the medicine accounted for except for three extra bottles for Papa. I put in a call to his doctor to check on any changes that he may have made. The labels look a little different than the others. Geeze, these people need to get their act together. People could die if they take the wrong stuff. I take Papa the medicine that I know he needs to take and his glass of water. Now finally I can get to my own problems.

Whether Cash is right or wrong, he has never given me a reason not to trust him, and I was out of line asking him to leave. I'm going to walk over there and admit that I was wrong. "I'll be back in a couple of minutes, Granny. Do you think you'll be all right? I can send Margie over if you feel anxious."

She waves me off and I go brush my hair and at least look at myself in the mirror. I hope I can get this straightened out. I don't know what I was thinking.

CASH

I've always been a true believer in respect and trust. Relationships do not work without those two things. True love can't exist without them, either. I'm most frustrated, though, because I thought Bailey and I had this connection, these inner ideals, why we just clicked.

I've come out here to this old barn to think, to put things into perspective. I don't normally trust so easily and I've let my guard down with her at the drop of a hat. I thought my judgment was better than this, but I'm logical. I can sit here and figure out a logical explanation to all of this.

I hear someone at the door of the barn. Turning, I see Bailey peeking through the crack between the doors.

"Cash," she says softly. "Can I come in please? I would like for us to talk."

She has the voice of an angel. It is enough to change my mind about being upset with her. She can't ever know that, though, because then I would look like a pussy.

"Come in, Bailey. You're always welcome anywhere I am, you know that." *I love you, and I want you forever in my life.* But it's just too soon to tell her this, besides the fact she doesn't even trust me anymore.

"Hey." She comes over and sits beside me on the loft steps. "Margie told me I would find you out here. She went over to stay with Granny and Papa for me."

That is my mom, always rooting for me.

"What do you want, Bailey? I happen to take offense to people not trusting me. I can't be in a relationship where there isn't trust."

We haven't talked a lot about my parents, but she needs to understand why this is so important to me.

"Cash, I'm so sorry. I lost my head for a few minutes. Please, let's forget this and start over."

She is genuinely apologetic for her previous actions.

"Bailey, I want you to know why trust and respect is so important to me. You know my mom and dad were going through a rocky divorce when he died, right?" I hate airing all our dirty laundry, especially to her.

"Right, that's when Clay and Oakley came into your life. Your dad had another life on the road so you don't trust people, right?"

Well, she has part of it figured out.

"It's not just that. He cheated on mom from the beginning. He would come home smelling of cheap cologne and would have lipstick smeared on his neck. I remember him coming home when I was young and making her cry. He loved to make her cry. He played mind games with her. He never loved her. He just wanted a place to lay his head while he was in town. He tormented her constantly, and she ended up in a mental hospital, Bailey. She tried to commit suicide when I was ten. She was in therapy for years. When he stayed away for a long time, she was happy, and I finally thought everything was good. Then he came back and started all his shit, just to file for divorce and leave her in tears. This is the happy version of the story for you. Mom has come a long way in her depression, but Bailey I would never do anything to lose your trust or your respect. I can't stand to see women hurt like that. I thought I'd shown you the kind of man I am, but apparently I've failed." Maybe she will understand. Hell, I don't know if anyone can understand the fuck-up my father was. Even living through it, I can't wrap my head around how he was half the time.

"Cash, I had no idea you and Margie went through all of that. You have never given me a reason not to trust you, I'm so sorry. Papa even said that he hit Hendrix."

She puts her arms around my neck, and I pull her in my lap. I feel all the tension leave my body and she kisses me. In no time, we are pawing at each other. The release of our emotions has worked us up into a frenzy. I take her by the hand and lead her up to the hay loft. I sit in the hay first, and I hold out my hand for her to join me.

She shakes her head, and slowly unbuttons her shirt.

I've never seen her look so seductive.

"Cash, I swore on my life that I would never have sex in a barn. It has been my number one rule since high school."

Shit, I've offended her. I thought some make up sex would make us both feel better, but I feel like a dick for expecting her to have sex in a barn. I love her. I can't treat her like a piece of ass.

"I wanted out of this town, and out of this lifestyle," she says.

When she takes the clip out of her hair and it falls past her shoulders, all I can think is I will love having my hands in her hair while I'm kissing her. Now, I'm really a dick. "Bailey, I'm sorry. We don't have to…"

"Shh, don't interrupt. I wanted a life for myself that I didn't have to worry about things like my family has always had to worry about in the past. Things like robbing Peter to pay Paul or not having health care."

She has taken off her shorts and panties. All she has on now is her shirt hanging loosely open in the front.

"You've changed me, Cash. You never asked me to change, but you've shown me how good it can be to be cared for by a person. During the last

three months, you haven't tried to take over and fix my problems. You've helped me find ways to work them out. You helped me become a strong woman. The best thing that has ever happened to me is you moving across the street. You're my whole life now." Bailey caresses my face.

Her eyes are so bright.

"I see what my grandparents have, and I see that in us. I love you, Cash. I want to love you in the barn, and anywhere else you want to love me. This is me giving you my heart. Be careful with it, I've never given it to anyone else."

"Sweet Cheeks, I love you, too. You had me the moment you opened your front door, and then when I saw how much you cared for your grandmother in the hospital. I had no idea, at the time, you would wiggle your way so fast and so deep into my heart, but here you are." I tap my chest. "When I'm away from you, all I can think about is you. I start missing you from the moment we say goodbye. I can tell you a hundred different ways how much you mean to me, how much I love you and still not explain the way I feel inside. I'm far from perfect, but with you by my side the world is a more beautiful place. I love you, Bailey. I want to marry you some day, when the time is right. You are mine, heart, body, and soul. I never plan on ever letting you go."

Tears are running down her cheeks, and she crawls into my lap. One of my favorite things is holding her all curled up in my arms. We stay this way for a little while, and we share gentle kisses. Soft touches and more words of love. We talk a little about the future, and I decide I'm getting her a ring. We can have a long engagement or do whatever makes sense. I love her and I want the whole world to know it.

"Well, are you gonna teach me the fine art of taking a roll in the hay, or do I need to Google it and teach you?" she asks.

I love that she makes me laugh. She leans back and unbuttons my jeans. I get my shirt over my head and she goes to remove her shirt.

"Leave it on, you're sexy as hell like that."

She gives a sultry laugh.

"Lay back, cowboy, this cowgirl needs a ride." With that, she gives my chest a push.

Bailey

Journal Entry: I love barns. I didn't realize how much character they have. Their sweet aroma. Sunlight casting shadows into the corners. They have to the most perfect places in the world. I had never thought of barns being intimate. They have always been smelly, half falling down places. Cash's barn is old, but I love his barn. I would live in his barn. It's almost magical in there.

I went into the barn so unsure of what to expect, how he would take me not believing him. I was totally expecting to grovel for days, hell for weeks, but Cash lovingly explained to me why trust is so important to him. He has always treated me with kindness, love and respect.

Cash had to get ready for work so I left him with a smile on his face and hay in his hair. I never knew hay was so sexy, but everything on Cash is sexy. We are going to have to revisit the barn soon because I have some plans.

When I get back to the house, Granny and Margie are talking about some of their favorite recipes. Margie is telling her some of Cash's favorites, and Granny has a pen out making notes.

"Did the doctor call?" They both shake their heads at me. "What are the two of you up to?"

Granny wears her little mischievous grin, and Margie's cheeks turn a nice shade of pink.

"We are just talking about exchanging recipes. What are we having for supper anyway? Why don't we have the Wilsons over?"

The little fixer is at it again, I see. She thinks she is sneaky. I play along with her because it makes her happy when she thinks she has gotten something over on me.

"Sure, they can come over. I was going to order a pizza, but I can order two of them and make a salad. Did you want me to make something for dessert, too?" I haven't even considered supper because it's not even lunchtime yet.

"We can't serve guests a bought pizza, Bailey. You can do better than that. Let's see." She glances down at her notes. "What about grilled chicken? You can use that indoor grill Kathy Rose got me for Christmas last year." She looks over to Margie and beams.

They don't know Cash and I have made up. They are trying to get me back in his good graces through his stomach. He does love to eat. But I'm going to have a little fun with them. "Granny, you and Papa don't like grilled chicken. I wouldn't want to make something you don't want to eat. That's kind of rude, don't you think?"

"We can just eat the vegetables. If you hurry up, you can get a pot of pinto beans going. I would love a good country meal tonight."

Margie is nodding.

"Granny, you know I'm not any good cooking cornbread. Mine always flops. Besides, beans need to soak overnight." I sigh. It's the truth. Cooking beans is an art I haven't mastered yet.

Granny looks at Margie hopefully.

"I can walk you through my recipe, Bailey. It's foolproof," Margie says.

I don't have much confidence that I can pull it off, but they seem excited about this so I go along with all of it. "Okay, I would love to learn a good cornbread recipe, Margie. Are there any other requests for this dinner or can I decide on my own what to serve?" I raise my eyebrows.

"You make anything you want to make, Bailey. You are an excellent cook." Granny looks at Margie when she says that instead of me. "But you need to hurry up and get those beans on or they will never be ready in time." I'm about to get her good. "Well, then I'll just go get some canned beans at the grocery store when I pick up the other items we'll need." I'm holding my breath so I don't laugh.

Their mouths hang open a little.

I better let them off the hook before they catch a fly. "I'm only teasing y'all." I laugh my way to the kitchen. I see some major Googling in my near future.

CASH

I want to surprise Bailey, and when I make my mind up on something, I get tunnel vision. I don't want to wait. I want to get the ball rolling today. I feel like I've known Bailey forever. I love her with every single beat of my heart. I've got plans to make. I text Lizzie to see if she can help me out.

> *Me: I need your help.*
>
> *Lizzie: Oh, no! What did you do?*
>
> *Me: What makes you think I did something?*
>
> *Lizzie: You're a guy. You all screw up eventually. Your brother is driving me crazy. Get him to leave me alone and I will help you.*
>
> *Me: Deal, can you meet me about 3?*
>
> *Lizzie: I guess. What is going on, Cash?*

I call Lizzie and let her in on my plans. She is more than happy to be my partner in crime.

I don't know what is up with Clay, but we've been hanging out a lot, so I feel like I have a pretty good grasp on his character—honest, and would do anything for anyone. He has this huge heart for helping kids with disabilities and is in the middle of setting up a ranch that will use horses for therapy. He's explained a dozen times how the horses will help the kids. I don't understand everything he tells me, but I donated money and offered to volunteer when the place is up and going. He is a standup guy, but when he gets around Lizzie he turns all cheesy. I need to teach that boy how to swagger. That's what big brothers are for, right? It's about time I take my job seriously. If he would turn that voice and those guitar skills loose on her, she'd be putty in his hands. He has more of our dad's natural talents than I did. He even has a band and they played gigs in Nashville before he and Oakley decided to move down here to be close to us. I can't believe the whole damn band followed him. He has to be pretty awesome for that to happen.

The rest of my workday drags on. I have a working lunch. Dawn picks me up a sandwich and I eat at my desk. I want to get as much accomplished as possible since I am leaving early.

Dawn is a keeper. She runs a tight ship, and I would be here several more hours a day without her. If I could get her up to par on a little bookkeeping, I wouldn't have to hire a full-time bookkeeper, but I can't keep up with all of the finances anymore and they're piling up.

I call Clay like I promised Lizzie since she'll help me out in a few hours.

"Hey, Clay. What's up, dude?"

"Man, I've been working my ass off. When are you and the little lady coming out to see the progress?"

He is proud of the work he's doing. He plays local bars at night to make ends meet, but his true passion is these kids and making a difference in their lives.

"Soon, man, soon, I promise. Hey, I've been meaning to ask you what is going on between you and Lizzie? You know she and Bailey are practically sisters."

"Hell if I know. She won't give me the time of day. I don't even think she knows my name."

I laugh. He is helpless. "She knows you're a cheesy ass. You've got to stop with those stupid ass pick-up lines."

He lets out a big breath. "Most girls think they're endearing. She doesn't? That's the problem? I love my pick-up lines. They're funny, and I like making people laugh. I really don't mean them as pick-ups. Hell, I've said them to Bailey."

I didn't know he was laying them on my girl too. "Yeah, about that, stop it. Find another way to be a comic genius, ya hear me, bro. The girls think it's stupid. Trust me on this one. If you really want to get to know

Lizzie better, I'll ask Bailey to give you some hints. I think Lizzie is a take no shit kind of girl. I happen to think a lot of her, so if you're not ready for that, back off."

We make some plans for a guys' night and get off the phone so I can finish up and meet Lizzie.

I'm bouncing my knee, tapping my pen on the desk, and I keep looking at the clock. I should have never tried to work today. It's not like I'm nervous. I just want to hurry up and do this. I'm excited and anxious. Besides, Bailey in the barn this morning was one sexy sight to behold. That image is fresh in my mind, not the work on desk.

I turn off my computer and get ready to leave. There isn't any reason to stay here. I'm not able to concentrate. It's an hour before I'm supposed to meet Lizzie, but I'm going to ride over and start the process early. "Dawn, I'm leaving for the day. I have some things I need to take care of, but can you take a look at the invoices? See if you can organize them. They are becoming a problem for us. I don't want to hire anyone else until we get them caught up and organized, even if I have to work double shifts for a month."

"Cash, go. I'll work on the bookkeeping." She comes over and pushes me toward the door.

Bailey

I've been on my favorite food blog this morning, Southernplate.com, and I have my shopping list ready. That southern girl, Christy Jordan, is awesome! She not only has great recipes but sometimes even great advice on life in general. She at least has a good story to go with her recipes, plus she gives step by step instructions with pictures, and every once in a while she will have a video lesson. She is a college girl's best friend. Her dishes are simple but so yummy. The best part, to me anyway, is she is from northern Alabama, too. That's a win-win in my book!

I've found a no soak method for the pinto beans, so that's happening. I'm making a loaded potato salad, grilled chicken, bacon wrapped green beans and old fashioned chocolate pie for dessert. The chocolate pie was my other grandmother's recipe and my daddy's favorite. I'm going to attempt Margie's cornbread, but I don't have high hopes. Everything else should turn out good though, not as good as Granny's of course, but better than Momma's. That's not saying much. Momma didn't get Granny's talent for cooking. I guess it skipped a generation. Momma would kill me if I ever told anyone that. She's the kind of cook that opens up the can and sticks it in the microwave. I didn't get any cooking lessons from her, in fact, now I cook for her. I think I've spoiled her.

The doctor's office finally called me back. They didn't order Papa any new medicine and they aren't aware of any oxygen therapy for dementia patients. They told me that adding that to his daily routines would probably agitate him. They are very concerned about why I would be experimenting with his treatments and how I got extra medicines. They didn't seem too convinced with my explanation and they will be taking a look into this. They talked to me like I was an idiot, don't they think I'm more concerned about him than they are. I will stop by the pharmacy and see about the extra meds that were in the bag and the oxygen tank. If the doctor didn't order them, how were they filled? This is all so confusing. I wonder if it is an old prescription that was mistakenly filled. But then why would the labels be different?

I call out to Granny and Margie, "You guys need anything while I'm out?" They have been in there plotting some more. I can hear a lot of whispering, but can't make out what they're saying.

"Did you get those beans on, Bailey?" Granny asks.

What is it with her and these beans? I know she likes dry beans but gee-whiz, give me a break already.

"Yes, ma'am. I have them in the crock pot." I know that isn't her normal method of doing them, but Southernplate's way looked so much easier. This girl is all about easy, as long as it still tastes good. "It's a new method I've learned about. It works wonders." I hope. I head out the door before she can complain about my methods of cooking.

There are a couple of other stops I want to make while I'm out real quick. I want to be prepared for our next rendezvous in the barn. Plus, I would like to get a trim and a pedi. I think I will call Lizzie and see if she will meet me. I put my phone on speaker so it's easier to talk and drive.

"Hey, girl, I'm out running errands. Wanna meet for lunch and then go get our toes done?" I ask. "I have so much to tell you. Papa apparently hit Hendrix in the nose this morning. Hendrix blamed it on Cash and it turned into a fight. Anyway, I'm going to run a couple of errands and then we can go."

"Slow down, Bailey. I can't go, I have other plans this afternoon."

She always goes with me. I'm thrown off and a little disappointed. "Other plans? You never have other plans, what are they? Can't you do them afterward? Don't you want to know what all happened?" This isn't like her at all. "Lizzie, is something wrong?"

"No, Bailey. I just made plans with another friend, that's all. We're allowed to have different friends."

She laughs, but that kind of hurts my feelings. "Yeah, I know, Lizzie. It's okay. I really don't have time for all of that anyway. I'm cooking dinner tonight for Cash and his momma. I should probably get what I need and

head back." That's the honest truth because I really don't have time for all of that anyway. I was just excited to be out of the house.

"We will plan a girls' day soon, okay?" She sounds almost apologetic.

"Sounds great, Lizzie," I say. "I'm at my first stop. Call me later, okay? Love ya, girl!"

"Love you too, Bay! I'm so happy for you, bye." She hangs up.

She's so happy for me? Sometimes, that girl confuses me.

Later, I stop back by the pharmacy and they said the oxygen didn't come from them. I show them the three bottles of pills, and they look up Papa's medicine in their records. There isn't a record of them dispensing this medication. The numbers on the bottle don't match any in their system. They ask if they could keep them and examine them further. Since I want answers on how these meds got into our bag and what exactly they are, I leave the extra medications with the pharmacy. I don't even want them in our house. They have Papa's name on them and say they are prescribed by his doctor. I leave my cell number with them and thank them for their time.

CASH

I walk into our house, and Mom is on me quick. Telling me we need to go to the Jacksons' because they've invited us over, and Bailey has been cooking all day. Mom doesn't notice the package in my hand and I don't mention it since she is in a tizzy right now.

"I'm half an hour earlier than normal. Do you think I would have time to change clothes and clean up a bit?" I smile and put an arm around her.

"I didn't even notice the time. Sure, go ahead."

We walk over to the Jacksons' house. The food smells wonderful, but I don't notice anything else when I see my girl looking all hot in a pair of jeans that hug her ass just right. I go over and give her a small peck on the cheek. We keep everything very PG around her grandparents. They don't want to see me all over her. That wouldn't be right. I bend down a little and whisper in her ear, "Hello, beautiful. Your ass looks great in those jeans. Makes me want to get you out of them."

She puts her arms around my neck. Sometimes she doesn't play fair when I'm trying to keep things respectful. She gives me a kiss on my lips, but she manages to keep the heat down.

"I've missed you all day. I didn't text you because I knew you were late getting to work and probably busy."

"Sweet Cheeks, I always have time for you. You can call or text anytime you want. I will always be there for you." I look up, and mom is watching the exchange with a satisfied smile on her face.

"Let's eat before everything gets cold," Granny calls out.

We all gather around the table and join hands to say grace. As we are passing around the food, we hear a knock at the door. When Bailey gets up to answer it, she tells everyone to go ahead and eat.

I can't see the door from here, but I can hear clearly.

"Hendrix, what are you doing here?" Bailey asks.

"I just need to talk to you. There is something you need to know about that redneck. He isn't good for you, Bailey. I care for you, love you and only want the best for you."

That little fucker. I pick up my napkin from my lap and scoot my chair back.

Granny puts her hand on my arm and holds up one finger. "Let's see how she handles this first," she whispers.

This will take a little self-control, but I'll sit here unless things escalate.

"Hendrix, I love Cash. The sooner you realize that things are completely over between us the better. I thought at one time I wanted the high heels, the BMW and all the stuff you consider high class, but you can keep it. I'd much rather have Cash. He knows how to treat me like a lady. I like my cowboy boots. I always have. That's just me—it's who I am. If you don't mind, we just sat down to dinner—"

"Oh thanks, Bailey, I don't mind if I do."

I hear him come into the house.

When he rounds the corner, he sees me, and the smirk falls from his face.

"Hello, everyone. Thanks for having me. Sorry I'm late."

He is priceless, acting like he was invited all along.

"Henry, I don't remember inviting you. This is just for our neighbors tonight." Granny isn't giving an inch.

He laughs. "Oh, Mrs. Jackson, you always make me laugh. I love your funny side."

The nerve of this guy. Bailey is way too nice because she brings him a plate and silverware. When I finally put this guy in his place, I'm going to have fun doing it.

Bailey sets everything in front of him and goes back to get him something to drink.

I see he has his nose all cleaned up. Asshole.

"Mrs. Jackson, everything looks and smells lovely." He smiles. "I didn't know you were back to your cooking."

"There's a lot you don't know, Henry."

She leaves it at that, but I can hear the animosity in her voice. She has never come right out and said she doesn't like him, but hell, he has to

know. I chuckle under my breath. She has a way of saying, "Go screw yourself," but like a lady, Hendrix will be lucky if Granny or I don't stick a fork up his ass.

Bailey brings him a glass of tea and sits down to make herself a plate.

"So, what all do we have here to eat?" he asks, taking inventory of the table.

"Grilled chicken, beans and taters." Granny cuts her eyes over to him. "That's the kind of food we eat out here in the sticks."

I snigger a little. She is trying to annoy him.

"That sounds really good to me, Granny. I love home cooked food," I say.

He has taken small helpings of everything. I look at the huge piles on my plate compared to those on his. I guess he's trying to keep his boyish figure. "This grilled chicken is really good, I've never had any like this before."

Bailey blushes a little. "That's my secret recipe, we can't have plain grilled chicken around here." She grins at me, pleased with herself.

"You made this, Bailey?" Hendrix asks. "I didn't know you could cook. This is scrumptious. You really need to give me the recipes for mother, or you can just cook them for me again."

He is full of shit.

"Did you not hear the part about her recipes being secret or has all that hair goop gotten to your brain?" asks Granny.

I need to let Granny know how much I love her.

Hendrix just laughs. "Good one. I'll have to remember that." He is picking at his food.

"Everything is great, Bailey, and your cornbread turned out wonderful," Mom tells her.

And it is.

We finish up the meal as soon as possible, in hopes Hendrix will leave. He doesn't take hints, or he ignores them rather.

Granny says she thinks Papa needs a break from so much stimulation and asks Mom to help her get him to bed. "Henry, I'm glad you got to see how good of a cook Bailey is. Goodnight. Cash will see you out."

That again is how Granny tells you to get the hell out of her house.

"Yeah, Henry. My girl is good at a lot of things." I pull Bailey in and stake my claim, right here, in front of everyone. After I release her, I go open the door and look at him expectantly.

"I guess that's my cue to leave." He walks to the table where Bailey is clearing dishes. "I'll see you later. I've got a surprise for you." She looks at him with her eyebrows drawn together.

"Hendrix, I don't want anything from you. Please leave."

My girl is standing up for herself. I love it.

"You heard her, pretty boy, it's time to go," I tell him.

He struts over to me with a smirk on his face. "It's not over between us, redneck. There's no way I'm letting scum like you take her away from me," he whispers as he goes out the door.

I want to go fucking crazy on his ass, but that is what he wants. He keeps taunting me so I will make a scene, but I'm a bigger man than that. "What you don't seem to understand, Henry, is that she wants a man not a boy. So if you want Bailey, you have work, both mentally and physically. Even when you get to be a man, you still won't be able to please her with your one inch wonder." I shut the door in his face and go help Bailey do the dishes. I feel much better now.

Bailey

Hendrix keeps coming over wanting to help me with any and all things. I only allow this because he has really done so well turning himself around. He is no longer the self-centered guy I once knew. He is more caring, and comes over in the early afternoon before Cash is home to help with whatever chore I happen to be doing. Today he is helping with yard work, which is so unlike him. Normally, he hires people to do this kind of stuff. He borrowed a pickup truck from someone and brought over enough topsoil and mulch to do the flowerbed and the little beds around the house too. I want to keep encouraging this change in him, maybe I can teach an old dog new tricks after all.

We have been out here spreading the topsoil for a couple of hours in the heat, and he isn't complaining. He is doing manual labor and he isn't fussing about sweating.

"Hendrix, what made you want to do this?"

"I can tell that this flowerbed has come to mean a lot to you since you've moved in and I wanted to help you make them beautiful."

"That's really sweet, Hendrix." I look across the street and see Cash's truck in his driveway. "Oh, Cash is home early today. I'll get him to come over and help us."

He glances at Cash's house. "I could really use some water, Bailey. Would you mind getting me a glass?"

"Yeah, I could use a glass too. I'll be right back." I get us both big glasses of ice water and bring them out. I see Cash making his way across the street as I hand Hendrix his glass of water.

Hendrix takes his water with one hand and pulls me in for a full body-press hug with the other. "Thanks, Bailey."

"What the hell, Hendrix! Don't touch me like that. I told you, friends only." I push him away.

Cash is in the yard now, and he's not very happy. "Why the fuck did you have your hands on my woman?"

I can see Cash is controlling himself, but who could blame him if he did hit Hendrix.

"I was just thanking her for bringing me the water. I meant no harm. I know she's yours now. Chill, boy."

Cash gets into Hendrix's face. "I think it's about time that you stop coming around here. Your help isn't needed nor is it wanted. So take your skinny fucking ass and leave. I don't want to see you here." Cash reaches over and straightens Hendrix's collar then pops him on his cheeks like he's a kid.

Hendrix breathes heavily through his nose and talks through gritted teeth. "You know, I don't remember asking or needing your permission to be here. The last time I checked, your name wasn't on the deed to this property and I don't see a ring on Bailey's finger."

This is getting intense, and I'm not sure how to stop them.

Cash tilts his head and lowers his voice, "It doesn't matter if there is a ring on her finger or not, Henry. We are in love, and I love her family. I will do everything in my power to keep you away from them. I don't trust you."

"You don't have to trust me, redneck. Bailey, I don't want to start anything here. I'll go in and say goodbye to your grandparents then I'll be on my way." He thrusts his shovel at Cash and goes into the house.

"Bailey, I think his biggest problem is that you're with me and he thinks I'm beneath him. I don't even trust him alone with Granny and Papa. He isn't a good guy and he is out to hurt you or them."

"Cash, if you only knew how much he's changed. He's so different than he used to be. How can I tell him to not come over here when he's paying for their care?"

If she could only see through his bullshit. "Think about some of the stuff that's been happening here lately. It doesn't add up. Wake up, Sweet Cheeks. Please. Before something happens."

Suddenly, I'm thinking, "What if Hendrix had something to do with the medicine and oxygen?" I can't stand the thought of him being here a minute longer. "Come on. Let's go inside. I don't like him being alone with them, either."

We walk inside the house, and Granny is nowhere to be found. I hear something in the bedroom. We head in that direction. Hendrix comes out in a hurry. His eyes are down and he isn't watching where he's going.

"Hendrix, where are you off to so fast?" Cash asks.

Hendrix ignores him and turns toward me. "Bye, Bailey. I'll see you later. Be sure to call me if you need anything, sweetheart." He has some nerve. If Cash doesn't punch him, I will.

"If she needs anything, little fucker, she will come to me. Now, get your ass out of here before I change my mind and knock your teeth out."

That's my man.

Cash thumps Hendrix's chest.

"Look, trash, you keep running your mouth all you want, but in the end we will see who ends up on top," says Hendrix.

I want to slap the smirk right off of Hendrix's face. "Hendrix, you need to leave. I don't want any more drama around this house. My grandparents have a hard enough time as it is."

"Well, you heard her, Cash. No more drama. Let's go." Hendrix waves a hand at the door.

What? Does he think since I made them both leave last time, I will make them both leave again? "I didn't say anything about Cash. I said for you to leave, Hendrix. Don't come back if all you want to do is try to start a fight. I don't want any of that around here, ya got it?"

"Bailey, I'd never do anything to cause you a moment of stress, Sweetheart." He brushes his thumb across my cheekbone.

Cash grabs his wrist and twists it. "I think I've told you to keep your fucking hands off of her or I would knock your teeth out."

Hendrix doesn't flinch, even though I know he must be in a lot of pain.

"No, you said you thought it was about time for me to stop coming around. You didn't say anything about me touching her. In fact, I thought you might want to share."

He has gone too far. Cash grabs Hendrix's throat and calmly walks him backward to the door. I go around them to open the door. Cash steps out with Hendrix and gives him a shove.

Hendrix stumbles a little but doesn't fall.

"If you ever touch Bailey again, I will tear you a new asshole. Is that clear enough for you, pansy ass prick?"

"We'll see about that." Hendrix turns and heads to his car.

I wrap my arms around Cash and we watch Hendrix leave.

"Bailey, I've controlled my temper, and bit my tongue for the last time. Please don't expect me to not pummel him into the ground if he touches you again. I can only take so much, and I've reached my limit." He puts his arm around my waist and kisses the top of my head.

"If you do, just don't do it in front of my grandparents. Please take it outside. I do think he deserves a good ass kicking though."

CASH

What is it going to take for Hendrix to get it through his head I will beat his ass if he messes with Bailey or the Jacksons? After we go inside, we walk into the Jacksons' bedroom. Papa is laying in bed, looking at the ceiling, and Granny is coming out of the bathroom.

"What happened? I heard a bunch of fussing out here."

Granny looks over to us with concern.

"Hendrix keeps hugging on me. He's pushing Cash's buttons to start a fight with him," Bailey says. She bends over the bed checking on Papa.

His eyes are dilated, and he is drooling.

"I was in the bathroom for about twenty minutes, and now I come out and your Papa is all spacey. What happened to him while I was in the bathroom? He was having such a good day, all happy and talking to me." Granny says.

"Hendrix came to tell you guys bye, and we came in a few minutes afterward because we didn't trust him in here without one of us," Bailey says.

"When we came into the house, Hendrix was coming out of here," I add.

"Bailey, he is kind of scaring me. I don't think I want him over here anymore," Granny admits.

"Cash told him not to come back here anymore. So, do you think he did something to Papa?" Bailey asks as she feels his forehead and looks closer at his eyes. She checks his pulse.

She looks to me with a worried look on her face. Surely, he wouldn't do anything to Papa? Why would he do something to him? What would he have to gain? All of those questions really don't matter at the moment because we need to figure out if Mr. Jackson is okay.

"Papa, are you okay?" Bailey asks. He doesn't respond. "I think we need to call his doctor."

"Alan! Alan, can you hear me?" Granny is down by his ear.

I call mom on my cell and she comes right over. Despite everything that has happened to her, when something like this takes place, she is level headed and good under pressure.

"They have left for the day but I left a message with the answering service," Bailey says as she comes back into the room.

Mom comes in and goes straight to Papa looking him over. "I think we need to carry him to the hospital," Mom says.

"Bailey, I think Margie is right, we need to call 911," Granny says, her brow furrowed.

I take out my phone and make the call.

"Have any of you noticed that he doesn't seem to be taking full breaths?" Mom asks.

"I've noticed that his breathing is a little shallow," Bailey says.

We stand around his bed anxiously waiting for the paramedics to arrive. They came in about ten minutes last time. Granny gets into Papa's field of vision and talks to him. Bailey holds his hand, and tears well up in her eyes. Mom and I keep giving each other concerned glances.

I wish we had moved here earlier and I had the opportunity to get to know Papa before the dementia robbed him of his body and mind. Watching him slowly get worse through Bailey's eyes has been heartbreaking. It's like a long goodbye because we are losing a little more of him each day. I wonder how long it will be before he doesn't know his family any longer.

The paramedics arrive, and Bailey and Granny both have fear in their eyes. Mom and I step out of the room, but I stand in the open doorway listen to everything.. I'd do to anything at all in a heartbeat to make things better.

"How long has he been this way?" one of the medics asks.

"Maybe thirty minutes or so now. What do you think could have happened? He was fine and then all of a sudden he was like this," Bailey says.

"I'm not sure, how long did you say he has had dementia?" The guy looks up at us as he listens to Papa's heart.

"About three and a half years, right, Granny?"

"Well, that's when the doctor actually confirmed it, but I think he has had it longer. We started noticing little things six or seven years ago," Granny says.

"What medications is he on?" the medic writing down all the vitals asks.

Bailey goes to the kitchen and comes back with a basket full of medicine. The guy goes through it bottle by bottle writing everything down. He gets to one bottle, and he shows it to his partner.

"When is the last time you gave him the morphine?" He looks at Bailey.

I step back into the room because I'm not liking where this is going.

Bailey holds her hand out for the bottle. She looks at the label then the pills inside. "I give these to him right before bedtime. They are supposed to help calm him down so he can sleep." She hands the bottle back to the paramedic that is questioning her.

"Are you sure you didn't accidentally get confused and give them to him early?"

He gives Bailey a stern look. I think he speculates Bailey of overdosing him on purpose.

"Look, mister, if my granddaughter says she didn't give it to him, then she didn't give it to him."

Granny's bear claws are coming out, protecting her cub.

He holds his hand up to ward off Granny. "Okay, ma'am, we just see morphine used a lot on people that are in their last stages of life to make their end more comfortable. Higher dosages can lead to shortness of breath."

"Do you want us to take him to the hospital? We can take him in, but it is really up to you. Personally, I think this is just a sign that he's slipping into the last stage of dementia and you need to do everything you can to make sure your time with him now counts."

The cocky sounding asshole makes it sound like Bailey is keeping him drugged all the time.

Granny looks at Papa with silent tears running down her face.

"No, if we feel like he needs to go to the hospital, we will carry him ourselves." I step up and take charge of the situation.

"Okay, then all I need is to get a list of everyone present and a signature saying you are refusing medical help for Mr. Jackson."

He's making me mad and this isn't turning out to be a good afternoon. I give him everyone's name and as caregiver, Bailey signs the paperwork. It's not long before they are gone.

"I'll go and pick up something for everyone to eat." I say. "Bailey, make a list of what everyone would like to have." I have to do something to be useful.

Mom brings in an extra chair so she and Bailey can both sit beside the bed. Granny sits on her side of the bed next to Papa. Watching the love she has for husband, how she tenderly cares for him, even when she isn't exactly capable herself, is so gratifying. I see why Bailey admires them both so much and wants that type of devotion from her life partner. I want to be the one she spends her life with and the one who gets the opportunity to be loved like that by her.

Bailey

Two Weeks Later

Journal Entry: I'm so glad tomorrow is Friday, Cash has taken the day off, and we are going away for a long weekend. Margie will spend the weekend with Granny and Papa. I'm glad she and Granny have become close friends. I like Margie too.

I need this time away. The last couple of weeks have been a nightmare. A few days after Papa's episode, we had a visit from the Department of Adult Protective Services. I had been turned in for elderly abuse. Someone reported that I had been not only taking advantage of my grandparents, but I was physically abusing them and I was also dispensing extra medication to Papa.

Papa was coherent that day and told them that I wasn't even big enough to hurt him. Granny was furious. She demanded to know who had called in the report, but they wouldn't tell her. She said it had to have been the paramedics, but it could have been Papa's doctor's office or even the pharmacy. They are actually investigating me, but that doesn't bother me because I have nothing to hide. I love my grandparents and I would never do anything to hurt them. So, they can investigate me all they want, but I would like to know what happened too.

We have been making good use of the barn. On my trip into town a couple of weeks ago, I picked up the shortest pair of Daisy Duke shorts I've ever seen in my life. I wore those and a barely there red checkered top that tied at the boobs. My boots completed my outfit, and I tied my hair in a low side ponytail. I packed a blanket and a picnic and went to the barn where Cash had been working all morning. When I walked in, he almost dropped the hammer. I was playing up the whole farmer's daughter scenario. I love that no matter what I come up with, he picks right up and runs with it like everything was planned.

Things have been crazy around here so when Cash mentioned a getaway, I was thrilled until he clammed up. He won't tell me where we're going. I don't even know what to pack. He said it is a surprise, and we are leaving Friday afternoon.

He did ask me to dress nice for dinner so now I have on a dress and my boots. I packed casual clothes and some new lingerie I bought just for this occasion. All of my essentials, which have gotten less over the last few months, fit in a small bag. I'm all set, ready to go when Cash pulls up in his truck with Margie. She comes in with her overnight bag, and Cash has a mischievous grin on his face. I can't wait to spend the weekend with him. He looks great all dressed up, but it doesn't matter what he has on, he looks great in nothing at all, too.

"Hello, beautiful, are you ready to go?" He pulls me in for a small kiss.

"I'm ready, if you are handsome." I turn to Margie and Granny. "Margie, you have my cell number, right? Call me if anything happens." I give them both a kiss and a hug. I'm so giddy I'm practically bouncing. "Bye, love y'all!"

Cash picks up my bags, he says his goodbyes and we are out the door.

Once we are on our way, I ask, "So, are you going to tell me where we are going now?"

"Patience, Sweet Cheeks, patience. Don't you like surprises?"

Ugh, he has been this way all week. "Casssh, you're not being fair. I'm going to see where we are going anyway." I give him pouty lips and puppy dog eyes.

"Alright, I didn't want to have to do this, but you really leave me no other choice." He sighs and pulls into a parking lot then he opens up the center console of his truck.

"Hey, is that my lucky bandanna? How did you get to that?" He is full of surprises today. "It's not dark enough for us to play around in the truck, Cash." My man does like to play. I love it!

"Yes, this is your blindfold, and no this isn't for play, Baby Doll. Remember when you told me I could take a turn and blindfold you? Well, I'm taking my turn tonight. You're not going to be able to see where we are going. Now, turn around and let me tie this on you. Oh, and if you don't close your mouth, I'm going to give you something for that, too."

I'm speechless. This makes me more excited. Bring on the surprise! "I'll play. You know how much I like our games." I lick my lips, giving him a devilish smile.

We drive for what seems like an hour. When we finally get to our destination, he still doesn't want me to take off the blindfold. I really don't want to walk inside somewhere with this thing on. I don't protest, though because he is being so sweet in wanting this to be a surprise.

"Just stay seated, I'll be right around to help you out."

I can hear his door opening and closing. He opens my door, and I only hear crickets and birds chirping.

"Here, take my arm, I won't let you fall."

I guess he is really going to make me wear this inside. I take his arm and I can tell we are walking on grass.

"Stand here for just a moment and let me get the door."

I hear a creak, and I smell a familiar aroma. I reach up and take off my blindfold. We are at the barn. He takes my hand and we step inside.

He has transformed a section into a beautiful dining area. He had to have someone help him. Candles in little votive holders are tucked in several places, and tiny lights hang from the rafters. In the center of the table is a large mason jar with wildflowers. On the table is a linen tablecloth with a burlap runner. He has thought of every little detail. "Cash, this is absolutely stunning—the most beautiful place I've ever been in my entire life." He did this for me. No one has ever done anything like this for me before, and I feel loved, honored.

He leads me over to the table, and that's when I notice it is our picnic table. He helps me sit down and puts a bandanna in my lap for a napkin. My guy has turned up his country charm tonight. I'm going to reward him real good tonight for all of this. He is going to be one very lucky guy.

CASH

The look in Bailey's eyes as she takes in the barn is precious, and it is my job to keep it there. I think this is the last thing she was expecting for tonight. She has been trying to get clues from Mom and me all week. She was adorable, offering me sexual favors in exchange for information. She has been excited for this weekend, and I have too. There were many times I wanted to forget this plan and get to the end result.

Dinner goes well and now on to stage two. I hit a button on the remote that is in my pocket and the music I've had piped throughout the barn plays. King George is singing our song, "Give It All We Got Tonight."

"May I have this dance?" I take her by the hand and lead her to the space I have designated as the dance floor. I sing along with him again, just like I did that night on that back road when we danced under the stars. I hope all of these little touches aren't lost on her. She has probably figured out what's coming. The anticipation has to be eating her alive. It is me. I hold her to me and breathe in her honeysuckle-scented shampoo. George finishes our song, and I ask, "Are you ready for dessert or would you like to dance more?"

"I'm ready for whatever you're ready for. I want this night to last forever, Cash. You have swept me off of my feet. Who knew you were this romantic? I mean, I knew you were romantic, but tonight you've pulled out all the stops."

She looks lovely with the dreamy look in her eyes. I really want to take her upstairs and get her out of this dress right now.

"There are more good things to come, Baby Doll. What are you ready for next?"

"I want the next good thing."

I knew it. She is on to me. "You do? What do you think that would be?" I ask.

"I don't know, but I'm ready for it. I just don't see how you're going to top all of this."

"Why don't we have dessert first and then we will go upstairs? I've made us a bedroom upstairs so you won't have to sleep on hay." I go over to where Lizzie set up our dessert. I owe her big time. I think she must have known the significance of bandannas as napkins. She asked if she should bring a cooler the next morning with orange juice. I'm sure as close as she and Bailey are, Bailey told her about my fondness for oranges now. I bring out homemade Italian Cream Cake and set it in front her, but I sit beside her this time so I can start this process.

"How did you know this was my favorite dessert? You have gone to a lot of trouble for this weekend. I've noticed all the improvements you've made to the barn, I'm glad you decided to keep it." She leans over and gives me a peck on the cheek.

"I've had a lot of help preparing all of this. There has been several people involved to make this weekend special." I take her hand. "When you stepped off the elevator that night in the hospital, I wasn't thinking about a long term relationship, but I did think you were the most beautiful thing I'd ever seen in my life, and I wanted to get to know you better. The compassion you have in your heart for everyone around you makes you even more beautiful on the inside."

I click the remote in my pocket one more time. The chords to Lonestar's "Amazed" plays, and I take her back to the dance floor. This time, I sing her the whole song myself. She lays her head on my chest, and when the song finishes, I get down on one knee. I take the ring out of my pocket. She is in tears with her hand over her mouth.

"Bailey Grace Reynolds, you are the love of my life and you're my best friend. I want the whole world to know how much you mean to me. Will you marry me?"

She doesn't say yes. She doesn't say no. She stands there and cries. Taking a deep breath, she says, "Cash, I want to be your wife more than anything else in this world."

Whew, she had me worried there for a minute.

"But…"

No, no but, why does there have to be a but?

"I have my grandparents, and I've promised to be the one who will take care of them. I love you with everything I have to give. You have all of me, but I can't move them out of their home and into your house when it's built."

I give her a smile. If that's all she is worried about, it has already been taken care of. I put the ring back in my pocket for the time being. "Bailey, look around you. Do you think I would overlook any of the details?"

She looks at me like I've lost my mind. I know she wants specifics and that isn't what I want tonight to be about, but for her not to feel like she is abandoning her grandparents, she needs to know how they will be taken care of. For her peace of mind, I tell her what my momma and her granny have been cooking up the last few weeks. Mom is going to move in with the Jacksons and take care of them on a regular basis. She's been over there all day everyday anyway. Bailey will become the backup. Bailey looks relieved as she knows they will be in good hands, and she'll be right across the street from them anyway.

"Cash, you really have taken care of all the details. Do you know what it means to me that you thought to take care of Granny and Papa, too? How did I get so lucky to find a guy like you?"

"The two of us meeting was fate, Bailey. We began somewhat as friends, though I did have other intentions in mind. I think us falling in love was inevitable. I didn't know why I was waiting on a relationship until I met you. Now, I know, having a relationship with anyone else wasn't right because you're my soulmate." I tell her and genuinely mean every word.

"I love you so much, Cash. I can't imagine my life without you. I'm so glad you came along when you did. I would be a broken mess right now."

We dance for a few more minutes then she looks at me seriously. "Cash, are you going to give me my ring now?"

"You haven't said yes."

A wide grin spreads across her face. "Do you want to ask me again?"

"Hey, Bailey, I've been thinking. I love you and you love me, right? So why don't we make things all official and get hitched?" This made her giggle. I love to hear her joy.

"Well, you know Cash, I was hoping to marry a cowboy. You wear a hat sometimes, so I guess you'll do. Yes, I'll marry you."

"I'll do, huh?"

She nods and holds out her hand.

"I might need to reconsider my options, since 'I'll do'."

She playfully swats me on my shoulder.

I get back down on one knee and take her hand. "Will you marry me and let us grow old together? I want to sit on the front porch with you in big rocking chairs and sip sweet tea while we enjoy the cool breeze. I want to give you a love like that forever."

"Yes, Cash, yes, I will marry you."

I take the ring out of my pocket and slip it on her finger. "I want a forever like that with you too." I bend down to scoop her up in my arms and carry her up the stairs.

"What about the candles, Cash? I don't want to be in the middle of something and have the barn catch on fire."

"They're battery operated, Bailey. How did you not notice that?" I laugh.

"I was only paying attention to you."

She gives me a heart-stopping kiss.

Bailey

Cash carries me up the stairs. He has really out done himself. He even has a bed set up in the loft. I guess he wanted it to look like a real room as much as possible. This man knows no limits, and he has gone far beyond anything I could ever ask for.

He sets me down gently on the bed, and slowly removes my clothes. The music very softly drifts upstairs, and a soft glow bounces off the window. He has more flowers, the bed has the softest linens, and I notice he added a little curtain to the top of the window. The scent of lavender is in the air and I feel the faintest of breezes.

He reaches for the button on his shirt, and I say, "Let me, please."

He drops his hands, and I replace them with my own. I slowly peel off his attire, piece by piece. I bend down to get his socks and take my time licking my way back up—the start of his reward for all of his hard work. I get to his inner thigh crease and I spend a little extra time in that area. He offers no complaints. I'm not sure why he tastes better than anyone I've ever been with. Maybe because he eats well and takes care of his body. I don't mind giving him pleasure. In fact, I enjoy it, and I know with Cash I will receive my own in tenfold. He is much more giving than taking. "Lay on the bed, handsome. I want to devour my fiancée."

He pulls me into his body. "I love to hear you say that." He says in a growl.

"I want to devour you, or lay on the bed?"

"The fiancée part, but don't make me wait long, Bailey, please." He lays down, pulling me with him. "I can't wait for us to start our lives together."

"Why don't we finish celebrating tonight, and talk about that later. Right now, I want to show you how grateful I am to have you in my life."

"I can live with that."

"I thought you might find that agreeable. Now, you just lay there and relax." I take my time kissing and licking him everywhere. Teasing him, sending him into a frenzy. Then I make him sit up on the side of the bed and put his feet on the floor.

"Sit up?"

He looks confused and disappointed.

"Yes, Cash, sit up."

"Okay, if you say so."

I climb on his lap and slide down on his dick. "Now lean back a little bit and hold onto my hands. I'm going to lean back too." We made a V with our bodies, and I grind on him. Damn, it isn't easy to move in this position. He helps me by putting his hands on my back and actually bouncing me a little. This angle makes his penetration much deeper. He feels so good inside of me. He moves faster and is hitting my G-spot with every thrust. This is supposed to be more for him than me, but he is always a thoughtful lover. He sits upright and puts his arms around me, almost cradling me. This changes the angle of penetration and wakes up more desires. I moan softly and bring myself up to a sitting position. There isn't any vacant space inside me; he has taken up every inch. He is moving me even faster now, and I feel the tingling in my belly. I know it won't be long and I'll show him how much he pleases me. The tingles run down to my core and the throbbing sensation takes over.

"Let go, baby. Give me those sweet juices."

I throw my head back and I can't control my moans anymore. They are getting louder. "Ahh! Baby! Oh, uhh, Cash! You're so..." I tighten around him and then I explode. My legs are trembling, and Cash is kissing me tenderly.

"I'm so what, Sweet Cheeks?" He picks me up then turns us, and gently lays me on the bed. He pulls me to the edge. Lifting my hips up, he lines up with my entrance and slides into me again. I wrap my legs around him. I lift my hips meeting him thrust for thrust.

"Holy fuck, Cash. More, faster."

He moves one of his hands to my center and strokes me which quickly starts another fire. A small sheen of sweat breaks out on his brow. He is gearing up for his own release. I pulse once more, and I feel him doing the

same. He pushes me over the edge and I climax again. He releases his own. He collapses onto the bed, and I move up by him. I cuddle up to his side and lay my head on his chest. I give him a peck on the cheek as we catch our breath.

CASH

Three Months Later

We finally get confirmation that the investigation on Bailey for elderly abuse has been closed. They found her in no fault. She was relieved even though she knew she didn't do anything wrong.

Bailey and Lizzie have been busy planning our wedding. I told her I would pay for everything because I know her parents don't have a lot of money, and I want her to have the wedding she has always dreamed about. She wants to keep the ceremony small and intimate and wants to have it in the damn barn. I apparently made her think I could work magic in a short amount of time.

I've been busting my ass to get this barn up to par because she didn't want me to tear it down and start over. No, it has to be this barn that really looks like shit in the bright sunlight, but she loves it. I've had a bathroom installed and added more fans for circulation. I made a bar area, and added a couple more windows for natural lighting. She said this can be my man cave afterward, so I better make it the way I like.

Even though I have offered to pay for everything, Bailey insists on having her cousins help her make decorations and some of the food for the reception. She said since only family and close friends would be attending, she didn't need anything fancy. She has been to several weddings, and the more simple ones were the ones that touched her the most. I put her on my checking account the week after our engagement, and I told her to take as much as she needed.

We cleaned out a bedroom that was being used for storage over at the Jacksons then delivered to people things Granny wanted them to have. Mom has been bringing things over slowly and spending even more time with the Jacksons to give Papa time to adjust.

Clay has a charity event planned for his equine therapy ranch next weekend. We have volunteered to help him, and Bailey talked Lizzie into helping too. She loves horses so it didn't take a lot of convincing. He has worked hard to get this place up and running.

Clay is smarter than I gave him credit for. Not only can he sing and play a guitar, but also he has a brain and he looks a lot like me. I want to help Lizzie see what a great guy he is, but Bailey said Lizzie can't be pushed. You have to put things in front of her face and hope she opens her eyes. That's next on my horizon. Help Lizzie!

I've been in my office all day going through the financial records, trying to get them in shape to go to the accountant. Dawn is helping me, but really she has enough on her plate as it is. Invoices aren't my forte. I need to be looking for that bookkeeper, but I want to get a good system in place before I hire one.

Dawn buzzes my office to let me know Bailey is on the phone for me.

"Hey, Sweet Cheeks, how's your day?" I answer the phone.

"Great, I've gotten so much done." She rattles off a list of accomplishments.

They all sound the same after a while. If I offer a "mmmhmm" every once in a while, she's happy. "Good, I'm glad you were able to get all of that done." I say when I hear a lull in the conversation.

She laughs, "Is all of this that boring to you? I bet you don't even realize what you agreed to."

"I'm sorry, I'll listen now."

"What are you doing?"

"I'm trying to get our financial books in order before we hire someone to do this full time." I sigh and lean back in my chair. My desk looks like something exploded. "Sweet Cheeks, it looks like I'll be late tonight, and probably the rest of week. I can't believe I've let this get in this much of a mess."

"Why haven't you told me this before now, Cash? You do know I'm only a couple of semesters away from having my degree in accounting? I can

help you with this, or better yet, I will come to work with you and do it for you."

She sounds excited. How can she be excited over this kind of shit?

"Bailey, that would be great, but I don't want you to have to do that. It will take me several days, but I will get it done."

"I'm on my way. I'll see you in half an hour. Then, I will come to work with you tomorrow and finish it up."

She hangs up. She didn't tell me bye or she loved me!

She can't see my desk like this. I need to tidy up quickly. "Dawn!" I don't even act all professional and use the intercom. "Dawn, I need you. Hurry!"

She runs into my office. "What's wrong? What happened?"

"Bailey is on her way to help with the books, and she can't see my office like this." I wave my hand at the mounds of clutter.

She laughs, "Is that all? I thought something was really wrong. Don't you think she'll figure out you're horrible at this when she comes and digs into everything?" She shakes her head, "Come on, I'll help make it look neater at least."

"Thanks, Dawn, I appreciate the help." We work in the office until Bailey walks through the door, then Dawn excuses herself to get back to her own work.

"So where do you want me?" Bailey asks me as she gives me a hug.

"I want you beneath me, I even need you there." I whisper in her ear.

She reaches up to kiss me and then playfully slaps my arm. "Behave! Where would you like for me to work on your books?" She looks over at my desk. Her eyes get big, "Cash, how long have you let this go? Why haven't you told me before?"

I shrug and try to look pitiful in hopes she will take mercy on me.

She tells me what she will need, and I get her all set up in the spare office. She gets busy in her accountant mode, all serious. She waves me off, and tells me to leave her alone.

Bailey

It's funny how my big strong man can handle all the little details of major projects, but can't manage receipts. He has too much on his plate. If I can get him organized, I should be able to keep him in good order by coming in and helping him one day a week.

After about three hours of inputting information into the accounting program, I've noticed he has some of his personal household expenses in with the business. I make a pile for those, too. I have almost everything separated; organization is the key. I come across a receipt for the rehab center Granny was in, and I examine it further. Behind the receipt, there is a hand written note from Granny which states she and Papa want to be put in a nursing home should they become too much of a burden for one person. The statement was witnessed by Cash and Margie. What. The. Hell. He paid for Granny's care? Nursing home? Have they been lying to me this whole time? Taking care of poor helpless Bailey? She can't do anything by herself.

I am infuriated. If he wanted to help, he could have at least told me like Hendrix did. He wants trust and respect, but he isn't showing me any right now. However, the thing that worries me the most is the hand written letter from Granny. I'm so hurt by all of them. Why would they keep all of this from me? I've got to go. I need to be somewhere I can think.

I pick up my purse and walk out of Cash's office. I don't stop when Dawn calls out her goodbyes. I can't stop. If I do, I will breakdown in front of her. I push the front door open with force then get into my Jeep and drive. I drive a little too fast. I know I have a temper, but I can't help it. I inherited it from Momma and Granny.

The texts roll in from Cash, and then from Lizzie. I don't want to talk to them. I want away from all of this. I send my own text. Then I turn off my phone. I want to go somewhere that I know I can vent, and nobody will be trying to change my mind. Sometimes you want to blow off steam and not to be coddled. I know the place to go—a place where I can find the answers I need.

CASH

Bailey left the office without a word to anyone. She isn't answering her phone from any of us, and she hasn't gone home. Granny hasn't heard from her and neither has Kathy. I don't know what happened to make her leave like she did. I question Dawn, "Did she say anything or give any indication of where she was going?"

Dawn stands there shaking her head. "She hit the door hard and left, Cash. She didn't even make eye contact with me."

I open the door to the spare office and look around to see if she left a note or a clue, something. Two neat stacks of invoices are on the desk, a stack for the business and a stack of my personal bills. I sit with my elbows on the desk and my head in my hands. There isn't a note anywhere to be found. Something has upset her. I go over everything in my head.

I'm not sure how long I sit here staring at that desk, but I finally notice the invoice on the top of the personal stack—the one for the rehab center. Then I see the note of Granny's wishes—the only way she would accept our help. I've been meaning to tell Bailey that mom and I are the ones taking care of the Jacksons' medical expenses, but she was being so headstrong on doing it herself. Then when she thought Hendrix was paying, I let her believe it. I'm not sure what has made her so upset. So I was making payments to help them out. I really don't understand the problem. Why the hell is she not answering her phone? If she would at least talk to me, I could explain all of this.

Finally, her phone goes straight to voice mail. Stubborn woman. Which is what she is. A damn stubborn woman. I don't know whether to track her down or just let her go. Anyone who would get this mad over this has to be a little crazy.

When I find her, I'm going to say my piece. If she still wants to be a brat after that, so be it, but she will hear my piece. I tell Dawn I'm leaving early. I pick up my keys and I'm gone. I rack my brain over the places she might go. There is only one place I can think of, but I pray to God she isn't there. If she is, I won't be responsible for my actions.

Bailey

I pull up and wonder why I'm here. I shouldn't be here. I've calmed down, and I can see reason now. Well, I can see some reason. I'm still a little upset about all of this. I'm as aggravated by Hendrix as I am by Cash. But I don't think it isn't anything we can't talk through.

I walk up to the door where he is waiting. "Hey, Sweetheart! Come in. What did that asshole do to you? I will kick his ass. I'm so glad you're back."

"Hey," I say, looking down at my feet, "I'm sorry I bothered you. I was temporarily insane. I'm not here to take you back, Hendrix." I look at him and smile a little bit.

"Do you want to talk about it?" Hendrix asks.

I shake my head and the tears flow again. He pulls me inside and closes the door. He takes me in his arms for a hug and I let him for just a minute or two.

"Hendrix, why did you let me believe you were the one paying for Granny and Papa's health care?" He stands there looking at me like he's been caught.

"Bailey, it was the only way I got to see you and spend time with you." He takes my hand. "Please know I would do anything to be with you. If you want me to give up all of my money, if you want a house right beside your grandparents, I'll build you one. Whatever it is, Bailey, give me a chance to show you I've changed."

"You're too late, Hendrix. It's over between us. I would like to remain friends, but you can't do things like you have been. I'm going to marry Cash, I love him."

He rocks back on his heels with his hands in his back pockets. "I know that, Bailey. Just know, if anything ever happens, I would like my second chance. I'm so sorry, Bailey. I do love you and I think you've really changed me." He kisses my cheek.

He can be so sweet when he wants to be, and I smile up at him. "Thanks, Hendrix, I hope you have changed because I think you have the potential of being a great boyfriend for someone." Oh my God. I've got to pee so badly. "I need to use your ladies' room."

"You know where it is."

I go to the one in his master suite because I'm so accustomed to using that one. I need to hurry up and get out of here so I can confront Cash about all of this, too. When I come out of the bathroom, a couple of pieces of paper on his nightstand catch my attention. One has a familiar color pattern, so I go over and take a peek, I'm so nosey. Un-fucking-believable!

CASH

Lizzie gave me his address. I hope she isn't there, but it's one of the first places I check. I pull into the parking lot scanning for her Jeep. *Shit.* I hit my steering wheel because there it is. I pull in a couple of spots down. It can't go down this way. I won't allow it. If nothing else, she is going to hear what I have to say.

I'm out of the truck and at his door before I can change my mind on anything. I go to knock, and Hendrix opens the door. I give him my best "go to hell" look and ask through gritted teeth, "Where's Bailey?"

He opens his door up wider for me to come in. "She's freshening up. She should be out in a moment."

I swear if he smirks at me one more time, I'll knock it off his face. I've been wanting to do that for a while anyway.

He takes his thumb and wipes the corner of his mouth. "So, you screwed up?"

That's it, that's all it takes. He meets the business end of my fist.

"Cash, what are you doing?"

I hear Bailey, but I'm furious she ran back to him, I don't even look at her.

Hendrix gets up and puts out his hands. I hit him in his gut, and his knees hit the floor.

"Hendrix, why do you have the number to the Center on Aging by your bed and these blank prescription labels?" Bailey asks.

"What the fuck was she doing in your bed?" I hit him again busting his lip.

"Cash, stop it!" She gets between us. "We only talked, and I was leaving to come talk to you."

Holding his gut, Hendrix is gasping and struggles to his feet. "Bailey, I heard about your grandfather's overdose on morphine and I called for them to check on him. Those labels, I can explain. Just call off your dog and I will explain it all."

"You were the one who reported Bailey? You are the one who put her through all of that? Did you give Papa the morphine that day too?" I give him an uppercut to his chin and land the next one on his temple. The asshole isn't fighting back or trying to protect himself.

"Bailey, you ran back to him! How could you run over here? If we have a problem, we talk about it. You sure as hell don't run over to your ex's house for comfort." I turn away to calm myself down.

"Look, man, you can have the bitch. I'll give her to you. She's not even worth the trouble." Hendrix stands.

"You'll give me to him? I'm not a piece of property that can be traded or sold off to the highest bidder, Hendrix." Bailey walks over and knees him as hard as she can in the balls. When he bends over in pain, she punches him squarely in the nose.

"Either you both leave or I'm calling the cops." Hendrix cries while he is on the floor holding his crotch.

Bailey shakes her hand from her badass punch she delivered. I notice drops of blood on the plush white carpet and more on his shirt. I turn to leave because I've seen enough. Bailey is right behind me.

"Cash, wait. I was using the ladies' room and then I was planning to leave."

"It doesn't change the fact that you ran over here, Bailey."

Bailey shakes her head and reaches for my arm, but I shrug her off.

"I came to ask him why he took credit for something you were doing for me."

She tries to get into my arms for a hug, but I can't do that right now. I'm still too raw with pain. She was in his bedroom. I want to know the truth. "Is that all that happened?" I have to know if he touched her. If I need to kill him or not.

She searches my eyes. "Cash, I love you, I would never do that to you." She smiles weakly. "Let's go so we can talk about this somewhere privately. Please." She rubs my arm.

I still don't like this at all. We do need to talk, but I need to cool down first. "Bailey, I'm going home. I need to think about all of this. We can talk later."

Bailey is in shock. She hasn't moved a muscle. I want her to get in her Jeep and leave, but I want her to do that on her on accord.

I get in my truck, my eyes never leaving Bailey's and hers never leaving mine. This still might be over. That's not what I want but it may be inevitable.

Bailey

Hendrix bringing extra medicine and provoking Papa makes perfect sense now. I'm sure Hendrix gave Papa extra morphine, and he admitted calling that agency on me. I'm glad Cash kicked his ass, but I had to get my punches in, too.

I'm torn now. I'm upset at what Cash kept from me, but I want to go to him. Only, he's mad with me. I want to talk to him, but he needs space. I can be patient, though. I will wait and let him come to me. Meanwhile, I have a little lady to talk to about her note.

I pull into our driveway, but I don't see Cash at home yet. When I go inside, I find Margie and Granny playing a game of cards.

Granny looks at me then says, "Margie, I think Bailey and I need to have a talk, if you could excuse us."

"Sure thing, Addie. I'll go home. Call if you need me." She walks over and gives me a hug. "It will all work out."

They must already know how I messed up. How I went and pushed away one of the best things in my life. The one person, who wasn't my family, who loved me for being me. I have a history of making a mountain out of a molehill because of my temper. I want to be Cash's everything, and now I'm probably his biggest mistake.

Granny makes her way to me. "Bailey, I want to talk to you. I want you to understand why I wrote up that letter and signed it. The letter wasn't meant to hurt you or bring you pain. Those are my wishes when the time comes. I don't want you to waste some of the most important years of your life tied down out here. If you want to go back to college, get married, or whatever it is, baby, I want you to do it. I want you to be happy, I appreciate everything you've done, but you need to live your life. When we are too much for Margie to handle, I want to be put in a nursing home. Will you please promise me that you will do that for me?"

I have full tears running down my face.

She pulls me in. "Shh, baby girl. There isn't any reason to cry, go clean up and make back up with my soon to be grandson."

I cry harder. "Granny, that's just it, I don't think he wants me anymore." I shake my head. "When you mess up like I do all the time, you can't keep a good guy."

"Cash loves you, Bailey. I can see how much he loves you. How he respects you and all of us really. He will see reason. Besides, I thought you were the one mad with him."

She glances at me confused. I'm trembling all over, dammit, for allowing myself to get that wrapped up over all of this. "I went to Hendrix's house to confront him about taking credit for paying for all of your medical expenses. I decided, about the time I got to his door, I shouldn't even be there, but he already was at the door holding it open. He pulled me into his apartment." I get up to go get a glass of water. "When Cash arrived and found me there, he hit Hendrix several times. I found Hendrix was the one that called and reported me. I kneed him in his... uh, privates and then popped him in his nose." Granny's eyes are wide. "Cash didn't want to go talk. He wanted me to leave him alone. I think it must be over. I can't take all of this. My anxiety is on overload."

She pats my head. "Go lay down for a while. Put some music on and see if you can't take your mind off of it for a few minutes."

"Okay. I love you, Granny, and whatever you want is what I want too," I whisper to her. "I'll be in my room, call me if you need me." As I go to my bedroom, I hear the matchmaker get on the phone. To call her partner in crime, I have no doubt. I would like to hear what all is being said, but I'm sure it will hurt too much. I lay down to wallow in my self-pity. I'm allowed to. I wished I knew what was on Cash's mind. Only if that Magic 8 Ball that Lizzie and I used to play with really worked so it could tell me what to do.

CASH

I'm not mad with Bailey. I'm hurt. It takes a lot to acknowledge that a little five foot nothing woman has hurt me. I think her running to Hendrix hurts more because I love Bailey, and I thought all of this was behind us. Not all of life is pretty. Sometimes things hurt. But it's how we react to being hurt that matters. Sometimes we grow from it, and other times it tears us down. I'm determined to grow from this and come out with a stronger relationship. But Bailey has to understand, this is the last time she runs off and doesn't talk to me about what is bothering her. That may have worked when she was a kid and dating young pricks like Hendrix, but that behavior doesn't work for me. These are things that Bailey and I both need to work on, together.

I'm pacing the barn because I have all this built up energy I need to let out. I go to work on the barn. A hammer, some nails, and a few pieces of wood should help calm me down. I need this physical labor.

Mom comes out with some water. "Hey, Cash. I thought you might be thirsty. What are you out here doing?"

"Just working on the barn, Mom. Working. On. The. Barn." I say each word as I pound in another nail. I take the glass of water.

"When you get this, whatever this is, out of your system, there's a young lady across the street that's hurting too." She looks at me all sad.

"When I get done with the barn." I call over my shoulder as I hammer another nail. Sweat is dripping down my face and back so I take off my shirt and wipe my face with it.

"No one is perfect, Cash, and you can't hold out thinking there might be someone else out there who is. You've got to focus on becoming the right man, no matter, if it's Bailey or someone you meet tomorrow. You know we all make mistakes, and it takes a strong heart, Cash, to continue to love someone that hurts you. It takes a bigger even stronger heart to forgive and let things go. Forgiving is a gift you give yourself. It won't change what happened, but it can shape the future. Think about that while you're beating those poor planks to death." She turns to go back in the house.

She always does this shit to me, gives me some mumbo gumbo then leaves. One of the things I learned from how my dad did things is to let go of things that you can't change. There will be bad days in my life, but with bad days, you keep fighting until you come out on the other side. Those days, on the other side, will be the best days of your life. I wonder if that is why mom kept fighting through all the shit she endured during all of those years. She knew the best days were ahead of her. Mom is a smart lady. She got me thinking in the right direction. I love that woman. She has always been my rock, even when she needed one to hold onto herself.

I put Bailey up on some kind of pedestal and thought she was perfect and ideal. That we would always have the perfect relationship. That we were invincible. Good thing we are going through this now and not after we are married.

I'm wasting my time being angry and hurt out here. The sooner I work things out with her, the quicker I will be happy again. I pick up my shirt, and go get a shower. I can work out the rest of this shit in there.

Bailey

Journal Entry: Right now, I feel like a vise has been wrapped around my heart and is tightening as each minute passes. I feel so alone and hurt all over. Why did I have to be so stupid?

I'm angry that Cash didn't listen to my explanation. This could have been solved so easily. I won't accept that this is over. It can't be. He is the only person who can get in my head and fix it. The dull ache inside intensifies with each breath I take. The constriction is so tight I feel like blood is no longer coursing through my body. I feel like something has died in my chest. Maybe my heart? Is it possible for your heart to actually die? My heart might officially be dead. The horrific part is the whole mess is my fault. I have no one to blame other than myself. I nailed my coffin shut all by myself this time.

I'm like a book that has been highlighted with all its mistakes. It has bad reviews and needs to be rewritten. The pages are crumbled and ripped and lay scattered, begging to be put back together. No one can read the words because the paper is soaked with tears, and the ink is smeared. Cash can make the book whole again. He is the editor. He knows how to overhaul the passages. Only he doesn't want to read the story. No one can read me except Cash. He can save us. But he has thrown us into a fire due to my flaws.

I'm not sitting around here while the man I love decides we are over. I'm going to fight with every ounce of courage I have. I'm not giving up on us, and I'm not going let him either. I believe we have something that doesn't come around often. I can't imagine losing him.

I put my journal away because I can't write anymore. Cash loves me. Not only does he tell me, but he shows me time and time again. A lot people base love on how much sex they have. Making love is the most intimate thing you can share and is as essential in a relationship as trust, honesty, respect and all of the building blocks required to construct a healthy bond. We have a connection that goes beyond sex. You can have sex with anyone. What I have with Cash is based on what I love about him as a person. Who he is on the inside. What you would call his character. Who he is as a person is as important as the sex. If you don't love a person's character, too, then all the sex in the world won't make your relationship work. I've never had this type of relationship before with anyone else. I'm only twenty-two and maybe I wasn't supposed to have these kind of feelings before. But now, I've met my soulmate. Enough of this moping, I need to pull myself together.

These miserable sappy songs I'm listening to make my heartache worse. They have to go. No more doleful country songs. I turn on some pop which is bound to give me a pick up. Crap! Taylor Swift comes on and she doesn't know if she is country or pop. I press next, Maroon 5. There we go. I'm going to get up and get moving to the beat. Perk myself right up so when the time comes to talk to Cash, I'm ready. Sugar comes on and even though it's kind of a breakup song, it's so upbeat, I'm a little more energized.

Then one of my favorite indie artists, Falyn, comes on my playlist. She has this great bluesy voice. She soothes my soul. She makes think a little deeper.

I hear a soft knock at my door. "Come in." I turn off my music and sit up on the bed.

Cash comes in, and my heart drops to my stomach.

"Can we go talk somewhere, please?" He holds out his hand to me. I will go anywhere he wants me to go.

I take his hand and give him a kiss, "I'm so sorry, Cash, I was wrong. Thank you for everything you have done for me and my family. I'm truly blessed to have you in my life, and I won't ever forget that. Never. Again." I kiss him a little deeper and his hands go into my hair, I can feel the tension leaving my body.

"Come on, Baby Doll. Let's go talk."

He takes my hand again and leads me out of the house. We walk across the road and get in the truck. I was hoping we would just go to the barn and make up but it can't be that easy. We drive around for a little bit and listen to some music. Cash pulls in to a park. I love this place. There are hiking trails, a playground and a grassy area by a pond. He takes a blanket out of the back of the truck after he helps me down from the cab. We head out to the pond. Night is falling, and shadows are dancing on the water. He wraps the blanket around us then he sits, bringing me into his lap. We are facing the water, and I see the tiny ripples made by the wind. I lean back into him, and we spend a while in the stillness. Tranquility washes over me. I turn and I see it has him, too.

A leaf floats down every now and then. We are having a late fall. The full limbs of the trees on the other side of the pond are evidence. The reds, oranges, and yellows make the trees look like flowers. The trees give me hope because even though all their leaves fall and lose their beauty, they are preparing for a new set. Even though we have gone through this difficulty, maybe we are only preparing for our own new beginning.

We put our foreheads together. Sometimes, I guess you don't have to say anything at all to make everything right.

"Bailey, I'm sorry, too. I have been meaning to tell you mom and I were paying for all of the expenses, but the time never seemed right. I love you. If you can forgive me, I'll spend a lifetime showing you how much you mean to me. If the way we spend our time defines who we are, then I want to spend my time making love to you. You are who I am and all I ever want to be. You make me a better man, and I hope I make you a better person too. I promise from here on out, I will tell you everything. No more keeping secrets."

He gets me in my heart every time. You'd never think this big, strong man wouldn't be so good with sentimental words.

"Cash, I promise to not let my temper get the best of me. I promise to come to you and tell you when you piss me off. As long as we fight every once in a while, it means we still have something worth fighting for." Gee, that didn't sound as pretty as his speech.

He kisses my forehead.

I never thought a kiss on the forehead could make you feel so loved. We sit here, happy to be with each other for another ten minutes. "Cash, can we go back to the barn now?"

A wide grin spreads across his face.

"Isn't the best part of fighting all the making up?" I give him a tiny smile.

"That sounds like a brilliant idea. This time, we'll let hay get in your hair. You can explain that to your Granny."

We stand up and he pops my butt.

I turn, jump up wrapping my legs around his waist and give him a proper make up kiss.

"You kiss me like that again and we won't make it back to the barn."

"I don't want anyone else to ever have your kisses. They're all mine."

"I don't want you wrapped in another's arms. Your body is all mine to hold and cherish."

I think he must be a descendant of Romeo because he always knows the right words to say to melt me into a puddle. He walks back to the truck with me wrapped around him and I give him kisses all over his face.

"Bailey, I can't see where I'm going." He laughs.

"Does it really matter as long as we are together?"

"Yes, we need to get to the barn. Now."

Yay for makeup sex!

CASH

Today is the charity event for Clay's ranch. He is doing a name reveal and having all kinds of activities set up for kids with disabilities. From one spectrum to the next, he loves these kids and just wants to help as many as he can. He thinks he has at least one activity that each kid will like. If not, maybe they will like just being around the horses and learning how to groom them. If all else fails, he said they can play in the dirt. He seems to have it all organized down to a science.

The November air is crisp, just the way I like it. Bailey wants me to cuddle with her more. With the nippy weather, the girls have on University of Alabama hoodies, hounds-tooth printed gloves and matching scarves. They do look cute, but I'm not sure if they dressed for warmth or to make a fashion statement, I'm just glad Bailey didn't cover her ass with a bulky coat. I would hate to miss one of my favorite parts of her body, all day.

We arrive at the ass crack of dawn. The girls have dozed off, but the crunch of the gravel under my tires wakes them up.

"Why?" Lizzie whines.

"It's for a good cause," Bailey says.

"Oh, I know that. But why? Why does it have to be so early?"

Lizzie complains, but I don't think she means it. She has a tough exterior, but in there somewhere is the true Lizzie. She has to be peeled back layer by layer for her heart to show. Besides, she and Bailey were raised together. They have to be a little alike because I know for a fact that my girl has a huge heart.

Clay has a group of people here today that will be volunteering with him on a weekly basis. Several professionals who will be using the facilities for therapy with their patients will be here too. I watch him as I walk up, and I feel a sense of pride. We didn't grow up as brothers, but I'm glad we are in each other's life now. "Hey, Clay, where do you want us?"

He looks up from hanging a sign on a fence post and waves a friendly hello.

"Hi, guys. I can't thank y'all enough for all of your help and support. Bailey, you doing our accounting for us will save us a lot of money." He gives Bailey a hug and picks her up off the ground as he does it. "Lizzie, you look mighty fine this morning. Damn, I'm glad I'm not blind. Could I tempt you in joining me for a cup of coffee?"

Lizzie rolls her eyes. "Does that cheesy shit ever work?" she says under her breath and yawns.

"Why don't we all go get a cup?" I pipe up before Lizzie turns him down cold.

She leans over to Bailey and whispers something.

"Would you happen to have cocoa, Clay? Lizzie and I don't care for coffee."

"Of course I do, Bailey. Cash called me a few days ago to make sure I had something besides coffee to drink." He winks. "Besides, I have to take care of my future sister-in-law."

To say the staff break room is bare boned would be a compliment. Not an extra dime is spent in here. A couple of safety posters are on the walls along with a duty roster and a few awareness posters for the different disabilities that the ranch will be focusing on. In the center of the room is a second hand table with some mixed matched chairs around it. An ancient Mr. Coffee is in the corner with real coffee cups, sugar, and a spoon.

"I love what you've done with the place, Clay." Lizzie laughs, looking around.

He looks at her seriously.

"I'm not spending money on anything that isn't a necessity. If anyone wants a fancy coffee, they can go spend their own money, not the money for the kids."

That is the first time I've seen him go defensive. My little brother has passion.

"Hold the sugar please because you're sweet enough for the both of us," he tells Lizzie as he watches her make a cup of cocoa.

I raise my eyebrows at him, letting him know he's being cheesy again. Lizzie just scoffs at him. More volunteers arrive and he moves away to greet them.

"Lizzie, you could try to be nice to him. It wouldn't hurt you." Bailey says.

"I'm not offering him an ounce of encouragement. There isn't any reason to fan the flame." She shakes her head.

"I want to welcome everyone and thank you all for coming out." Clay claps his hands to get the attention of all the volunteers. "I'm glad everyone could come out bright and early this morning. We still have several things to do before the kids arrive for the festivities. First, I want to reveal the name of our ranch." Clay pulls a sign from behind the table. "Welcome to Crossroads. I hope we will be the crucial turning point for some of the kids, and they learn to cope a little better with the help of a horse. These horses are such a blessing to the families of these kids, and to watch the kids start to bond with the horses is just incredible. They learn so much by brushing and feeding the horses. Sometimes, that can be transferred to social and communication skills with other people in life as well. That is just one facet of wonderful programs like I hope this one will be.

Our main thing today is safety. I know you all watched the videos and have taken the required training courses, but please think safety first. If you're not used to being around horses, you need to partner with someone who is. I have an assignment roster here for the jobs that need to be done. Some of you already signed up for jobs, and some of you I assigned to jobs based on your experience level. This is my assistant, Denise. She allows me to act like I'm in charge and know what I'm doing. If you have concerns or problems, you can talk to either one of us. Thank you." Clay motions for us to come over. "I want y'all to meet this angel. Isn't she adorable? This is Denise, my assistant." He introduces us all and we all shake Denise's hand.

"It's really nice to meet y'all," Denise says.

Denise's southern drawl is thicker than any of ours. Clay puts his arm around her shoulders, talking about how great she is and the girl is beaming.

"Clayton, you can just go on and on with those sweet words." She laughs and puts one hand to her chest.

Denise is a looker, or would be if I wasn't engaged and all. She has long legs, a tiny waist and big doe eyes for Clay. Can he not see what is right in front of him?

"Lizzie, I have you working with me in the stable." Clay announces to our group. "Denise and Bailey, y'all are setting up the front office. Cash, I need you to finish hanging up the warning signs."

"Clayton, I thought I was going to help you in the stables." Denise whines and actually puckers her lips.

Lizzie looks at Bailey, and they both have to cover their mouths to keep from laughing. Denise does look kind of like a duck.

"I don't have time to train you today, Denise. Lizzie has experience working with horses already and I could use her help. You will be working in the office mainly anyway so I want you to get it the way you like it, sweetheart." He gives her a pat on the back and dismisses her.

"Lizzie and Cash, if you will come with me, there is a good bit to be done. Cash, the first signs need to be hung in the barn." He turns toward the barn without another word. Lizzie and I follow him into the barn. He gives me instructions for the signs first, then he and Lizzie walk further into the barn.

"Are you and Denise dating?" Lizzie asks Clay.

"No, but I would like to be dating you. I'll even cook you dinner, and then you can cook me breakfast," he tells her with a wink.

"Look, Clay that shit might work for some silicone Barbie doll like Denise, but not me."

Whoa! I'm glad I'm over here for this because that was some funny shit right there. I laugh, but I stop when they both look at me. "I'll be over here with the signs." I clear my throat then walk away putting up the signs around the stable. I can't hear their conversation anymore, which is too bad. How can I help Clay if I can't hear what he is doing wrong? Everybody should be in love like Bailey and me.

The love of a good woman will change a man and make him see things differently. When we get old and our bodies change, and our hair turns gray, Bailey will still have that good heart. I fall in love with her over and over again each day.

If it's true that everything happens for a reason then I'm glad Bailey dated Hendrix. It showed her the difference between a boy and a man. A man that worships the very ground she walks on. You have to weed through the bad seeds to find the one that will make the best fruit.

People say my generation has lost romanticism. Well, not all of us have. I want Bailey to feel like my queen, so if that means writing her a love song, then I'll do that. If it means taking her on picnics in a field of wildflowers then slowly making love to her for the rest of the day, I can certainly handle that, too. Holding hands while we walk, sweet kisses, and even sweeter

words are all things my girl deserves. If that makes me pussy whipped, I'll be the happiest pussy whipped person who ever walked. It makes me happy to see her happy.

43

Bailey

We have busted our asses all morning getting everything ready for the charity event this afternoon. At the last minute, everything comes together. When children arrive with their families, they join in the various activities. The main attraction is the horses, but I think our booth comes in a close second. Lizzie and I are running the funnel cake booth. I was supposed to do this with Denise, but Lizzie traded with her. Cash and Clay are doing the pony rides, and Denise is at the donation booth. The other volunteers are scattered out doing other games and activities for the kids. The kids were invited to participate free of charge. Clay wants to be able to offer these services free for anyone who can't pay. So fundraising will be a way of life for him. That and his music.

"I can't wait until tonight to hear Clay sing. Cash says he is phenomenal, that he puts him to shame." I tell Lizzie, and she rolls her eyes at me. "If you roll your eyes at me again, I'm going to pop you up the side of your head with this spatula. What has you all pissed off today?" I laugh.

"Nothing, I'm not pissed off. I'm just tired from getting up so early."

She sure could have fooled me. We work the stand in silence for a few minutes. All the kids who come up with their parents for a funnel cake are so cute. Some are really shy and that's okay. They get their treat and are off to the next fun stop.

"How is Denise? Was she nice to work with? She seems so fake to me." Lizzie says.

"She was really sweet, I think she has a huge crush on Clay. She wants to double date with Cash and me."

Lizzie stops what she is doing and stares at me for a second then picks up the dishcloth and wipes the counter top.

"You're not interested in him, are you, Lizzie?" Earlier today, I thought I saw a spark of interest in her eyes, but she doesn't like the way he comes off with his joking.

"Me? Oh my goodness, Bailey, how can you even think that? He and I together would be like water and gasoline. That just wouldn't work. I don't fall for that crap. You're the hopeless romantic, not me. I'm balls to the wall, call 'em as you see 'em, don't take no shit, rocker chick. He is a little too good and a lot too country for my taste. I bet he doesn't have any tats. He wouldn't know what to do with me." She laughs.

"Sounds like you've been thinking about it a lot if you've got all that figured out." I lift my eyebrows in challenge.

"Shut up, Bailey." She turns around and busies herself.

"You like him, don't you?"

"He's not my type, Bailey. You know I like my guys a little rough around the edges. One who knows how to take charge and give it... Oh, never mind Ms. Hopelessly in Love. I don't like the sweet and gentle."

"Lizzie, you never know how someone will be until you give them a chance."

"Bailey, he is too sweet and mushy. I want hard and bad."

Night finally falls. Cash thankfully brought a blanket for us to sit on and has it up front and near center stage. Clay has a stage set up under a huge tent, and his band has their gear all ready to go. I didn't realize how official they were. Their equipment looks expensive to my untrained eye.

Cash pulls me close and snuggles me, I love being in love! There isn't any place I would rather be. There isn't anything better. Maybe I am a hopeless romantic. What's wrong with that?

"Is he going to sing our song?" I'm sitting in front of Cash with my back leaning against his chest.

He reaches down and kisses the tip of my nose. "You're going to have to wait and see, Bailey." He looks over and asks Lizzie. "Does she try to sneak peeks at her Christmas presents too?"

"Yes, she is horrible. She can't wait to give gifts, either. When she buys something, she will either give it to you early or give you so many hints that you know what it is."

They are both laughing at me.

"See if I buy either one of you anything for Christmas." They gang up on me constantly, but I love that they get along. It makes things so much easier, especially since Cash will be part of our family soon.

Clay comes onstage and does introductions of his band members and thanks everyone for coming out and for their donations. The band starts playing their first song. Lizzie has been on her phone since we sat down, texting with friends. She looks up with a shocked look on her face and leans over to us.

"Why is he singing a Nine Inch Nails song?" she whispers to me.

I shake my head, "This is by Johnny Cash, and he was a legend. That's who my man candy was named after."

"Bailey, I know a Nine Inch Nails song when I hear it, I'm not stupid and I know who Johnny Cash is too. I watched "I Walk the Line" with you, remember?"

She huffs at me and picks her phone up and starts typing. She turns her phone toward me.

"Cool. Nine Inch Nails covers this song, too," I say.

"Nine Inch Nails doesn't cover this song. Trent Reznor who *is* Nine Inch Nails wrote the freaking song. That makes this amazing." She looks at me like I'm stupid.

I shrug and pick up my phone then show her Johnny Cash's version.

She watches Clay on the stage, not taking her eyes off of him.

"What do you make of that?" Cash whispers in my ear, then proceeds to kiss down my neck. He knows that drives me wild. I've already threatened to take him into Clay's office and make use of that desk. It is just begging to be used.

"I think if you keep kissing my neck, you are going to become an official member of the porta potty club." I sigh. He can keep it up. I don't mind at all. He can take me right here in front of everybody. My inner kink goddess is open for business.

"That's disgusting, but I wasn't talking about that." His fingers are playing in my hair.

He is keeping everything PG here in front of all these kids, and I want to jump him right here, right now. I already forgot the question he asked, he distracts me so easily. "What was your question then?"

He motions over at Lizzie who looks mesmerized by the music.

"She likes good music." I turn a little bit, "Do you want to know what I like?" I lick my bottom lip, getting ready to pounce on him.

"I would like to call my brother, Cash, up here." Clay announces from the stage. "He has helped make all of this possible and I want to thank him. Cash, would you come up here, and bring Bailey too?"

I'm going to kill Clay. I do not get up in front of crowds. He is a dead man.

Cash takes me by the hand and leads me up to the stage. Everyone is clapping for us, but they are merely being nice. Cash takes the microphone from Clay and one of the volunteers brings out a stool for me to sit on, but I don't plan on being up here long enough to need that. I smile at him as a thank you but hop onto the stool anyway.

Clay jumps off stage and goes to sit by Lizzie.

WHAT. THE. HELL. Then our song, "Give It All We Got Tonight," starts playing and my man is singing to me. Hot tears are rolling down my face, I have the sweetest most romantic man alive, and he loves me. He looks into my eyes the whole time. Everything else slips away and it's only Cash and me. We are out here in the late autumn air, and my heart is so full of love for this man. How could I ever think I wanted to leave a life like this? This is perfect. Leaves are in full color. Lightning bugs are out brightening up the night with little twinkles. A cool breeze gives me gooses bumps and the man of my dreams is singing me our song. When Cash finishes the song, he gets a standing ovation, but we are too busy to notice. I'm right where I want to be, where I need to be, wrapped up in Cash's arms. Right where I'm supposed to be.

The End

LOVE ME ~ WITHOUT REGRET

Chapter 1

Lizzie

"How about him, he looks like he would have a big cock?" Aubrey checks out the guy at the end of the bar.

"I would break him, he's too little," I muse. None of these guys are really my type, they are all too "good" and I like rough around the edges. We need to head out to another bar, but I have ulterior motive for being here.

Aubrey and I reached the bar about an hour ago and I'm ready for the band to start playing. Even though this place is hopping, there isn't anyone here that is really doing it for me. We get our new drinks from the bar and test them with our swizzle sticks. I don't mind going home with someone but it will be on my terms. There won't be any date rape going on with this chick unless it's me doing the raping, with a willing participant.

"Have you gotten picky? What's been wrong with you here lately, you're going soft." Aubrey downs her drink. So, I down mine too, ready for round three. Who will be the lucky guy that will get to buy this round? Damn there isn't anyone interesting here and I wore my favorite outfit.

I have been saving up for this pair of ankle boots for a couple of months and they looking fucking hot on me. They aren't going to go to waste tonight. These are so steampunk! They are black leather Hades Oxfords. They lace up and have three buckles on each side, with five inch metal heels. They also have some cool metal gear work on them too. They are totally kick ass. They go perfect with my black, leather, barely there, mini skirt, and my black tank with a Harley and skull cut out on the back. I don't know why I'm wasting how good I look here. Almost everyone else is in denim, freaking redneck. I mean I dress that way too but OH MI GAWD! Can these people not wear something different? My makeup is heavy tonight with thick black eyeliner, flicked up on the sides. My lips are ruby red and full. I'm ready for some action, but I'm in the wrong bar for that tonight.

"We are just in the wrong bar Aubs, let's wait to see if this band is any good and we'll leave."

"You were the one insisting we come here tonight." She crosses her arms and checks her watch for third time in the last thirty minutes.

"They should be on any minute, let's get on the dance floor so we can get a good view."

She shrugs, "Whatever, but you don't really like this kind of music, so what's the big deal?

There is a huge dance floor with a stage centered against one wall. The lighting is fantastic for the performers. The speakers and sound system is top of the line, I wonder how this bar can afford this kind of equipment.

There are table and booths lining one side of the dance floor. They are extremely cozy, with little candles flickering on each of them, casting a romantic glow. The lights on that side of the room are turned down low, crating the idealistic atmosphere for setting the mood. On the other side on the dance floor are a few pool tables. High top tables and barstools are scattered haphazardly, thank goodness that everywhere has gone to non-smoking now, so there isn't a heavy layer of smoke in here.

The announcer comes on the stage, "Please welcome to the stage, the band we all have come to love, Shades of Regret." Girls all over the bar comes to the dancefloor, screaming like these guys are famous or something.

"What kind of name is Shades of Regret? Aubrey looks annoyed.

"Here," I pull a twenty out of my bra, "go get us more drinks." She is going to have to quit that whining, I can't put up with that shit. I mean Bailey doing it is one thing but, anyone else grates on my nerves. Aubrey is my best friend outside of Bailey. Bailey is so far up Cash's ass, I surprised she doesn't smell like shit. I can say that because I love her and she is like my sister but Aubrey better watch her damn mouth. I'll jack her up if she says another word about Bailey, because I ain't playing. She was complaining earlier that Bailey never came out with us anymore now that she was engaged to Cash. I'm glad Bay found her soulmate, not everyone is that lucky.

He takes the stage, I'm sure he won't recognize me dressed like this, so I can get my fill of looking without him going all cheesy on me.

"Thank y'all for coming out tonight. We appreciate all of our loyal fans, ladies." He winks at a group of girls to the right, of center stage. They act like a bunch of stupid ass teenagers going crazy over the latest boy band. "The boys and I are playing for our favorite charity tonight, Crossroads Ranch. So ladies, if you like what you hear, come by and fill our jar with your change." He turns and nods to the drummer.

I hear the opening licks to 'Rusty Cage' by Soundgarden but only it sounds country. I have to say, if I were to listen to country music, it would be this kind.

Aubrey comes back with my vodka and cranberry, I take out my little tester stick and swirl it around. Normally I'm a beer kind of girl, but tonight I needed something stronger if I'm going to pull this off. It really shouldn't be too hard, seeing he is already after my pussy and all. I'm just going to make it easy for him, this one night. Get the easy going country boy out of my system and go on to my bad boys, I wonder how he is going to like my Nefertiti. It normally drives guys wild, but you never know. Bailey and I got them together but when she started date the guy before Cash, he took it out, saying it was trashy. I loving refer to him as 'A Joke". I couldn't be happier that she is rid of him.

"Who is that, is he the reason you wanted to come? They aren't half bad." Aubrey points to the lead singer.

"Just shut up and listen to music, ho." I grin at her.

"I call dibs" She is lusting after the lead singer too.

"Like hell you do." Has she lost her ever loving mind? He does look exceptionally hot tonight. He has on perfect fitting blue jeans, a black t-shirt with a long sleeved button up shirt left hanging open. He has on a baseball hat and cowboy boots, he has grown a little bit of a beard since I saw him last. It looks good on him. The whole look makes him appear a smidgeon more rugged. It's doing wonders for my libido, like it needed any help.

"We will let him decide on that." She replies, lifting her chin.

Yes, we will let him decide. Next song is 'Heavy is the Head', I swear I've heard this song somewhere. Man, I do like the way he sings. He plays a few more songs equally as good. You wouldn't exactly consider him a country sing, he's more southern rock to me. I love dancing to this music, it can certainly get me swaying my booty.

I look back at the stage and we just made eye contact, at first he looks thoroughly confused. Recognition appears, then a sly little smirky grin shows up on his face.

"We are going to take a little break and we will be right back." Clay says and jumps off the stage and heads my way, good boy, you might get rewarded.

"Lizzie? You look different, I like it." When he gets through eye banging me, he said, "Come on let me buy you a drink." Just as he was about to put his arm around my shoulder, Aubrey butted her way in between us.

"Hi, I loved your music, I'm Aubrey!" She leans over and hugs him. Aubs better keep her hands to herself, dicklicker. "Was that country?"

"Oh, Hey there! Is your hand heavy? Let me hold it for you." Clay politely removes her from humping his leg, and take her hand to give it a kiss. "I'm Clay, are you a friend of Lizzie's?" She is eye drooling all over him now, she needs to back off.

"Yes, he is my friend, Cheesy Ass." I say as an introduction. "You do sound impressive tonight." Lifting my eyebrows, I commented with a tiny giggle. "Who knew you had it in you?"

"What? I'm sorry, I didn't hear you. I know you didn't just give me a compliment." He howled, watching me roll my eyes.

"I thought you sounded amazing" Aubrey is flirting shamelessly. "You guys should go professional."

"Thank you, Are you the moon? In the dark you still shine bright." Aubrey laughs her ass off and touches his shoulder.

"Aren't you the charmer? Lizzie hasn't told me about you, I guess that means either your bad in bed or she hasn't gotten you to bed yet." I fixing to whop this bitch's ass, I give her my, you had better back the hell up look. She doesn't have the same telepathic communication abilities as Bay and I do, so she is thoroughly lost.

"How about that drink? I don't have long on my break?" He suggests, deflecting the conversation and turning red.

"I guess, if it will get you to stop bothering us?" I wink at him.

We make our way to the bar and he puts his hand on my lower back, guiding the way. I do feel little sparks shoot up my spine but that probably the amount of alcohol I've consumed tonight.

"What will it be ladies?" He knock his knuckles on the bar.

"I'll have a Bud Lite, Aubrey?" She is standing on the other side of Clay and she keeps fondling him, I don't know why he doesn't just push her off of him. It's just sickening how she is trying to hang on him.

"I'll have whatever your having Clay." She is batting her eyelashes at him.

"One Bud Lite and two bottles of water," he turns back toward me, "are you guys going to watch the second half."

"Yes we are, I drove and I say when we leave" Aubrey does her bob thing, she doesn't realize that was part of the plan. I have been stalking the band's Facebook page this past week, incognito of course. Yeah, you're looking at "Mary Woods", sweet country girl, a.k.a. my alter ego.

"I guess I'm stuck here then, I just hope you don't go singing any whiny, country music on me now." I tell him, as I take a pull on my beer. I turn around leaning my back on the bar.

"Not a country music fan? Are you and Bailey even friends?" he chuckles and leans in closer to me.

"Wait, are you Cash's brother? This is Cash's brother?" She is looking back and forth between us.

"Yes" We say in unison.

"Oh." Aubrey backs off a little now, I confided in Aubrey after Clay's charity event, that I thought he was cute. I mean he is attractive, in a cowboy sort of way, if you're into that sort of thing. Personally, I'm not into cowboys. Quit being repetitive Lizzie, who are you trying to convince anyway?

"I think I'll leave on that comment, let me know before you ladies leave Lizzie." He gives us both a small one arm hug. Then he is gone, back on stage for the second half of his show.

I watch his ass all the way back to the stage. Mmm, mmm, mmm. Why does he have to look so stimulatingly fine, I exhale and wonder.

"Lizzie, why didn't you tell me who he was? Stupid Ass ho, you know I wouldn't have been all over him." She shakes her head and taps her fingertips on the bar.

"Aubs, it's no big deal. I think he's sweet, that's all. He is so stupid with those crazy pickup lines." I state flippantly, waving her off.

"Lizzie, I can tell when you're all stormy in your panties over someone, your just lying to yourself." She is as deranged in the head as Bailey.

"Have you been franchizing alongside Bailey? I swear she is determined to have a double wedding." I huff out like I'm exasperated.

"Just think Lizzie, the sooner you get it through your thick skull, the quicker your cobwebs get cleaned out!" She laughs.

"My cobwebs are cleaned out regularly, thank you very much. I don't need him for that, he is sexy and has a seductive voice, that's it. We are friends, end of the story." I state firmly, turning my attention back to the stage.

"If you believe that Lizzie, you're more stupid that I thought." She is getting cocky now.

"Watch it, let's dance, there's a couple of cute guys over there." I need to get my mind off of a certain tremendously sexy vocalist.

We sauntered our way to the guys and danced near them. The dance floor is crowed, there is every kind of dancing imaginable going on. These guys are okay looking, they will be fine to dance with. They looked better from a distance, that's fine for now. Aubs makes eye contact with one of them and gives him a wink. They come over and start dancing with us from behind.

"Hey sexy, I'm Preston. You sure know how to move that fine ass of yours." The guy whispers in my ear.

"'I'm Lizzie, thanks." I say glancing backwards with smile, at Preston who was now trying to dry hump my ass. He took that as him invitation to put his hands on my hips. This music is great for dancing, and I'm feeling the effects of the alcohol, I've been downing all night. He wraps his arms around waist and pulled me into him. We were both moving in sync to music, his hips following my movements. Then I feel him start to grow hard, I breakaway and put a little distance between us. I move up a little closer to Aubs.

Aubs and I are having fun dancing sexy with each other. Preston dances close but he keeps a safe distance for a couple of songs. Then I see the guy Aubs is with lift his chin up to Preston. They both move in on us and sandwich us up. Preston isn't as aggressive as he was before, so I continue to dance with him.

I hear Clay announce this was there last song and they were going to do one for the true country fans. The band changes to a country two-step song, and Preston grabs my hands and starts spinning me. I don't normally two-step, it's not my cup of tea, so I beg off. I start to make my way back to center stage. He pulls me back, getting forceful and I don't play that way. Game over.

"Hey, where are you going?" He say through his teeth, keeping a tight hold around my waist and tries to kiss me.

"Let me go cowboy, this isn't my beat." I smile, but turn my head before he can kiss me.

"Awe baby why don't we get out of here, we can go home and dance in the sheets." He doesn't take hints, I'm going to have to lay it out flat for him.

"Listen, I'm not going home or anywhere else with you, for that matter. You are going to spank your own monkey tonight. Now, if you don't remove your hands from me, I'll have to kick your ass for you."

He glowers at me and pulls me into him. "You can kick my ass in bed all you want to."

I stomp on his foot, so he lets go of me. I take a step back and give him a right hand jab to the chin. Just hard enough to know I mean business. His eyes go wide and he rubs his chin, I caught him off guard to say the least. I swing around to leave but he catches me by my hair yanking me down. Son of a bitch that hurt, he's had it now. I get up ready to take battle but he's being pulled away by the bouncer. I still want my last lick, I trot over to them and punch him in the gut, as hard as I can this time.

"You fucking bitch, I'll find you and when I do, you'll regret that." He threatens. I start to say my comeback and get all in his face when I'm picked up and hoisted over a shoulder.

"Oh yeah, you bring it on anytime time butt muncher." I still get my retort in, even if I can't see him any longer. I twist around and struggle to get down from this guy's hold. I refuse to be manhandled and whoever this is, carrying me over their shoulder is going to have hell to pay. They will be suffering from my wrath as soon as they release me. I look down at this guy's ass and I know exactly who it is now.

Chocolate Gravy

A special thanks to Christy of Southernplate for allowing me to use her name and recipe in my book. I really do love her website. Http://www.southerplate.com

Ingredients

     1 cup white sugar

     2 T flour

     1 T unsweetened cocoa powder

     1¼ cups milk

     1 tablespoon butter

Instructions

1. Combine everything except butter in a heavy saucepan. Bring to boil, stirring constantly to prevent scorching.

2. Once boiling, cut the heat down and stir for a minute more (it will get pretty thick rather suddenly). Take off heat and stir in butter.

3. Pour over biscuits. I tear my biscuit up in a bowl first and then pour it over.

Recipe by Southern Plate at

http://www.southernplate.com/2009/05/
chocolate-gravy.html

My Papa made this for breakfast, all the time, but he used water instead of milk. Like most people of that generation, there wasn't any measurements wrote down, he would always say 'that much' and show me an amount he had put in the pot. He was the one who cooked breakfast, so Granny could sleep in a few extra minutes.

Bailey's and Cash's Playlist

https://play.spotify.com/user/1273789225/playlist/
4Rx8ciDH5cSXSTBodRPWkI

Give It All We Got- George Strait

Amazed – Lonestar

Southern Girl – Tim McGraw

The Mona Lisa – Brad Paisley

Boondock- Little Big Town

Who I Am With You – Chris Young

Sugar- Maroon 5

Just a Moment – Falyn

All Of Me- John Legend

Sweet Home Alabama- Lynard Skynyrd

Love Like Crazy – Lee Brice

Thinking Out Loud – (Country Version) Dylan Scott

Acknowledgments

Wow, I really wrote a book! Who would have ever imagined that, not me. I'm just a small town girl from Decatur, AL.

I have so many people to thank that helped me make this dream a success. I'm sure if I got down to it, I could fill another book. I know this will be long, but hey, it's my first book. I know my Granny and Papa would have been so proud of me for this accomplishment. I wish everyone could have known them, they were awesome to grow up with.

I first need to thank my husband Jason for putting up with me for twenty-three years. Believe it or not, I know it has been a hard job at times to get along with me. I love you, I cross my heart. I never chased you down mall, please quit telling people that.

Brett, I love you. Thank you for teaching me new things all the time. I have a fresh outlook on life because of you. You are always so kind and it makes my day to talk to you. Hurry home because you are greatly missed. I even miss your pranks, I bet you never thought you would hear me say that.

Braxton, you have always been the bright spot in my life. You have the biggest heart (and the laziest bone when it comes to cleaning your room) and you're the most loving person I've ever met. I love you, I won! You give me the best hugs, and I don't want you to finish growing up. Can't you stay with me forever and be a little boy again?

To my editor and friend Lorrie Anson, you will never know how much your help is appreciated and your friendship is valued. I'm so thankful we met. You're my word genius.

Amy Wiater, thank you for being a dear friend and stepping up when I became consumed by this book. I owe you more than this thank you. Thank you for simply being you. I'm so fortunate to call you my friend. I double checked your last name.

To my writing partner Dawn Stanton, thank you for keeping me focused and motivated, I couldn't have done it without you. You made this journey fun, who knew that suggestions through Facebook Messaging could be so helpful. That's what we do!

Kay Lindy, you are my rock girl. We are in this together and we got this. Thank you for listening to my doubts and my pity parties. #TeamRindy2016 for the win!

Rick Veal, thank you for all of your help, tweaking (no not twerking) and beyond. You even made me love vampires and trust me that was a feat. You're my book guru now!!

Melissa Shank, there isn't enough words in the English language to express what you mean to me. Thank you for sharing with me your first-hand knowledge on Grapefruits, and educating me on that fine quality video. You rock with your ideas! I know one hundred percent, I would have never had the courage to write a book if we hadn't have met. You are the sister I never had. (You're my joke!)

Kathy Isaacs, thank you for letting me go on and on about this book and reading and rereading. Thank you for making me part of your family, I love all of you! I appreciate all the confidence you have in me, when many times I didn't have any in myself. Thank you for loving my kids too, that means the world to me. Thank you for not judging me for my sometimes poor decision making skills.

Denise Veach and Cindy Wilson, it is true what they say that true friends can go months or even years without talking and pick up where they left off… we never miss a beat. Love you girls. Denise, also thank you for reading and rereading.

Donya Claxton, meeting you was another great point in my life! Thanks for reading and all of your help. You're an amazing friend and I feel a kindred spirit in you.

Dina Littner, wow! Who knew when we met, you would be helping me so much. It was supposed to be the other way around. Thank you for all of your help. I can't wait to actually meet you one day. You rock!

Maggie Adams, I'm so glad that I came across your book. I not only love your writing but I love you too. Thank you for being a great friend and fellow freak! Don't change anything about your books, I love them just the way they are.

A.D. Eliis, thank you for opening my eyes to the world of indie writers, and becoming a dear friend to me. I love your books, keep writing great heartwarming stories. You inspire me. Thank you for showing my son that he is truly a gift.

Jude & Platypire Reviews, you're the first blogger who took a chance on a newbie indie author. You're a great sounding board and you've answered so many questions and taught me so much. You're such a blessing.

Mom, thank you for giving me a love for reading, love you much! I know we didn't always get along when I was growing up, and I'm sorry that I'm just as hard headed as you! Neither of us like to give in very much, thanks for letting me win most of the time. You got your wish, I have a child just like me.

Dad, thank you for being all the things I needed and always being proud of me. I'll always be your baby girl. Love you. You're the best daddy a girl could have ask for and I'm so glad you chose to be mine.

Dusty, love you. You'll always be my little brother, thanks for reading and encouraging me. I wish we could go back to when you were little and dance to the Beach Boys. I miss when you thought I was cool, maybe one day, I can get to that status again.

Uncle Robert, thanks for sharing stories about Papa and Granny. I love you, your favorite niece!

My cousins, thank you all for being great friends growing up.

Marty, I love you like you are my brother even if you did try to kill me when I was five by running over me with your bicycle.

Angel and Troy, I always felt like you were more like my niece and nephew. I wish we ALL could go back to how things were before Granny passed away.

Liz, thanks for being a friend, "cousin" and sounding board. Plus all the other stuff that is way too long to mention.

Mercedes, I love and admire your strength. If I lived closer, your boys would be rotten.

Sidnee, you are a turkey and I know I'm your favorite cousin.

Niketa Little, you are a sassy mess. You will be a character one day. So glad we met.

To all of the authors in Waking Up Indie Authors, thank you guys for your support and answering the million questions! There is way too many of you to name, but please know, I appreciate each and every one of you.

Beta readers, bloggers and reviewers, thank you to everyone who helped me! Much love to you all!

Vic, thanks for being a great cover model. You're beautiful, inside and out and Kristy Rodgers, thank you for taking an awesome picture.

Deb Jones Diem, thank you for giving my book once last look and being an apostrophe nazi.

Last but not least, my real life Lizzie! Thanks for being my inspiration for my Lizzie. You're an amazing young lady. Stay true to yourself. Stay sassy, you're perfect just the way you are! Don't ever change for anyone, if they can't accept you for who you are, then they don't deserve you.

Thorns & All

About the Author

Renee Kennedy grew up in Decatur, AL and has been married to her high school sweetheart for 23 years. She currently lives in the Houston, TX area with her husband Jason, her son Braxton, and one very spoiled Yorkie, Chico. She also has one son that is serving our Country in the military, Brett.

She loves living in Texas but she'll always be a Bama girl and that is where her heart remains. Renee has always been an avid reader but never dreamed of writing a book, until reminiscing about her grandparent's love story, Bailey's story popped into her head. Her grandparents played a significant role in her life growing up, so sharing a little piece of them with the world, helps keep them alive in her heart.

When she is not reading or writing she loves to cook and try out new recipes. You can often find her hanging out with her family and friends or stalking her own favorite authors.

Chico, her mini Yorkie, runs Renee's house and her so his every need must be catered too, after all he is her 3rd baby.

Goodreads:
https://www.goodreads.com/author/show/917787.Renee_Kennedy

Email: renee@author-reneekennedy.com

Website: http://www.author-reneekennedy.com

Facebook:
https://www.facebook.com/Reneekennedyauthor

Piniterest: https://www.pinterest.com/authorreneekenn/

Twitter: https://twitter.com/realreneewrites

Instagram: https://instagram.com/realreneewrites/

www.ingramcontent.com/pod-product-compliance
Lightning Source LLC
Chambersburg PA
CBHW060151180626
46813CB00007B/2695